CONVENIENTLY CONVICTED

IVY ASHER
RAVEN KENNEDY

Copyright © 2020 Ivy Asher and Raven Kennedy

All rights reserved. This book or parts thereof may not be reproduced in any form, stored in any retrieval system, or transmitted in any form by any means—electronic, mechanical, photocopy, recording, or otherwise—without prior written permission of the author, except in cases of a reviewer quoting brief passages in a review.

This is a work of fiction. Names, characters, places, and incidents either are the products of the author's imagination or are used fictitiously. Any resemblance to actual persons, living or dead, businesses, companies, events, or locales is entirely coincidental.

Edited by Polished Perfection

Cover Design by Covers by Christian

For Dom, we love you more than Pop Rocks and tail flicks.

1

B*ounce.*
    With my back on the bed and my legs spread-eagled up the wall, I toss the bright yellow stress ball right between my feet. I keep bouncing it back and forth to myself while I lip sync to the nineties music that's playing out of the headphones attached to the portable CD player resting on my stomach.

I like colors, so the ball and blue CD player are two of my favorite things in here. It helps to make up for the rest of the drab surroundings. My hair does the job too, since it's a bright ombré with orange at the roots and yellow at the tips.

I've tried to bedazzle my jail-issued inmate numbers that are printed over my breast pocket, but the guards didn't like that too much, and they made me take it off. Such a drag. So I've resorted to just coloring it purple instead. Nothing in the rule book against that.

The walls and floor all around me are boring gray concrete, no doubt suffused with some kind of magic—just like the silver cuffs around my wrists. Not that I'd try to break out of here. That would be stupid.

Bounce.

My CD skips, the words to "No Scrubs" by TLC getting all choppy on me. Damn. I'm going to have to bribe another guard for a new CD soon, and sometimes, I get stuck with some questionable ones. I just had to listen to "My Heart Will Go On" by Celine Dion for a week straight before I got this new CD. It was torture.

I hit the forward button until "MMMBop" by Hanson plays, and I smile. Such a classic.

I'm humming happily to the lyrics when I hear footsteps rushing my way. I pull down my headphones, letting them rest against my neck so I can listen. Yep, someone is definitely coming.

I tilt my head backward until it's hanging off the side of the bed, just as someone reaches my cell. I study him upside down, but even from my vantage point, I can see that the dude is not a guard from this paranormal jail I'm currently residing in. I know all the guards in this place, and he's not one of them.

I cock my head, looking him up and down. He's wearing some major stealth clothes, all black, armored, and uber boring. He's tall and damn scary looking, with a wicked scar down his left cheek.

"Cut yourself shaving?" I ask before digging into my pocket and grabbing a packet of Pop Rocks candy. I dump some onto my tongue, and the grains immediately start popping like there's miniature gunfire going off in my mouth. It's like an adrenaline rush and a candy rush all in one.

"Are you Sinclair?" he asks, ignoring my question.

"What?" I call around the insanely loud popping going off in my mouth.

Frustration crosses his face. "I said, are you Sinclair Denali?"

I hold my hand up to my ear. "Can't hear you!"

A tic in his jaw pulses with irritation, and he leans his face closer to the bars. "Stop eating that shit and tell me your fucking pack name!"

"Geez, no need to yell. I'm sitting right here," I tell him with exasperation. "And I think the word you're looking for is *lounge*, not pack."

"What?" he snaps, confusion taking over his purpose-filled gaze.

I've gotten him so wound up that he's nearly turning purple, but I just happily crunch the rest of the candy in my mouth and swallow them, enjoying the little pops as they travel down my throat.

"Lounge, Assassins R Us. A group of lizards is called a lounge. Not a pack," I explain as I lick my lips, searching for any stray sugary morsels.

He lets out a giant huff. "The general term for any group of shifters is *pack*," he argues, like I'm some bratty five-year-old that needs to be put in my place. "Are you Sinclair Denali of the Denali *pack* or not?" he asks again, glaring at me as he hits a hard *K* on the word.

"Yep, that's me," I finally admit, ready to move onto the next phase of this little game we're playing. I'm *very* familiar with this game. I've been forced to play it quite a few times already.

I stuff the remainder of the candy packet back in my pants pocket. I have to ration these bad boys. I have sentencing later today, and if all goes well, I'll be headed to Nightmare Penitentiary—the supernatural prison. That place is like the holy grail of prisons for our kind, and the security is top notch, so bozos like this dude won't be able to pay me a visit. At least I hope not.

"Good. I'm here to break you out," the Liam Neeson wannabe announces. His chest puffs up with his words, and I can just tell that he wants to put his hands on his hips and let the Superman vibes waft all over me. I bat them away, and it's my turn to exhale an exasperated huff.

Not again.

I frown and sit up, my poor stress ball falling to the floor from my inattention and my CD player forgotten on the bed. I stand up and walk over to him, and man, he's even uglier up close. His face looks like he's in a permanent scowl, his eyebrows are almost grown together, and his fanged teeth are in serious need of orthodontic work. "I'm pretty sure breaking out a prisoner is against supernatural law. Or human law, even. Lots of laws across the board. Super illegal, man."

"Alpha Bowen hired us to retrieve you."

As soon as I hear that name, I quickly spin, scoop up my stress ball, and lie back down on my bed, stretched up legs and all. "Like I told the last guy, no thanks," I say before opening my pop candy again. This calls for some serious sugar. "I'm good."

I go back to bouncing and sugar popping.

Bounce. Bounce. Bounce. Pop. Pop. Pop.

The guy gapes at me from the other side of my bars. "*What?*"

I tilt my head back again, sighing when I have to swallow my candy prematurely. "I said no thanks," I repeat slowly, rolling my eyes.

You'd think Alpha Bowen and his hard-on for power could hire smarter cronies. I run my gaze over the dim-witted version of Assassin's Creed...hmm, guess I'm giving him too much credit.

"As much fun as it is to explain this for the fifth time since I got myself locked up, I *want* to be in here. It's exactly the stay-cation I've been looking for," I tell him.

I watch his face, waiting for the bewilderment to crawl

over his features just like it did with every other Prison-Break-Barbie that came before him...*and there it is.*

I wish these dudes would just take a hint already. I'm in here because I want to be. Well not *here* exactly, I'm waiting to get to Nightmare Penitentiary, but who knew the wheels of justice took so fucking long to turn? I mean, how long does it take to throw the book at someone?

I'm hoping after my sentencing today that I *finally* get transferred, and then Alpha Bowen and his lounge of over-muscled fuckwits won't be able to get to me anymore.

I still can't figure out how Bowen found me in the first place. I was so careful not to leave tracks. The not knowing gives me an itch that skitters just under my skin and makes my tail twitch with irritation. It makes me want to run, but I'm *so* close. Just a few more hours and I'll be out of his reach, *and* out of reach from my own lounge.

There's a long, awkward pause, like the henchman wasn't expecting this at all. Don't they talk to each other? If he'd just chatted with Henchman One through Four, he'd have known all of this already.

"You're saying...you *want* to stay in jail?" he inquires, his face scrunching up like the words are sour in his mouth.

"Ding, ding, ding! What do we have for our winner, Bob?" I reply cheerfully.

The cell goes quiet, all except for the steady bouncing of my ball against the wall. I clear my throat. "Um...you should probably go," I point out. "Don't want to get caught and end up where I am, right? Well...unless you want to hide out too. But let me just tell you, it takes *way* longer to get punished than you think it will. I mean, I broke *so* many laws! What the hell is taking them so long?" I shake my head. "The paranormal judicial system needs some serious work."

He blinks. I bounce.

During his silent gaping, the prison alarms start going

off really loudly and red emergency lights begin to flash. I point at the flashing lights and gesture for him to run along. "See? You better hurry up."

I pull my borrowed headphones back over my ears and blare some Backstreet Boys to drown out the noise. I sigh and shake my head when the militia reject starts to fiddle with the lock on my cell door instead of making a break for it like I told him to.

Suddenly, there's an explosion of magic and sulfur, and my door bursts open. Sitting up, I cough and glare, waving my hand in front of my face to try and dispel the black glittering smoke that's now filling my cell.

Dammit. I was having such a nice day today, too.

Scarface runs up and grabs me, and that's when I stop being Miss Nice Cockatrice.

One second, he's hauling me to my feet, and the next, I grab his wrist, spin faster than he can blink, and I pivot. Using my momentum and strength, I lift him clear off the floor and flip him over, sending him crashing onto his back. His head smacks against my metal bed frame with a sickening crack, and just like that, the dude is out cold.

"Maybe next time, you'll listen to me," I tut as I dust off my hands and lie back down on my bed.

Getting comfortable again, I grab one of the magazines that I keep stuffed under my thin mattress. Flipping to the article the guard Paul told me about, I'm just getting to the part about how chandeliers are a necessity in creating an awesome she-shed, when two prison guards come running in. They take one look at my open cell door, the magic smoke still polluting the air, the unconscious male on the ground, and turn gaping looks at me.

I give them a bright smile and point down at Scarface. "Hey, Paul. Could you clean that up for me? I think he wet himself."

Paul lowers his gun and pulls off his SWAT-style helmet. "Another one?" he asks, jerking his chin toward my uninvited cell guest.

I shrug my shoulders and give him an apologetic smile. He shakes his head and nudges the unconscious jail-breaker with his boot. "Damn. We need to up our security. We aren't used to so many supernaturals trying to break someone out of here," he says, scratching the back of his neck as he frowns in thought.

"Yeah, it's very disruptive," I tell him.

He grunts in agreement. "Good thing your ride is here," Paul mentions casually as my unwelcome cell guest groans loudly from the floor.

I squeal and start clapping excitedly, which startles both guards. "Yes, finally!" I shoot up from my cot and thrust both arms out, ready for the required shackles whenever a prisoner is being transported.

Paul releases an amused chuckle, and Terrence—the other guard in my cell right now—gives me some judgement-laced side-eye as I giggle and wait like a kid on Christmas morning for the cuffs to click into place.

I'm *finally* going to be sentenced and booked into Nightmare Penitentiary. I can't fucking wait.

My knee bounces up and down rapidly. The movement jingles the links connected to my tail chain, my ankle chain, and my wrist chain. I'm two people away from freedom, and it's so close I can almost taste it.

The armored car ride over here was thankfully uneventful. I was thoroughly searched by a dour female guard once I arrived, and then I was grunted at by the most useless lawyer I could find. After all that excitement, I was led to this side room where all the other prisoners are waiting for their time in front of the judge.

"Judge O'Vine likes it when you look nervous," a large wolf shifter to my left announces.

I turn to her, ready to announce that it's not nerves but eager anticipation that has me all bouncy, but she keeps talking.

"He likes the contrite pretty ones, so you should be fine. Mind your manners and don't let any foul language sneak out. You'll have probation in no time," she adds, looking me over like she can read my rap sheet with just a glance.

I offer her a sweet smile and start compiling a list of swear words to use in my head. I should've gotten that neck tattoo I was planning on, but there just wasn't time. Damn my matriarch for fucking with things and throwing me off schedule.

The dirty door in the yellowing tiled room suddenly opens, and I look up. "Case 11764," a deep voice calls.

I shoot up out of my seat like a rocket. "That's me!"

The wolf shifter next to me snickers, and I can almost hear the accusation of *rookie* in it. I ignore the aural jibe and square my shoulders, trying to look as rough and unapologetic as possible.

I'm escorted into a room that looks like it was decorated by a woodchuck. Every inch of it is some different form of lacquered or polished wood, and shiny mahogany benches sit atop a duller floor of the same material. A waist-high partition separates an empty viewing area with two tables, and I breathe a sigh of relief that no one is sitting there waiting to either break me out or speak on my behalf. That would be super inconvenient.

I take a spot behind a table next to my toadstool of a lawyer, which is difficult, because they have my tail chained down to my legs, and it makes sitting awkward. I look down at the yellow, orange, and red feathers that tip my scaled tail and make sure they're all accounted for. Nothing I hate worse than losing pretty tail feathers. They're a cockatrice's pride and joy.

I get myself settled as much as I can and look up to find a —surprise, surprise—mahogany judge's bench. A massive black-robed figure shuffles papers as I take my place, and I can't help but stare at Judge O'Vine because the dude is a massive minotaur.

I've never seen one in person before. I'm completely taken aback by just how gargantuan he is. I run my surprised green eyes over his furry arms and his serious rack—of horns, that is.

I'm tempted to immediately shift my hair until it's blood-red, instead of the ombré yellow-orange that I love, but I decide to wait. I'll keep that as the pièce de résistance in case my sailor mouth and *give no fucks* attitude doesn't get the job done.

The prosecutor clears his throat. "Sentencing case 11764: The Supernatural People against Sinclair Denali, a female cockatrice shifter who has been convicted of: Breaking and Entering, Grand Theft Auto, Indecent Exposure, Disturbing the Peace, Public Endangerment, Reckless Driving, Evading Arrest, Assault, Assault with a Deadly Weapon—"

"It was a glitter bomb," I scoff, rolling my eyes. "How is a glitter bomb classified as a deadly weapon?" I demand, internally smiling when the judge glares at me and slams his gavel down twice.

"The defendant will remain silent until all charges are read," he warns and then turns back toward the suited man reading off my offences.

"Damaging Public Property, Defacing a Monument—"

I chuckle at that, and the judge's horned head snaps

back to me, his eyes alight with promises of retribution if I ignore his command to be quiet again.

I got you right where I want you, bull boy, and I haven't even had to drop any T-bombs yet.

The prosecutor looks back at the file in his hands. "And lastly, Fraud."

Judge O'Vine gives a terse nod and then looks back to me. He takes me in more thoroughly, and his eyes fill with confused interest. He turns to the prosecutor. "Did the jail get new uniforms?" he asks while studying my bright purple scrub outfit.

Wow, talk about unobservant. I've been standing here for almost four minutes and he's just now noticing my sweet threads?

"Not that I know of," the prosecutor answers.

The chains clink as I raise my hand and wait to be called on. The judge eyes me for a beat before dropping his chin. I take that as a sign to go ahead and explain. "I'm a cockatrice, right? I'm sure you know how much my species *loves* color. But check this, it turns out that I have this super awesome ability to change the color of things that have extended contact with my body," I tell him, running my chained hands down my bright purple uniform.

He just looks at me.

"I can do clothes, shoes, underwear, my hair and my feathers, my nails...pretty much anything if it touches me for long enough. I once made out with a boy in eleventh grade for so long that I turned his skin green, which was awesome because it's, like, one of my *favorite* colors."

I lift my hand and put it to the side of my mouth like I'm about to tell the judge a secret. "Downside, though? He wasn't a great kisser. I kept thinking if I kiss him the way I wanted to be kissed, he'd catch on, hence the long make out session, but he didn't get the hint. He kept doing this fish out of water thing with his tongue, and that just doesn't work for kissing. Well, not unless he's kissing someone's cli—"

"Enough!" Judge O'Vine shouts, cutting me off. He shoots me a disapproving look and then shakes his head like he's trying to clear it of something.

I try not to roll my eyes. What a prude. He's probably a flaily tongue kisser too.

I look down at myself while the judge takes a second to collect his thoughts. I like my purple jail scrubs. I picked the color just for today. It complements my shamrock green eyes and the pink undertones in my otherwise peachy-bisque pallor. My citrus hair is luscious, layered, and on-point, while my long lashes and nails are black, because in my opinion, that's *always* the best color combo for lashes and nails. It adds just the right amount of drama and badass to really get you through anything. Color is very important. Get the wrong combo, and it can totally ruin your day.

A throat clears somewhere in the room, and I pull my thoughts away from my outfit and colors.

"What do you have to say for yourself in regards to your crimes?" Judge O'Vine asks me, like some disappointed father who expected more from me.

If he only knew who my mother was and what she and my father were all about, he'd know I'm too far gone to be affected by that attempt.

The lawyer looks at me from the corner of his eye as I open my mouth to answer. "In my defense, Your Honor, the ice cream truck was left unsupervised, and it was hot. I was just helping out by driving it to the park. I would've been happy to pay for the ice cream I gave away, but no one gave me a chance," I explain. "Next thing I knew, the police were tearing into the parking lot, and it's only natural to want to get away from that. If anything, it's their fault that I evaded. They spurred my fight or flight response."

"Is that so?" the judge drawls.

"Yes. And I object to the Reckless Driving charge. The ice cream truck couldn't even go over forty. The cops are the ones who ran me into the side of the bridge. So if anyone should be charged with damaging things, it should be them."

My lawyer sighs and rubs his fingers over his brow as his hairline begins to get a bit dewy with sweat.

"It's true," I insist. "After that, jumping off the side of the bridge was the only way to get out of the wrecked truck. I didn't know there was a sign posted saying not to jump off the bridge. And if I hadn't stripped out of my wet clothes, I probably would have caught pneumonia."

Honestly, all of this should be self-explanatory.

"Sidenote, telling a woman that her naked body is *indecent* is rude," I add, holding up a finger at the prosecutor. "And I kissed the cop, I didn't *assault* him. He's the one who slipped *me* the tongue. If he hadn't distracted me with that move, I would've remembered the glitter bomb and warned him," I explain, sure to insert a shit ton of irritation in my tone and exasperation in my features. From everything I researched, a sure fire way to piss off a judge is to defend bad behavior and blame other people for your actions.

Of course, I had bigger plans put in motion for how to get imprisoned, but when my matriarch announced that my mating had been moved up by several months, desperate times called for desperate measures. The ice cream truck really was just sitting there like a fucking gift from the ether. It was just asking to be put to good use, and I'm an opportunist.

The bullish judge stares at me like he's waiting for me to say more. *Hmm, how to end this...*

"Oh yeah, and you're a shit-for-balls, ass hat wearing prude, who probably can't kiss for shit!" I say.

My lawyer winces.

"Fuck all the fucks, and cover them in cunt gravy. Cash me outside, cuz I ain't even sorry. Go blow your horn, you overgrown useless minotaur. How do you like them apples?" I spout off evenly, like I'm reading from the dictionary instead of trying to piss off the judge and extend my sentence as much as I can by being as foul and offensive as possible.

Judge O'Vine just shakes his head instead of becoming the level of irate I was hoping for.

Well, that's disappointing.

"Sinclair Denali, it's clear to me that you have some serious emotional and mental issues that need attention. I hereby sentence you to one year in Nightmare Penitentiary, followed by two years of probation where you will get the mental health support you are in desperate need of."

I stare at the minotaur motherfucker, completely shocked. *One year?* How the fuck am I only getting one year? Did he not hear the list of shit I did? I literally set off a glitter bomb in a human police officer's face before tackling his mouth with my tongue. And that was after I stole a damn ice cream truck and threw all the merchandise out of the window at unsuspecting children while blaring "Chain Hang Low" by Jibbs over the speakers.

I need more time than that, dammit! I fucking earned it fair and square!

Fear flashes through me, and I feel my lungs caving in, like they want me to hyperventilate. I can't be imprisoned for only a year; I need at least a solid five. I need long enough to get away, to be forgotten, and to become useless to the fucked up plans everyone has for me.

One year only manages to put a tiny little kink in other people's bullshit, and the probation afterward will make it hard as fuck to run. They tag shifters on parole, and the chip is a major pain in the ass to get removed. I'm not even sure if I have the contacts to get something like that done before my matriarch and Alpha Bowen would swoop in and forever ruin my life.

Reality kicks me in the gut like a minotaur's hoof, and I panic.

"Are you fucking kidding me?" I demand, as I hoist myself up on top of the table and spread my arms wide.

I almost lose my balance because my poor, beautiful tail is prohibited from moving, but I tighten every muscle I have and straighten up. All the guards in the room grow tense.

"*One year*? That's the best you can do? How the fuck did you get this job? I'm a motherfucking menace!" I bellow as I jump down from the table and hobble-run for the judge.

Judge O'Vine just leans back in his overstuffed high back chair and looks at me like I'm proving his point about needing mental help as I run at him. Stupid male doesn't realize I don't need that kind of help. What I *need* is to be locked away where no one can get to me. This asshole is ruining everything! I shift my hair to be blood-red and glare at him as I close the distance between us.

"Toro toro, you little bitch!" I scream at him, taunting him with the call that a bullfighter uses.

Judge O'Vine's eyes fill with indignant fire, and satisfaction floods me.

Yes, get mad, get even, extend my sentence...please!

I lift my hands to mock his curved horns, but I'm side-tackled by a guard before I can take another step. The impact knocks the wind out of me, which also makes it impossible to scream more offensive shit at the judge. I had a good *Your mother was bred in a barn, and your father was ridden by cowboys* ready at the tip of my tongue, but I'm forced to choke it down and gasp for air instead as I'm carried out of the room.

No! This can't be how it goes down!

I scramble to get out of the guard's hold, but it's solid, and the magical cuffs around my wrists, ankles, and tail make it impossible to shift into my cockatrice. The door closes behind me, and my chance at pissing off Judge O'Vine so he'll throw the book at me slips out of my fingers. I pull in deep breaths and fume at my luck.

Okay. Time to change tactics.

I immediately begin to look for ways to solve the problem. So they won't lock me up and throw away the key...yet. I'll just have to figure out a way in prison to change their minds. That shouldn't be too hard.

I hope.

2

It takes about an hour for me to get booked into Nightmare Penitentiary's system. Someone keeps hacking into the jail's systems and deleting my file, so they have to put everything in manually so that I can be transferred. Alpha Bowen and his annoying attempts to thwart what's about to happen will soon be in my past.

The booking officers versus my arresting officers aren't so different, except the arresting officers at least offered me coffee. These jerkoffs just ignore me when I tell them I could do with a caffeine kick.

Rude.

I sit at a desk with an overweight ghoul who has a very distinct lisp, waiting while he enters everything into the computer. He grumbles with every offense he has to add to my rap sheet. I guess all cops hate doing paperwork.

When he's finished filing all my charges, he leads me to a room where I change into my new Nightmare Penitentiary uniform which consists of a very drab gray ensemble. The guard points me to the lined wall that clearly displays height measurements. I get a little spring in my step.

"Oh, another mugshot!" I start running my fingers

through my colorful hair. "How do I look?" I ask, my lips a little duckish as I pose for him.

He levels me with a look. "Like a convict," he says dryly.

"But like a cool, hip convict? A pretty convict? Or like an understated, *she's probably a really good person beneath that pile of convictions* convict?"

"Are you for fucking real?"

I would admit that yes, I am, but instead, I decide to close my mouth because I don't think Officer Ghoul is in a very friendly mood.

"Heels against the line. Stand up straight. Hold this," he says, pushing the placard at me.

I grab it and turn it around so I can read it. "Look at that, it has my name on it and everything."

I get in position and straighten my new uniform shirt, but I frown down at the gray color. With a thought, I use my shifter ability to change its color. It's a rare gift for my kind, and it does have its limits. Certain things have to have contact with me longer in order to change. Like shoes or really bad kissers.

For some reason, I can only shift my hair and tail feathers into shades of orange, yellow, or red. I suspect those tones are my natural color spectrum, so it restricts what I can do, but I love those colors, so I don't feel restricted. Oddly enough, I can't change my eye color at all. They're a bright emerald green, and they always have been.

When I look down once again, the uniform is now a lovely lemon yellow. "There. That's better."

"No."

My brows pull together. "But—"

"No."

"It's just that the gray—"

"No," he says for a third time.

I sigh, making the fabric ripple with my skin until the

color leeches out and my shirt is gray again. "There. Satisfied? You just made my shirt go from happy to depressed."

"Yep."

He picks up a camera from a shelf behind him, and I quickly take position. I want a nice mugshot, after all. I decide to go for a demure half-smile because I know that once my matriarch sees this, it'll really piss her off. I'm basically smirking at her with a big *fuck you* in my eyes.

He takes the first shot, and then has me stand in profile, and I hear the click of the camera again. "Done."

"Can I see it?" I ask.

"No."

I sigh. "Can I at least keep my placard?"

"No."

"You should really broaden your vocabulary," I mutter.

"My shift is ending, and all I want to do is sit on my couch and drink a beer. So get your ass in the portal so you can be somebody else's problem."

"That's the spirit. Way to go above and beyond the line of duty."

Ignoring me, he leads me through the back and stops at an unassuming white door. "Go."

My heartbeat kicks up in anticipation. This is it. After all my planning, I'm finally going to the terrifying supernatural prison. This is so exciting.

I turn the doorknob and push open the door, coming face-to-face with the swirling smoke of the portal. I head forward without hesitation, confidently going straight down the middle. There's no way anyone can try to bust me out now.

With a smug step, I move out of the grasp of Alpha Bowen and my matriarch, and right into the clutches of Nightmare Penitentiary.

I step out of the portal door, and as soon as it swings shut, it disappears. I turn full-circle to look around. Immediately, I feel the damp cool air, which is so different from the stagnancy of the jail office. "Man, I am not in Kansas anymore," I mumble as I take in my surroundings.

If this wasn't a convenient solution to my serious life problems, I might take this opportunity to run. I don't have an escort, and surprisingly, the portal didn't deposit me inside the prison like I expected. But as I run my eyes over the damp flat landscape and the thick tree line in the distance, I gather that there's probably nothing surrounding this place for miles.

Good.

That should put a stop to the shenanigans that were taking place at the jail. It's a good holding cell for supernatural criminals, but it's not meant for anything long-term, and it's definitely not up to the task of keeping crazy ass alphas from trying to break out prisoners. But this place is.

I turn forward and take in the ominous spread before me. There's a large gothic gate about ten feet away with the initials *NP* wrapped in barbed wire.

Nightmare Penitentiary.

I made it.

The gate itself is iron and tall, and past it, there are massive buildings that look like a cross between a decrepit castle and a creepy mausoleum.

Thorny vines are overgrown and trailing up the stone walls, and there are some menacing gargoyles carved as sentries on the top spires. There's enough magic coming from the gate that it's giving me goosebumps. There's some serious power ingrained in that to keep the prisoners inside and everyone else out, which is exactly what I need.

Nightmare Penitentiary is an ominous fortress meant to keep supernatural people with all sorts of abilities and power on lockdown. It's the most intimidating and protected place in our paranormal world. Everything about it screams *scary*. There are even bats flying around as a dense fog creeps in all around me just to add to the terrible ambiance.

It's awesome.

I smile as the gate creaks open and a really terrifying dude walks out. He's wearing a long brown leather trench coat that has a distinct steampunk vibe to it and bulging pockets, probably filled with all sorts of weapons. He has a wicked glare and a cigarette hanging from his mouth that's making an odd amount of smoke trail behind him as he walks.

He stops in front of me, and I'm forced to crane my neck up to look at him. I've never wanted to wear platform shoes so badly until right at this moment. "Man, you could give a girl a real crick in the neck."

He ignores that completely. "I'm the Warden here. You'll be in Section One for the minor offenses. You even *think* about escaping, you will find yourself brought to the deeper levels, and trust me, you won't survive down there for a single day."

I pat him on the shoulder. "You don't have to worry your scary little head about me, Warden. I'm a big fan of your work here. I'll be the model prisoner, just as soon as I get my measly sentence increased."

He narrows his eyes and looks me over like he's not sure what to make of that. He takes a deep pull of his smoke stick. "Follow me."

"Aye, aye, Captain Warden, sir."

He turns and starts stalking through the gate, which creaks just as loudly as it shuts behind us. I know the magic is sealing me in, and I breathe a little sigh of relief. Our footsteps crunch on the cracked stone walkways as the Warden brings me toward one of the large buildings. I tap the doorway for good luck as we head inside.

Section One really completes the whole dreary vibe. Crumbling plaster, thick iron bars, and the sound of distant snarls. The Warden leads me down the corridor with questionable lighting, where I pass several inmates. I start waving at everyone as I pass them by.

"Hey!" I call to a gnome dude who's doing some crunches on his cell floor. He ignores me, and I turn and wave to a chick in the next cell across the way who has an iron blindfold clasped over her eyes and snakes for hair. "Oh, a gorgon!" I say excitedly as I step up to her cell. "I've always loved gorgons. Your snake hair is kickass."

She cocks her head, nose flaring as she faces me, unable to see because of her confined eyesight. "Fuck off."

"Well, that's not very friendly," I say with a frown. "We're gonna be neighbors, and we should form an alliance or something. You know, support girl power and all that."

Her blue snakes start hissing at me, and I hold my hands up. "Alright, geez. I'll go find someone else."

"Inmate 11764, get your ass up here," the Warden calls from ahead.

I hurry to catch up to him. When I spot a goblin picking at his gold-capped teeth as he sits on his bed, I stop again. "Hey there, can you please tell me what the coolest prison gangs are in this place?"

The goblin looks at me with disdain and then spits a piece of dislodged food at my feet. Ew.

"11764!" the Warden shouts in warning. He really has a problem with patience.

"Alright, you think about it and get back to me," I tell the goblin as I catch up with my line leader again.

He unlocks an empty cell and shoves the door open. Crossing his arms, he glares at me. "Get in and shut up."

"Cheers," I say brightly.

When I don't walk in fast enough, the Warden grabs me by the collar of my shirt and shoves me in. I feel a sting at my tail as I go stumbling in, and I spin to see the warden shoving something orange in one of his pockets.

"Did you just pluck one of my feathers?" I demand incredulously, looking down so I can inspect the damage. He totally did.

"For my collection," he replies ominously as he slams the door behind me, and a speckle of magical smoke bursts out from the lock to seal me in at the same time that the chains around my limbs and tail disappear in a puff.

He walks away, and I have no fucking clue what I'm supposed to make of that. Miffed, I pet the spot on my tail that's now a feather down before turning around to take in my surroundings.

"Ahh. Cell sweet cell," I say as I breathe in the nice stagnant air.

Seeing the extra prison-issued uniforms that are waiting for me on the bed, I gather them and set them on the small desk that sits at the foot of the bed on the same wall. I have a metal toilet and a small sink in here, and that about rounds up the decor. Directly across from me, I can see a wall and the very edge of another prisoner's iron bars, but at this angle, I'm not able to see the supernatural inside.

I release a relieved sigh. I settle back on my lumpy bed with my hand under my head, ready to live the Nightmare Penitentiary life.

Ah. I've never felt so free.

By the time the cell doors open for dinner, I'm starving.

I'm going to have to get my new system worked out here. The holding jail was super easy to bribe some guards and ally with other inmates to get the good shit. Like Pop Rocks candy and extra pillows. Luckily for me, I was pretty much made for this prison life. There's no way this place can be harder to navigate than my family.

I don't need my matriarch and patriarch to sell me off to be mated to a shifter who just wants me for the alliance and money. I'm not property to be auctioned off, and I'll be damned if I'm forced to become a trophy mate hanging off some douche's arm—or worse, under his thumb like I have been with my mat and pat my whole life. No thanks.

Unfortunately, when your lounge leader decides to mate you to someone, there is no telling them no. I'd be exiled, clipped, and stripped of the Denali name, and that's if I'm lucky. I'm *never* lucky, and my *no* would most likely be a death sentence, even though my matriarch is my damn mother.

But getting imprisoned? There's nothing my mat and pat can do about that. Shifter packs aren't above supernatural law. It can't be held against me, and there isn't fuck-all they can do about it. This is my self-induced vacation. The perfect way to get away from everyone trying to dictate or steal my future.

By the time I get out of here, Alpha Bowen will have moved on to someone else, and my matriarch's anger will have faded. Hopefully. Now I just need to make sure this vaycay lasts longer than a year.

I walk in line with the other inmates as we head down the drab gray corridor with a pretty yellow line painted down the middle. I let the movements of the other convicts direct me where to go. After passing the rest of the cell block and heading up a set of metal stairs, the herd of gray clad bodies spills into a large cafeteria room.

It's like the Great Hall in Hogwarts except with fluorescent lighting, cement picnic style benches, and it smells like toe-cheese. Okay, so it's not like the Great Hall at all. It looks like it's segregated by cliques and gangs rather than Houses. There are definitely no Hufflepuffs up in here.

I look around the tables, my eyes scanning over everyone. I see a dozen gorgons in the far corner, their hair snakes hissing at one another. They all start laughing as soon as I come in, like they can sense me even though they're all wearing iron blindfolds. I guess that group is gonna need more time to warm up to me.

There's another group of some vampires with a posse of fang bangers hanging all over them. Most of the vamps are forgoing the food completely and are just sucking on willing veins instead.

I don't blame the fang bangers at all. I've been bitten by a vamp once at a rave. I orgasmed on the dance floor just as soon as their sharp teeth pricked my skin. Vamp venom is a very powerful aphrodisiac, but the crash afterward is a bitch. It was like coming down from the highest of horny highs to dealing with the world's worst PMS lows. I ate an entire palette of cookie dough ice cream, texted my ex, and plucked out way too much of my eyebrows.

The fang banger option is gonna be a hard pass for me.

Turning around, I head to the buffet-style assembly line and pick up a red plastic tray and empty paper plate. The male in front of me turns around and growls when I accidentally bump into his back.

I roll my eyes. "Calm down, Big Bad Wolf. It was an accident."

"The fuck you say?"

Groan. Wolf shifters think they're such hot shit. They've

fancied themselves the public's favorite shifter ever since *Twilight* came out.

"Go huff and puff on your little piggy, mmkay?" I tell him with false sweetness.

The wolf shifter looks at me incredulously, and he's a big dude, but the way he's squinting at me makes me think he's a little slow.

I hear a female snicker behind me, and I shoot her an awkward thumbs up where my hand is still clutching the edge of my tray.

He, in turn, tosses his tray to the floor with a loud clack —needlessly wasting food, I might add—and faces me, rolling back his shoulders like he wants to intimidate me. "I will fucking crush you, lizard girl."

My eyes widen. "Oh, this is gonna be my first prison fight!" I say with excitement. I set my tray down responsibly and then rub my hands together and bounce from one foot to the other. "Alright, go ahead. I'll give you the first punch."

His bushy brows pull together. "Huh?"

I pat my chest. "Just not the face, okay? I've managed to go this long without a broken nose, and I'd like to keep it that way," I explain. "I know that might not sound like a big deal, but I'm very scrappy. I got in a lot of fights as a kid."

He hesitates, like he's not really sure what to do with me. We've created a scene by now, and the entire cafeteria has quieted down to watch our exchange. The workers serving the food ignore us completely though, and the guards stationed along the walls look like they're taking bets. I wonder if I can get in on that action?

"Just to be clear, what does the winner get?"

"What?" he snaps.

"Bragging rights? First turn at the toilet? You become my prison bitch?"

A new growl bursts from his chest, and then he charges

at me. I jump out of the way, watching as he spins on his heels, fury in his eyes.

But before he can pummel me, the same female who laughed earlier steps between us smoothly and tosses him a bored look. She's wearing the same gray scrubs as everyone else, and she has black dreadlocks pulled back at the nape of her neck, dark skin, and golden eyes. She also has a metallic-green tattoo of a tiny lotus flower beside her left eye that seems to shimmer slightly. "Beast, stop your growling and go lick your hairy balls," she tells him.

"Fuck off, Zen. This is between me and the lizard girl."

I crinkle my nose at the nickname and hold up my finger, leaning around Zen to speak. "Excuse me, if you're giving out prison nicknames, can it be something better than *lizard girl*? Because I can't work with that one. There's no amount of bedazzling that can make that look good on the ass of my pants. While we're at it, let's think up something new for you too. Beast is just so...predictable. And let's be honest, Belle and that library-giving hottie she's with really fucked with the terror that the name Beast used to evoke."

Beast seems to get irrationally angry at that statement and just starts growling at me like crazy. I blink at him as he starts frothing at the mouth, tawny hair breaking out over his skin.

"He's gonna get the collar!" someone yells out with excitement.

Sure enough, as soon as Beast starts shifting on all fours, some of the prison guards rush over and clamp a metal collar around his neck. His body pauses mid-shift. Everyone winces and oohhh's. It looks painful as hell, and a shiver runs up my spine at the sight of a shifter stuck in their shift. The unnaturalness of it messes with me, and I watch as he's led away like a stray to the pound.

The female, Zen, turns to me and shakes her head. "Damn, girl. I've never seen Beast hate someone so much at first sight."

I shrug and pick up my tray again. "I'd say that was a new experience for me...but I'd be lying."

Snickering again, Zen follows me as I continue back to the food. The rest of the inmates in line are still paused, watching me. They're blocking the goods, though, and I really am hungry, so I start to elbow my way between two of them as they watch me, shuffling over awkwardly. "I'm just gonna slide past you and get some of that coleslaw."

I serve myself, piling up the creamy cabbage deliciousness in one high mountain. I don't know what it is, but I just love cafeteria food. I flourished in elementary school. "Mmm. Perfect."

One of the cafeteria servers comes up and dumps down some tuna casserole next. I fill up the rest of the plate with that and some red Jell-O. I *love* red Jell-O.

Pleased with my collection, I turn to figure out what table I'm going to sit at, but Zen stops me as I pick out a small carton of milk. "Can I get some strawberry milk instead?" I ask the servers. The female in the hairnet rolls her eyes and dumps more plain milk into the barrel. I guess that's a no.

"Come on," Zen says to me. I notice she's opted for a plate full of cornbread. I respect that. "You can sit with me."

"Which one is your group?" I ask as I follow her.

"Does it matter?" she asks, cocking a brow at me.

I nod. "It does. It's very important to assimilate myself in the correct prison gang on my first day," I explain. "It has to be a group strong enough that the other gangs won't fuck with us, but not top dog because then that would mean we would always be fighting for dominance, and that shit is exhausting."

"You've thought a lot about this."

"Oh, yeah. I've been getting ready for prison for months now. I had to up my time table last-minute though, so I'm not as up-to-date on all the pruno recipes as I'd like to be, but it is what it is," I tell her on a shrug.

Zen eyes me for a beat before she chuckles and jerks her head in the direction of a cement picnic-style table with a matching cement bench on each side. Immediately, two inmates grab their trays and move, clearing the way for her. She gestures for me to have a seat, her golden eyes gleaming. I cop a squat and take her in with a new light.

Hmm, Zen is *someone* here. I can tell by the way the other inmates react around her.

I shove a massive spoonful of coleslaw into my mouth and chew while I wait. She'll either explain the deal around here, warn me, challenge me, or continue to size me up like she's currently doing. Surprisingly, I don't get a threatening or even a dominant vibe from her. But it's clear by the way others are side-eyeing her that she should be added to my *do not fuck with* list.

I try the tuna casserole next, and I can't help the face I make or the noise that sneaks out of my mouth. "So damn good," I chirp as I swallow the delicious bite down and immediately shove in another. I know I should be getting the lay of the land right now, but this is delicious.

Zen chokes on the bite of cornbread in her mouth and gives me an incredulous look. Huh, maybe the cornbread sucks here? I make a mental note to avoid it.

"What's your name?" she asks after she clears her airway of the offending bite. She opens a carton of milk and downs it.

"Sinclair," I offer around another massive bite of tuna casserole and coleslaw. Man, this combo is fucking glorious. "But if you're handing out nicknames, I'm a fan of

Rainbow Dash, because...color, and let's be honest, she's by far the best pony. Or, if you want to go the other direction, I'm a personal fan of Baby Shanks. Speaking of, can you point me in the direction of someone who needs to be shanked? I have a sentence I need to get tweaked. I also want to get a shank shack going. Think people would pay good money for some nice shanks in here? I need funds for snacks."

Zen stares at me like she's not sure if I'm serious or not. Why do people keep doing that? Is it so hard to believe that someone might actually *want* to be here? I mean, with food like this, it can't be that far-fetched of an idea. I take a bite of my pretty jello and groan. Yep, I'd shank a ho for this jello, no questions asked.

Zen smirks like she just heard that thought. She leans back and gestures over to something and starts to talk, but a flash of fluorescent green snags my attention. I watch as several guards enter the room and take up position where the guards who carried out Beast were previously standing.

Each of them wears crisp navy blue uniforms with their names stitched in white on Velcro-attached name tags over their left breast pocket. Their pants are tucked into black combat boots, and their waists are circled by utility belts with all kinds of goodies attached.

Some of them are beefy as fuck, and some are the definition of dumpy, but the one with the bright hair who's slowly circling the perimeter of the lunch room has my entire focus. His hair style is trendy, a short crisp fade on the sides and a nice disheveled coif on the top, but the color is blowing my mind. It starts out fluorescent green at the front and graduates ombré-style into a darker jeweled green tone, then into turquoises, electric blues, and finishes as a deep royal blue at the base of his skull.

Those colors are drool-worthy. But as my eyes track

down, I notice his tail, his scaled tail with the feathers on the end...just like I have.

Fuck.

I'm immediately drawn in and sucker punched. Because whoever this guard is, he's a cockatrice, and that is a serious fucking problem for me.

I don't recognize him, but that doesn't mean anything. My kind doesn't associate much with other cockatrices outside of our lounge. We have a get together every five or so years where lounges come from all over the world so we can keep an eye out for potential mates, but I've never seen this guy.

I'd remember him.

Bronze skin, forearms I want to lick, tall and muscled with a straight white smile, bright turquoise eyes, and fucking dimples. Dimples! What sort of female can go up against that?

I'm immediately on guard. My tail twitches with both interest and annoyance, and I sink down and hope I'll continue to go unnoticed by him. He lazily makes his way around the lunch room as my synapses fire off with all the possibilities that could explain his presence here.

Could he be an Alpha Bowen henchman? Or someone my mat and pat hired to get me out of here and bend me to their will? Is the ether blessing me with eye candy? Or is his presence a simple coincidence, and I'm reading into it because that's what I've had to do my whole life in order to survive? I simmer in my thoughts and paranoia, wondering what the hell I should do.

I stalk him like prey with my eyes as he moves through the hustle and bustle of the room. Fellow guards greet him as he passes and so do some of the inmates. More than one of the convicts in this room swoons and sighs as he graces them with a dimpled, gleaming smile.

I bet he smells good.

What?

I jerk myself away from those thoughts and try to figure out what to do. He's making his way closer to where I sit, while Zen is still chatting away, but thankfully, he still hasn't spotted me. I'm not sure what I'll do when he does. He's getting closer.

Will I see recognition in his bright turquoise eyes? *Ten feet away.* Attraction? *Eight feet.* A death sentence? *Six feet.*

Shit!

Just when I think I've finally escaped all the anxiety and stress, this fool has to walk in and ruin it. *Four feet.* Anger blooms in my chest as he gets even closer. *Two feet.* Nope. I can't let him fuck this up for me. I *can't*.

I meticulously fold my paper plate into a pie shape and move it and my milk carton to the table. He's right beside me now but still hasn't looked my way. I grab the empty tray with both hands, stand up, rear both arms back, and let 'er rip.

Smack!

He grunts as the tray makes contact with his head. I'm so fast that he doesn't even get a hand up to help protect his gorgeous face.

Shouting sounds off all around me, and I'm only able to get in one more half-cocked whack before something presses into my side, and my body lights up with pain.

I drop to the ground and fold in on myself, electricity and satisfaction surging through me. I clench my teeth as my vision tunnels, and all I can see are pairs of black combat boots as they step into my shrinking line of sight right before I pass out.

3

I smack my lips together to combat the dry cardboard thing currently going on in my mouth. A rhythmic beeping calls my attention, but the feel of cold metal around both of my wrists seems like the more pressing issue to focus on. I groan and work to force my heavy lids open. I blink the room into focus and then jump when I realize there's someone standing close to me...just watching. Creepy.

She has skin the color of cream with Kool-Aid red hair and brows. The intricate braids in her tresses and the pointy tips of her ears give her away as fae. But the vicious vertical scar that starts mid-forehead and runs down past her left eye, ending at the apple of her cheek, is *not* something most fae would have. Fae are vain as fuck, and they also have healers, so the scar on this female's face, along with the glint of mania in her jade green eyes, immediately sets off the beeping monitor that's recording my now rapidly pacing heart.

She watches me with cold interest. I'm not sure what to make of it. I test the cuffs around my wrists, and a clang fills the room. Yep, I'm definitely shackled to a bed.

"My name is Dr. Brina. You're in the medical ward of Nightmare Penitentiary," she tells me in her smooth feminine voice.

I look around at the gray stone walls and floor. I guess I'll just have to take her word for it, because nothing about this place—well, aside from the hospital bed and the heart monitor—screams medical ward to me.

"Do you often suffer from psychotic episodes?" Dr. Brina asks me, her head tilting in a creepy way as she waits for me to answer. She must read the confusion on my face, because she elaborates. "You attacked a guard...unprovoked."

Ah. That.

"He's a cockatrice," I tell her, like that explains it all. My voice is scratchy, and my throat hurts, and I look around hopefully for a glass of water, but there isn't one.

Her scarred eyebrow lifts in question. "You are the same species, and that is what motivated your attack?" she presses, clearly not understanding my explanation.

I shrug, not willing to get into it with a weird stranger who's looking at me like a bug she wants to pull the legs off of under a microscope.

"Well, you seem to be recovered," she tells me, and I can't help but notice the tinge of disappointment in her tone. She pulls a light from her pocket and flashes it in my eyes. I blink through the brightness, flinching slightly at the burn as my pupils contract.

"You had a few bruises on your ribs from where the guards kicked you, but those are all healed up now," she states in an oddly cheerful tone as she steps away. "Apparently, you slept right through that beating, so we'll have to make sure you're awake for the next one."

That announcement has my head snapping in her direction, and she gives me a wink as she walks over to the door and opens it. Fluorescent hair, angry turquoise eyes, and plump lips glower at me from the other side.

Shit.

"You'll learn very quickly here at Nightmare Penitentiary that the staff looks out for our own." She turns to the guard I brained with a cafeteria tray. "If you plan to beat her to the point of unconsciousness, I simply ask that you have her drink what's in the vial before she passes out. I'm sure she has very filling dreams, and I could always use a good meal."

The guard nods, but I'm completely lost as to what she means.

"Have fun," she calls over her shoulder as she steps out of the room. The cockatrice guard steps in and closes the door behind him.

For a moment, the two of us just stare at each other. There isn't a hint of bruising or a bump from where I smacked him with the tray earlier, so either I didn't hit him very hard or he's healed already. I try to stay focused on his eyes so that my gaze doesn't wander up and down his form, because this male is a *very* nice looking specimen. He's hot, plain and simple. My cockatrice wants to get to know his cock...atrice. And that's just plain dangerous.

I've learned that I can't really be trusted when it comes to attractive males. Or bright colors. I tend to do really stupid things when I come into contact with either. And this dude is both hot *and* colorful. He's like fucking neon kryptonite.

"Who are you?" I demand, trying to sound as haughty as possible even though I'm strapped down to a bed.

Instead of answering, he just crosses his arms and props his back against the wall next to the now closed door.

"Are you going to beat me to a pulp or what?" I ask, hoping that him not moving toward me is a good sign. I really don't want to be beaten up. Shifter bodies may heal quickly, but it doesn't mean we don't feel pain.

Silence.

He just stands there, watching me, the expression on his face unreadable. The lack of communication is really scraping my paranoia raw. I just want him to do *something*.

"Well, get on with it," I snap, my anxiety ready to burst out of my chest.

Still nothing from tall, hot, and colorful. Not even a tail twitch. He just studies me, but I have no idea what the hell he's thinking. It's unnerving and makes me feel completely vulnerable.

"Not interested in talking, huh?" I ask as I fiddle with the metal cuffs on my wrists. If he's not going to do anything, then I'm not going to waste my time. I won't just lie here and wait for someone to fuck with me. "Fine. I can talk enough for the both of us."

Using a jiggy-hip move that makes the male's eyes come down to my waist, I shimmy myself down the hospital bed until my feet are hanging off the end and my head is even with my hands. From this vantage point, I'm able to reach my hair, where I have a couple of pins tucked away. "We both know why you deserved to be smacked with a cafeteria tray," I begin as I dig through my orange and yellow hair, trying to find one of the pins to grab. "You were sent here by my mat and pat, weren't you?"

He gives me a blank stare.

"My matriarch and patriarch sent you here because they found out I got myself arrested and they want you to bust me out, right? Well, bad news for you, I have no intention of going anywhere." Finally finding one of the pins, I pluck it out, scraping my scalp and yanking out a few hair strands in the process.

I look over at him as I turn my head and snatch up the

pin with my teeth. He does nothing as I lean over and stick the pin into the lock of the cuff on my right hand. I watch him the entire time, like a challenge.

He's a guard at Nightmare Penitentiary. Dr. Brina insinuated that he came here to beat me, and I'm giving him a very justified reason to do so. Plus, I started it in the cafeteria.

I try to read his expression, but there's nothing. He's not giving away a single thought or emotion, just continues to watch me as I try to break out of my restraints. And his green and blue hair...dammit, I keep getting distracted by it. It's *very* bright.

I wrench my gaze away and continue to dig the pin in, which would probably take someone else a very long time, but I've always had a gift when it comes to picking locks. I've also had plenty of opportunities to master my skill. You'd be surprised how many times I've been shackled.

Finally, the telltale click sounds in my ears, and I grin with the pin still between my teeth as the handcuff pops open. Spitting it into my now free hand, I quickly get to work on the left one. "Hmm, if you were from my mat and pat, you'd probably be more verbose. My mat always likes the talkative types." I shoot a look over at him while I work. "So maybe Alpha Bowen sent you? But really, it doesn't matter much. Because the answer is the same. I'm staying here."

The second cuff pops off, and I sit up victoriously before swinging my legs over the side of the bed and popping the pin back into my hair. I get up and start looking around the room, wondering what exactly the good doctor wanted me to drink so that she could feed off my dreams. Fae are seriously fucked up supernaturals.

As much as I try to seem aloof about the male's presence, I'm completely befuddled, and I'm very aware of his presence. What the hell does he want? And more importantly, why the hell isn't he saying anything?

I run my hands over the vial that says, "drink me" and wrinkle my nose at it as I uncork it. "How very Lewis Carroll of her," I mumble before moving over to the sink and dumping the contents out.

Once the offending liquid is gone, I turn and face the male who still hasn't moved from his spot. "So? Who sent you?"

I don't expect an answer, so I almost flinch when his voice comes out for the first time. "No one sent me."

Sweet cockatrice's feathers, his voice is *sexy*. "Oh, good. You're not mute after all," I snark, though it comes out breathier than I would have liked.

I palm the now empty vial—this would make an epic shank—and move to the wall opposite the guard, mirroring his posture and his wall-lean. I'm almost certain I see a flicker of amusement in his eyes as I copy him, and his dimple ticks like he's working to keep it in place instead of allowing it to move and reveal his beautiful smile. But from one blink to another, his features return to unreadable stone.

"*No one*, huh? Who exactly is that a code word for?" I ask casually, swallowing down my scoff.

If he thinks this is my first interrogation rodeo, then he's in for a surprise. I know all about the half-truth tricks that won't change your scent or otherwise give you away.

"Is that what this is all about?" he asks, his head cocking to the side in a way that I find myself mimicking.

Stop it, Sin. No following the pretty colors and trying to make them do naughty things to you.

"You think that I'm here for you?" he asks. This time, there's no mistaking the amusement that lights up his turquoise eyes. He shakes his head and raises his eyebrows like my presumption is ridiculous. "I'm not sure what you've got going on outside, Sunrise, but from the sound of things, it's a lot of shit I couldn't give two fucks about."

I preen as the nickname Sunrise leaves his full lips. He's spot on. I pulled inspiration for the colors of my hair from the sunrise that dawned on the morning I crawled out my window and walked away from my lounge's land. I appreciate *his* appreciation for my colors. But when the rest of his words fall out of his lips, my appreciation dims dramatically.

"And I'm just supposed to, what? Take your word for it?" I ask, my hand tightening on the glass vial still in my grasp.

"As long as it means no more lunch tray attacks, I don't care what you do. I've worked at NP for years. Just know this is your first and last warning. Don't come for me again. You're a female cockatrice, and that fact alone has earned you the mercy I'm showing today, but don't push me to show you what life looks like without that mercy," he tells me, the warning sending a shiver scurrying up my spine.

His tone growls *don't fuck with me*, but the look in his eyes is almost begging me to. His relaxed posture against the wall and the slight tilt of his head is completely throwing me off. He's warning me away with his words, and yet also ensuring every color in his hair can be seen while maintaining non-threatening body language. He's reeling me in and simultaneously pushing me away.

Desire lights through me and also dims from the mixed messages, like I'm some fucked up strobe light. I'm impressed and irritated at the same time. I've never met anyone who made me want to lick every inch of their body until they worshipped me, and then promptly rip their head off. I study him for a beat. He could be telling the truth, or he could be a *very* skilled plant.

I tilt my head down and look up at him through my lashes. My bright green eyes are filled with contrition and my posture just a skosh shy of submissive. Two can play this game.

"Then I'm sorry for hitting you...twice," I tell him sweetly. I let my gaze rake over him appreciatively and keep my smile from going wider when I notice his pupils dilate. "Mercy looks good on you," I purr. "But I promise, you don't want to see me take mine off either."

I push off from the wall and move slowly toward him. His kissable lips part slightly, but his relaxed mien doesn't budge. All I want to do is nibble on him and find out if he tastes as good as he looks. He doesn't budge as I close the distance between us. There's no hint of worry. No tensing of his well-developed muscles. He's confident that between the two of us, he'd win. How cute.

I stop inches away from him and move my own head so he can get a good look at all the pretty colors in my hair. A smile twitches at the corner of his lips, but he tamps it down. I stand there and just watch him, giving him a little taste of the awkward silence he fed me earlier. I give his bright hair one last glance and then offer him a seductive smile as I lean in.

"You stay away from me, and I'll stay away from you," I declare, and then I crack open the door and purposefully rub against his side as I duck out of the room. The door closes with a click behind me, and I smile, unable to help it. I walk down the gray hallway, with no idea where I am in the prison. I figure someone will stop me at some point and tell me where to go. I hold up the Velcro name tag I just silently ripped off the cockatrice's uniform as I swing left around a corner.

I read the name that's been stitched on it. Well, Officer Rook, I think I'll ask around about you. I smile at my sleight of hand and picture him noticing the missing name tag later and wondering where it went. I chuckle at the thought and high five myself for my mad skills. Prison is going to be so much fun.

Now to find Zen and find out about that shank shack customer list I asked for earlier.

Wait...

I stop in my tracks. Grinding my jaw, I pull my other hand forward and stare at my empty palm for a blink. *That worm!* He stole the vial I had in my hand!

I shake my head, lost between irritation and mirth. What a shit. I chuckle, impressed by the ballsy move, and continue back down the hall in the direction I hope my cell is.

Touché, Officer Rook. Touché.

4

"I've seen some shit."

I nod in commiseration at the female wolf shifter where she sits against the chain link fence in our recreation yard. Recreation yard is putting it nicely. It's basically just a huge square of dirt and weeds and the occasional concrete piece broken off from where there used to be a sidewalk.

"You haven't seen shit," the gorgon with the harmless eyes counters. She doesn't hang out with the other ones or have to wear a blindfold, and they sneer at each other every chance they get. "Until you've walked in on someone shoving a sub sandwich up their ass, you're still a newb."

Someone else titters. "That was hilarious."

"Oh, go flick your clit. I've seen plenty of shit," the wolf, Sophie, says. "I've been in here longer than you have!"

The red snakes on the female's head hiss. "We've been in here for five years."

"So have I!" Sophie growls.

Zen's eyes shoot over to the female, and I see her lotus flower tattoo gleam beneath her eye. Just like that, the anger between the two immediately dissipates, and they sigh on a calming breath.

"Sorry, Sophie," snake-hair says.

The wolf shifter is too blissed out on Zen's zen power to reply. She tips her head back and breathes it in, her whole body relaxing. "I love that shit, Zen."

Our leader just smirks and continues to sit with her legs crossed as she retwists some of her dreadlocks. It seems like very meticulous work.

I wrinkle my brow in concentration as I continue to sharpen the small piece of plastic tray I have in my hand. I've become a bit of a shank connoisseur, and business is booming already. I've sold ten shanks this week, and it's only Thursday.

My first one was from a spork, and I simply sharpened the handle, but I've gotten more creative since then. For my second shank masterpiece, I plucked the teeth off a comb and stuck them in some toothpaste. I then let the whole thing harden overnight. I call that bad boy The Minty Hedgehog. I sold it for a hot fifteen bucks, which is basically a grand in here.

I've also used the end of a toothbrush, a piece of concrete, and a really colorful one made out of Jolly Ranchers. I kept that one for myself. I don't know how useful any of them will be, but no one seems to care. Apparently, just the illusion of protection is worth a pretty penny in here.

While the others talk, I hum nineties music to myself and sharpen the plastic with a pretty rock I found. I'm sneaking this rock inside with me later. I love rocks just as much as I love colors. I'm thankful for the rec time and being outside, and sigh in relief again at how relaxed I am. This is so much better than being at home, constantly hounded by my mat.

There are thirty or so inmates in the rec yard right now,

all of us getting our allotted sunlight time. A few of them are playing football, but it's mostly an excuse to throw a ball at the other team member's faces, tackle them, and then beat the shit out of each other. I didn't think the contact sport would be allowed in here, but the guards don't break it up, and the others that aren't involved just watch because it's entertaining as hell.

I've been here for a week now, and I've got a system down. I know which guards don't like my particular brand of humor. I know which ones still hold a grudge over my little cafeteria tray incident. I know that this place serves epic Sloppy Joes on Saturdays. I also have a tentative inmate group that I hang out with, courtesy of my good friend Zen. Well, maybe friend is a strong word. It's more like she tolerates me. But that's all I needed, because it gave me the perfect in.

Which is how I find myself in the rec yard every day, hanging out with Zen, the wolf shifter Sophie, a couple of water fae, the Medusa-wannabe with the broken eyes—she can't turn anyone to stone with her gaze, and yet, she won't let me pet her red snake hair either—and Joe. He's a troll who doesn't talk, but even though he's scary looking and has to go in sideways through every doorway because he's too big to fit, he's nothing but a big teddy bear. At least, I think so. He only grunts when I talk to him, but they seem like friendly grunts.

Zen presides over the whole crew, but she also has people outside of this little circle that she talks to on a daily basis. No one fucks with Zen. Not the other inmates, not the guards, not even the Warden, who I see from time to time. He always has a cigarette hanging from his mouth, and he's cloaked in shadows and smoke.

As for the prison guard, Rook, I've only seen him a couple of times since our weird ass meeting in the medical ward. I was fully expecting Dr. Brina to come search me out after she realized she wasn't feeding off my dreams, but luckily, I haven't seen her again.

And even though Rook hasn't bothered me at all, the other guards are a different matter. It's like they got all pissy just because I hit one of them. So sensitive.

They like to make their presence known every once in a while, but I take it in stride. The most they've done is shove me harder than necessary through doorways or trip me as I walk by. I can handle it.

With Rook, I'm still on my guard. I don't trust his presence here. Cockatrice shifters aren't all that common, but that doesn't mean it's not a coincidence. So I watch him carefully, though he doesn't pay me any attention whatsoever, even though I changed his name tag to read *Rookie* and put it back on his uniform when he wasn't looking. When people were snickering at him in the cafeteria, his eyes found me, and he arched his brow like, *Really?* I thought it was a win.

But overall, I'm still not sure exactly how I feel about him.

Movement by the doors that lead us back inside the prison catches my attention. I look over at the waving hand that belongs to a guard who I discovered has a situation I can use to my benefit. He looks nervous. I shake my head to myself as I watch him pace and wipe the sweat from his upper lip. I step away from my crew, tuning out whatever new topic is being discussed, and pocket my shank project as I start to walk over.

I approach the anxious guard, and he waves me around the side of the building where inmates aren't normally allowed to go. I look around to see if anyone is paying attention, but only find Zen's eyes tracking my movements. I give her a wave and smile as I disappear around the corner where I'm met by a manila folder practically being shoved in my face.

"Damn, activate your chill, Chuck," I censure as I step back, checking my face for papercuts.

"I got what you wanted. Just take it. Before someone sees," he tells me with a distressed catch in his tone.

"Chuck, you seriously need to just take a couple of deep breaths. It's not like I'm asking you to shove a sub sandwich up your ass for me. It's just some papers you printed for me to have a look at. No biggie," I tell him reassuringly.

Chuck opens his mouth to say something, and then his features fold with confusion. "Why would you want me to shove a sandwich up my ass?" he asks, taking a step back and looking me over with renewed concern.

I huff out an exasperated breath. "Apparently it's a thing, but I *wouldn't* ask, that's my point."

"But how would that even fit?" he demands, his hands dropping to cover his butt, clearly not focusing on the fact that no one has requested an ass sandwich from him.

Rolling my eyes, I ignore the question and instead open the file and read through what I asked Chuck to get for me. My eyes scan the pages, and then I sigh a little. Officer Rook's employment file isn't half as exciting as I hoped it would be. The dates in this file confirm that he's worked here for four years, and he's received two promotions. From what I can see, he hasn't had any complaints filed against him since he started here.

I flip through the copies of the reviews he's had and read through the lease agreement that Chuck printed off for the condo it seems Officer Rook rents. I glance quickly over the registration in the file for a 1970 Ford Bronco and then close the file, handing it back to Chuck.

It seems Rook checks out.

I look past Chuck in thought, but his nervous rocking

makes it hard to focus on other avenues I can discreetly check to be sure I'm not missing anything on the Rook front.

"You did real good, Chuck," I coo, and the man wipes more sweat off his upper lip and gives me a smile. "I appreciate your help and your *discretion*," I add with a hint of warning in my tone that this obviously needs to stay between us.

Chuck nods his head vigorously and shoves the file back up the front of his shirt.

"The next time that harpy gang comes into your wife's shop, tell her to say *shlecom*...and that Sinclair said hi. After that, they won't ask for the protection fee anymore, and they'll make sure nobody else messes with her. Her new flower business will be *blooming* in no time," I tell him, smirking at my pun. Chuck doesn't appreciate it though, he's too busy mouthing the code word multiple times to make sure he's got it right.

I know for a fact it's right, because I once got into a tussle with some of those harpies, but then we became fast friends once they realized I liked to cause mayhem just as much as they do. His wife will be under their wings of protection in no time.

"And that's it?" he asks me, his gaze growing a touch leerier.

I offer him a wide smile. "That's it, Chuck. Just a one-time thing like I promised it would be. I mean, we can still be friends, of course. And if a friend wanted to give another friend some Pop Rocks every once in a while, there'd be no objections, but we're square."

Chuck's Adam's apple bobs as he swallows down his nerves, and then in a flash, he hurries away from me.

Making friends is so much fun.

I wait a minute or so and then round the corner and head back toward Zen and the others, my mind taking in all the info about Rook. As though my thinking of him suddenly summons him, Rook steps out of a door that leads up to the tower in the corner of the yard where more guards keep an eye on the perimeter. He closes the door behind him and immediately looks up, his stare landing on me. We both watch each other for a second, and I ignore the heat that dips dangerously low in my belly.

Could he really just be a coincidence? Everything I've unearthed at this point says that he is, but I'm still skeptical. As much as I'd love to think the universe has finally taken pity on me and offered me this visual gift as an apology for all the years of fuckery, I can't let go of the feeling that it's too good to be true.

As he watches me, Rook wiggles his head from side-to-side, and the moment his movement registers, both of our eyes widen in shock.

Did he...Did he just head wobble me?

Rook's cheeks light up with a bright blush, and he shakes his head like he's somehow answering my unvoiced question. His hands flap up at his sides, and he looks even more distressed as he slams them back down and speedily starts to walk away. I watch him hurry through the yard and disappear around a corner, a smile creeping slowly over my face.

Oh my sweet color spectrum, he totally wobbled!

I recall the last cockatrice gathering I attended and pull up the memories of the dance that male cockatrices do when they're trying to intrigue a female. Yep. First comes the head wobble and then the arm or wing flap. Toss in some tail whips, and then the holy grail of color flashing, and you've got an interested male cockatrice.

Rook likes me.

My smile spreads even wider. So this attraction *isn't* just one-sided! He's totally been thinking about cocking my trice. Smirk.

After I saunter back to Zen's group and sit back down on my designated piece of broken concrete, I am looking mighty pleased with myself.

"Hey Lizard-bird, your tail is wagging."

I look over at Sophie and then down to my scaly tail. The orange and yellow feathers on the end are flicking back and forth like a pleased cat. Flustered, I quickly grab my tail and stuff the end of it into my pocket, inwardly chastising it.

Stop it, tail!

It's one thing for Rook to wobble, it's another entirely for my own instincts to start getting jiggy with an answering tail flick. Male cockatrices *love* a good tail flick. It draws their attention to our feathers. I snagged many a fella in my rebellious teenage years with my super bright orange and yellow feathers. I've been told that the plumage on my tail is fantastic.

Zen leans in. "You know, if you're looking for information, I have a better source than Up-Chuck over there."

I raise my gaze to her, giving nothing away. I'm really glad I have her as a sort-of-ally right now, but I wasn't born yesterday. Everyone in here is a criminal, Zen included. And inside prison, everything comes at a price. You can only count on yourself, and trust is just a banking term.

"I'll keep that in mind," I tell her.

A smirk kicks up at the corner of her lips. "You've got more than just a citrus grove sprouting out of that colorful head of yours, I'll give you that," she says before unfolding her legs and getting fluidly to her feet. "Walk with me, Sinclair."

It's not a question, and Zen isn't the kind of person you deny. I get to my feet, dusting myself off, and make sure my tail is still tucked securely into my pants pocket. I don't want to trip over it, and I can't trust it not to go all flick-happy in case I see Rook again. I'd rather keep the upper hand and make him think I'm not interested. Nothing drives a cockatrice crazy like a one-sided mating wobble.

Oh man, I'm going to have so much fun with that.

"So, Sinclair Denali," Zen begins as we make our way around the rec yard, keeping to the fence line. "I've heard some things about you."

AKA, she's been asking around about me just like I've been asking around about Rook.

"Yeah?" I say noncommittally. Several of the other inmates and guards watch us as we walk, but I have no idea if me walking alone with Zen around the yard is supposed to be significant or something. I haven't been here long enough to know all the ins and outs.

"Your lounge of cockatrices is a humble size but strong. Your matriarch and patriarch have ruled for over fifty years. You were set to be next in line."

"I was," I answer with a nod, not really knowing where she's going with this.

She stuffs her hands into the pockets of her gray uniform pants. "It's weird that your matriarch would sell you off to a rival pack leader for mating, instead of allowing you to choose your own patriarch to mate with within your own lounge and groom you for leadership."

Again, not a question, but Zen is careful with her wording. She makes it sound like we're just having a friendly convo, when really, she's showing me how much she already knows about me. I'm not sure if it's a warning, a challenge, or something else.

"Yeah, my mat and pat are a real piece of work." That's putting it mildly. I have a very...combustible relationship with my parents—my mat in particular.

Zen gives me a sidelong glance. "I've heard rumors that

the Denali lounge owes a lot of money. It's one of the reasons why you were given to Alpha Bowen. Maybe to settle a debt?"

Anger causes my feet to stop in their tracks and spin to face Zen. "Where did you hear that?"

Instead of being affronted by my snippy tone, she just shrugs. "Like I said, there's better sources to get information from than Up-Chuck."

I have no idea how she heard something like that, but it pisses me off. "That's bullshit. My lounge would never borrow money, especially not from Alpha Bowen," I say, although doubt trickles into the back of my mind.

Is *that* why my mat and pat drew up a mating contract without even discussing it with me first? But why? We had money of the white *and* the black variety. At least, I thought we did. Our lounge has always been stable. We have businesses and all sorts of schemes in place. Why in the world would they have been in debt? And why the fuck would they have reached out to Alpha Bowen for help?

The cockatrice alpha is rumored to be a power hungry whoremonger with a thirst for war with other lounges. Every year, he always takes over another cockatrice lounge, forcing them to merge into his own. The moment my mat informed me that I was to mate him, I knew that I was doomed and that I was going to have to be very creative in order to get out of it. That's why I chose Nightmare Penitentiary; I'm out of reach, but it's not a situation my lounge would be forced to go to war over.

"Do you have a point to this little share and tell?" I ask Zen, crossing my arms in front of me.

She breathes in deeply, closing her eyes slightly before opening them again. "Your anger is very potent. Tasty, too."

That catches me off guard. She must be some kind of fae

or demon to be able to feed off that. "What do you want, Zen?"

"Nothing," she says simply. "Yet."

I narrow my eyes. "Yet?"

"Mm-hmm. You think I took you in because of your bright hair and affinity for cafeteria food?" she asks, shaking her head. "Cockatrices aren't all that common, but they are wily. You could come in handy," she answers cryptically. "You also have a price on your head."

My eyebrows shoot up. "What?"

She nods in affirmation. "Seems Alpha Bowen wants you. Bad. He's offering a lot of money to the person who can break you out and bring you to him. And word in the prison is...there's someone on the inside who's taking up the offer."

A sick feeling churns through my stomach. I mean, I'm not stupid. I know that all the attempts to break me out were because of him. But I didn't realize he would get all obsessive about it. I mean, ordering his shifters to fetch me from jail is one thing, but putting up a breakout bounty on my head in Nightmare Pen? That's just crazy. And someone on the inside...that can only be one person. Rook.

"Thanks for the heads-up," I say before I start to turn around.

"Sinclair."

I stop, barely suppressing a sigh. I knew it couldn't be that easy. Nothing is free in here. Least of all information.

Zen steps forward to be in front of me once again. Her dark eyes hold mine, her lotus flower tattoo glimmering slightly in the sunlight. "The next time someone tries to break you out, we can help each other."

She holds my gaze meaningfully, and I nod. "Deal."

I'm not sure if she wants out or if this is an excellent enterprise opportunity, but as long as I get to stay in here, I don't care.

With a nod, she turns and walks away, and I let out a breath. Feeling my tail flick inside my pocket, I frown as my eyes immediately shift over and up, where I see Rook standing in the guard tower, looking down at me from the window.

I clench my teeth, digging my hands into my pockets so that I can grip my rebellious tail and hold it still.

Even if it is a coincidence that another cockatrice works here, that doesn't mean he hasn't heard about Alpha Bowen's price to get me back. And what better person is there to break out an inmate than a well-trusted guard?

I turn and stalk away, my footsteps angry as I kick up dirt behind me.

I lift my chin with determination. So that colorful hot fucker is going to try to make money by breaking me out? He can fucking try.

5

The lock release on the metal door of my cell buzzes like a hive of pissed off bees. I jerk awake and stare at the door as an over-muscled guard who happens to be on my *not a fan of me* list leans in. He glares at me, and I glare right back. He just interrupted an epic dream I was having where I rode the face of a mystery man while his tail did all kinds of delicious things with my ass.

I close my eyes, ignoring the expectant look on the guard's face, and try to invite the dream to come back and ravish me the way a girl deserves to be dream-ravished. Something slams against the metal bed frame that's attached to the stone wall, and I cover my ears from the ringing noise it creates.

What the hell?

I sit up quickly and eye the asshole guard with the smug look on his face as he reholsters his baton.

Dick.

"You have visitors waiting for you. Hurry up before we send them away," he snaps, his sand-brown eyes alight with the joy that threats and mistreatment must give him.

Wait. *Visitors?*

I wrack my brain for all of two seconds before I deduce exactly who might be waiting to speak to me. It's not like the list is that long.

"Yeah, go ahead and send them away," I tell him, not at all interested in speaking with anyone who isn't currently inside this prison.

The torturous light in the guard's eyes dims slightly and then lights back up like someone just poured gasoline on this fucker's messed up thoughts.

"On your feet, inmate," he orders, and I stare at him for beat.

Is he serious? First he threatens to send my visitors away, and now he's going to force me to talk to them just to fuck with me?

He rests his hand on the baton that's once again hanging from the utility belt circling his waist, the warning clear. I roll my eyes and stand up, pushing my feet into my prison-issued Crocs. I was up late last night chatting away to my new troll bestie, Joe, in the toilet and changing the black slip-on shoes into a tie-dye rainbow of color. I can't help but smile with pride as I stare down at my colorful feet. It's almost enough happiness to help me get through what I know is about to happen.

Almost.

I follow Sandbag—the loving nickname I just gave this sandy-eyed douchebag of a guard—out of my cell. I pass Sophie the wolf and the water fae, and I give them a tough looking chin jerk in greeting. I giggle at the thought of looking like a hard-ass, and Sandbag shoots me a glare over his shoulder.

Jeez. Someone needs to miss a dose of steroids or accept that the stuff is just going to make his shrinky dink even smaller, and then cheer the fuck up, because he is grumpy.

I'm buzzed through doors and led down unfamiliar hallways, and each time I have to stop and wait and get going again, my irritation and anger begin to boil in my chest. By the time I'm stopped just outside a door with Visitor Room marked on it, I have a solid mask of *fuck off* in place. Sandbag shoves me inside, and I snarl at him over my shoulder as he slams the metal door shut and leers at me from the peephole hatch.

I turn to find a metal chair, a phone attached to the wall, a thick scratched pane of plexiglass, and two people I have no interest in speaking to...my matriarch and patriarch. I stare at them with dead eyes and fold my arms over my chest, as if somehow the move will offer another layer of much needed protection.

My pat's ruby red eyes grow soft when he sees me, but my mat's green eyes do the exact opposite. She looks me over and finds me lacking...just like she always does. I think I've only ever witnessed a smile on her face twice in my life. Once was when my pat had announced that he acquired a rival lounge and that the alpha of said lounge—who had slighted my mat in some way—was no longer breathing. The second time I saw her lips tilt up with cruel happiness was right after she told me that I now belong to Alpha Bowen.

A fist slams against the metal door behind me, and I turn around to meet Sandbag's elated gaze.

"You'll stay in here until you talk to them," he declares, and I wonder if he's a sadist or if he's being paid off. Probably both.

I release a resigned sigh and then turn and walk to the metal chair. I sit down and pick up the phone receiver and slowly bring it to my ear.

Satisfaction blooms in my mat's eyes, and she stares at me for a beat before picking up the receiver on her side of the dirty glass barrier.

"Maybe I should kill your little pawn out there when this is done," I announce casually, hiking my thumb over my shoulder to point to the guard. "I've been looking for a way to extend my sentence, so if he doesn't return your calls after this, you'll know why."

My mat just blinks. "Fine. That'll save us from having to send him any payments for his services," she tells me just as casually.

Disappointment fills me. I look at my pat, just like I always do, pleading with my eyes for him to deal with her, because I just can't.

To say that my mat isn't maternal is an understatement. With her deep green eyes, hair, and tail feathers, I've always thought that she embodied the envy trait rather well. Nothing is ever good enough for her. No matter how green her grass (or feathers) are, she's always looking over the fence for something better, for *more.*

To outsiders, she probably looks like a stern, forty-something-year-old woman with an obnoxious hair color and thin lips that are permanently bowed downward. She looks tough before she even opens her mouth. Even her pristine pantsuit shows that she means business. Everyone in our lounge knows that she's the one that wears the pants.

My pat, with his ruddy complexion and red hair, eyes, and feathers, would probably look scary if it weren't for his unassuming posture and his easygoing attitude. I've never seen him yell, or swear, or cry, or even belly laugh. He seems to be stuck on one setting all the time: calm.

It's infuriating, especially when I was a hurting teenager who cried and begged for her father to step in, to speak, to do *something*. He never did. Not when my mat banned me from the house whenever I pissed her off, leaving me to sleep outside. Not during screaming matches between her and me. Not even when she sold me off to a stranger.

My pat is just...incapable of not deferring to her, and my mat doesn't have a warm or fuzzy bone in her body. We've never gotten along. Things got worse when I hit thirteen and stopped trying to please her. I realized that it was hopeless to get her to give a shit about me. There are a few things my mat cares about, but none of them are named Sinclair.

"Did you think getting yourself incarcerated would stop Alpha Bowen?" she asks, her tone and head tilt condescending. "He had his pick of potential mates. He chose you. He's not going to just let that go so easily."

"Clearly," I grumble and do my best to stare at her with pure boredom. "But word in the prison is that I'm a debt trade, not a power alliance like you pitched. Is that true?"

My mat gives nothing away as she shakes her head and hands the phone receiver to my pat, like she just can't be bothered with me anymore. But she doesn't answer the question.

My mind whirs with all the possible paths that could've led to the lounge being in debt. I still can't piece it together. It just doesn't make sense to me, knowing all the pots our lounge has their fingers in.

"What were you thinking coming in here?" my pat's deep rumbling voice asks me, pulling me from my thoughts.

I narrow my eyes at him. "I was thinking I'd just been sold off to the worst of our kind, all so that my matriarch wouldn't have to face a possible challenge when I came of age in a year. I was thinking that prison sounded like a better place than the lounge I grew up in. And I was thinking that since I wasn't in possession of parents who would protect me or look out for my best interests, it was time I stepped up and started managing that for myself instead."

My pat's red eyes drop from mine, and I know he felt that hit.

Good.

He loves my mat and bends over backward for her. Behind the scenes, he does that for me sometimes too, but if it's between me and her, he chooses her every time. It's time we both come to terms with that fact.

"Our arrangement with Alpha Bowen was in the best interest of you and our entire lounge," my mat announces after ripping the phone receiver out of my pat's hands. He just lets it go, and my heart falls even more. "We are second in power only to Bowen and his extensive lounge. If our forces combine, there isn't anyone who would be a threat to us, not even the Drakes."

At the sound of that name, I mock spit on the ground at the same time my mat and pat do. It's something all cockatrices do whenever the Drakes are mentioned. Bunch of fire-breathing, hoarding, dragon menaces. They think they're hot shit. Cockatrices and dragons do *not* mix.

"So you didn't sell me to settle a debt?" I ask.

My mat smooths a hand over her green coiffed hair, pulling back her shoulders so she sits up more rigidly in the metal chair. "The finances of the lounge are of no concern to you, Sinclair. That's lounge business handled by your matriarch and patriarch."

I scoff, making the noise louder than necessary just to get the satisfaction of watching her jerk the phone away from her ear. "If you sold me off to settle *your* debts, then I have a right to know."

"Actually," she begins primly. "You have no rights. Not while you wear that horrid prison uniform."

I look down at the gray fabric and turn it bright yellow without a thought. Not to please her, but because gray is my least favorite color. "Happy?" I ask with a snarky smile.

My mat just levels me with a look. The same one she used when she'd send me to bed without dinner. "Alpha

Bowen isn't happy, Sinclair. He knows you've thwarted his attempts to break you out from jail."

I shrug because I don't give a fuck. "Good. I'm not happy about being given to him or him trying to break me out, so we're even."

"No, we are not!" she shouts, slamming her palm onto the surface in front of her. My brows hike up at her burst of emotion. She leans forward, clutching the phone in her hand so hard that her knuckles go white. "You listen to me now. You will *not* get any time added on to your sentencing. You will behave yourself. And if you have a chance to get out of this place, you will take it, and then you will go to Alpha Bowen, because that was what was agreed upon."

Anger and dismay crawls up my throat. "I *never* agreed to that."

"We did," she counters, "as is our right as your parents and lounge leaders."

"Fine. Then you can consider me a rogue."

Their faces blanch. My mat's mouth drops open, and my pat breaks out into a sweat. I just stare back at my mat coldly, dispassionately, though my heart is pounding in my ears. So much blood and emotion is running through me that black circles appear in my vision.

Being rogue in our world is like throwing away your family, your friends, even your identity. It means no protection, contacts, home, alliances, and hell, not even a last name. And once you're rogue, there's no going back. No other lounge will take you. You're destined to live life shunned, to be a pariah.

"How could you...take that back!" my mat shouts into the phone.

"No," I say, shaking my head, because as terrifying it is to be a rogue shifter, I'm digging my heels in now. I've finally gotten to them. I've finally found the only button I can press, so I'm going to jam my finger on this motherfucker as hard as I can.

"Sinclair..." I see my pat mouth from the other side of the glass.

"If you go rogue, then Alpha Bowen will consider our deal null and void. He won't strike our debts off his ledger," my mat tells me, cutting off whatever my pat was about to say.

I grind my teeth. So I *was* sold for money. "Guess that's your problem."

I start to get up from my chair, but my mat's voice stops me before I can hang up the phone. "If you do this, you will be the reason for Denali's downfall. Our entire lounge will go bankrupt, Bowen will take us over instead of watching our backs, and your lounge, your people, will be gone forever."

I scoff. *My people?* Part of the reason she did what she did was to make sure they would never become *my* people. I try to focus on that, but despite my efforts, guilt pricks the backs of my eyes. Aside from my shitty parents, my lounge isn't bad. They're my family, my friends. "Then give me another option," I beg. "Please."

Her green eyes twinkle with my plea. She knows her guilt hit home. As much as I try to be the emotionless hardass that she is, I just can't do it.

Running away from my responsibilities? That's easy. I've been doing that my whole life, although I was half running and half being chased away. I knew at a young age that even though she went through the motions of setting me up to take over, she would never let it happen. She's not ever going to give up the reins.

After that realization, the running became more about fighting for control of my life. She wanted me to set the table, so I didn't come home until bedtime. She wanted me to make a speech at a lounge meeting? I claimed I had laryngitis. Running away was supposed to cure this stupid mate contract too. It was par for the course she and I always played. Except this time, it's different.

Prison was supposed to be a break from her and all the damn politics and messed up expectations. But this...this crosses a line that I might not want to cross. This is suddenly too much responsibility and I'm not sure my shoulders can carry it. I'm a sloucher, dammit. My posture isn't meant for these kinds of decisions. I don't want to obliterate my lounge. I just want to obliterate my mat's hold over me.

"This is the only option," my mat tells me coldly.

"Selling me off to a monster is the best you could come up with?" I shake my head. "Let me look over the books, maybe there's something there that you're just not seeing. I've always been good with numbers."

My mat's eyes turn hard as jade, and I know where this is going to go before she even opens her mouth to speak. She wants a solution to the lounge's problem, but only the solution that *she's* decided on. After all, it's not just the debt that she wants gone, it's me.

"Sinclair Denali, I am your matriarch, and you will do as you're told."

I stare at her for a beat and wonder how I could've ever hoped that she would someday care about me. My eyes move from my mat to my pat. I wish I saw some hint of defeat in his slumped shoulders, like he had fought for me but lost, but it's not there. He looks...unaffected.

Clearly, my mat and pat are a dead end on the *how to save the lounge* issue, but that doesn't mean there aren't other options. I just need to find out exactly what the debt situation is and why. Once I have that, I can figure all of this out on my own.

Hopefully.

Probably.

Maybe.

"No, I won't," I answer to her demand. There will be no sitting pretty and doing as I'm told.

I hang up the phone and push back my chair before standing up. My mat slams a hand against the plexiglass, but I ignore it. Another fist against the barrier echoes around me and then another, but I give them my back. I walk to the door and can just make out the high-pitched resonance of words being screamed at me. I let them bounce off my skin to land uselessly on the polished cement ground. Nothing either of them can say will penetrate. They raised me to have a hard hide, and they can be as mad as they want, but it's partially their fault that my thick skin now serves as my armor.

I don't pay any attention to the banging or aggressive noises. From the sound of things, my mat is attacking the barrier between us. I'm tempted to turn and watch the spectacle, but I know I need her hard eyes to be the last memory I have of this meeting. I need that image burned into my mind so I can find a way to get my lounge out of whatever mess she's created for them.

I raise a fist and bang on the door, waiting for Sandbag to come back and try to force me to stay here. I don't care if I have to gouge his eyes out through the little rectangle in the door, he better let me out. I'm not in the mood for any more bullshit.

I breathe through the adrenaline and anxiety that are forcing my heart to beat faster and my breaths to come quicker, but it's not sand-colored eyes that I see. It's a stunning pair of turquoise irises that take me in.

Rook looks over my shoulder at what is clearly my mat having a temper tantrum to end all temper tantrums. The yelling seems like it's getting farther away, and I can just picture my pat escorting her furious ass away and trying to calm her down. The noise fades, and Rook and I look at each other for a beat, me challenging, waiting to see if he'll open the door or just leave me to stew in all the animosity saturating the room. I hear the lock click open, and then he pulls me out of the chaos and wraps me up in comfort and safety.

Or shackles. Same thing.

I look down at the handcuffs and arch a brow as he clicks them around my wrists, the door closing behind me. "Is this really necessary?"

His lips twitch in amusement. "I thought it would be a good distraction," he says before fixing the last lock and then letting go.

My hands hang in front of me, the handcuffs firmly in place. "A good distraction?" I repeat dryly.

"Yeah, from your nice visit that seemed to go so well," he replies, hiking his chin up toward the empty viewing glass.

I turn to look and confirm what the lack of noise already told me—they're gone. My shoulders relax just a bit, and a sigh escapes my lips. That was one of the worst interactions I've ever had with my parents, and I've had some doozies in the past. Just as I feel the guilt and the emotions settle over me again, Rook suddenly holds up his black watch in front of my face.

"Timer starts...now." He clicks one of the buttons on his watch, and it starts counting up from zero.

He drops his hand, and I cock a brow. "Timer for what?"

"The handcuffs, of course. Let's see if you can get them off in under three minutes."

Three minutes? Does he think I'm an amateur?

I shuffle on my feet, feeling myself growing excited. Me

and my cockatrice always love a good race. "What do I get if I win?"

To my utter amazement, he shoves his hand in his pocket and pulls out a trio of Pop Rocks packets. My mouth instantly waters. "Deal," I blurt as I quickly raise my hands to my hair and pluck out my handy pin. My orange hair falls in front of my face, but I just blow it back with a breath as I get to work.

"You're a terrible guard," I point out. "Encouraging me to de-handcuff myself and whatnot."

"We both know you'd de-handcuff yourself anyway. Might as well make it interesting," he replies. "Besides, you said yourself that you don't want to leave this place, so I've got nothing to worry about."

He's got me there.

"Come on. Walk and unlock," Rook orders, amusement clear in his voice as he nudges my arm and forces me to walk back to my cell while simultaneously picking the lock.

It's a little bit tricky because there's *just* enough slack on the chain for me to bend my hand the way I need in order to dig into the lock on my left hand. Plus, the prick is making me walk at the same time, so I keep stepping out of sync and running into the wall or into him—which is basically another solid wall.

"You didn't ask what happens if you lose," Rook points out beside me.

I don't look up at him, because I'm very aware of my countdown, and there's no way in hellfire that I'm losing this bet. Not when I've been going through serious Pop Rocks withdrawals.

"That's because it doesn't matter. I'm not going to lose," I tell him.

A slow, rumbling laugh escapes his chest, and the sound actually makes me trip over my own feet. I stumble to a stop, momentarily stunned as I look up at his smiling face. Dimples. The fucking dimples! Just like that, my tail starts flicking behind me like crazy, trying to jerk around my body so he'll see my bright-colored feathers and pay attention to them.

I quickly reach behind me to try to stuff it in my pocket, but I can't reach with the cuffs, and my tail darts out of the way. I curse and spin around, trying to catch it like a dog chasing her tail, and I drop my pin in the process.

"Son of a bitch!" I dive for it, but a black boot comes down, landing on top of it before I can snatch it up.

I lift my head up, glaring at Rook from the floor, my tail still going wild behind me. He has the audacity to shine those dimples and perfect teeth at me like they're high beams. "Problem?"

"Move your foot!" I hiss.

Biting his bottom lip in a gesture that is *way* too sexy for a prison hallway, he shakes his head. "Your tail seems to be doing some very interesting things right now, don't you think?"

"No!" I snap. "It's just irritated. It's twitching in irritation."

He pretends to consider this while my tail sneaks between my legs and shakes at him like a crazed maraca that's begging to be shaken or fucked. I slap it away, and it goes back behind me and curls around my hip to sweep over the top of his foot like it wants to shine his boot. And I mean that sexually *and* literally.

Letting out a string of curses, I reach for my horny tail and manage to finally grab hold of it and stuff it into my pocket. The feathers bulge obscenely, gyrating around my pants like a hussy on the dance floor. So embarrassing.

Still on the ground between his feet, I glare at Rook

who's clearly enjoying this *way* too much. "Are you gonna move your foot now?" I growl.

"No, I don't think I will."

Fucking cocky ass cockatrice!

I glance at his watch, seeing that I only have thirty more seconds. I give him a sickly sweet smile. "Fine."

With a move that would make lightning jealous, I slam the heel of my palm up directly against his balls.

Bam!

A pained grunt flies out of his mouth, and he falls to his knees, his feet coming up enough for me to pluck the pin from the ground. While he's swearing and sweating and clutching his family rocks, I whistle a happy tune and quickly unlock the first cuff before getting to work on the other. With three seconds to spare, I pop off the second cuff, my whistling changing to mix with the beep of his alarm going off.

I swing the handcuffs around on one finger as I smile at his pained face. "I won."

Still clutching his cock rocks, he glares at me. "You can't fucking attack a guard!" he snaps, though I must say, his voice is a little more high-pitched than usual.

I shrug and get to my feet, so that this time, it's me standing over him. "Why not? You were standing on my pin, which was a total bastard-cheat move, by the way. Besides, I'm trying to extend my sentence. The opportunity presented itself."

With some effort and a lot of grunting, he manages to stand upright, though he's hunching a little. "My balls are not an *opportunity*."

"Agree to disagree," I singsong before I turn to start walking back to my cell. I have a smile on my face the entire way while he stalks beside me, and when we get there, he slams my cell door shut with a clang.

"Okay there, big guy?" I ask, spinning to sit on my bed.

"You hit me in the balls. What do you think?"

The intense scowl he wears makes me have to stifle a giggle. "Sorry."

He scoffs. "No, you're not."

I grin, unable to hold it back, and his scowl cracks. For a second, his eyes soften as he sweeps over my face. "You have a nice smile."

Taken aback, I sit up straighter, my smile falling. Even Rook seems surprised that he let that confession slip from his lips. For a moment, we just look at each other. I have no idea what he's thinking, but my stomach churns.

I forgot who I was talking to for a second. Zen pretty much told me flat-out that Rook is the person who's in cahoots with Alpha Bowen to try to kidnap me out of here. But for a few minutes, I forgot all of that. I even forgot about my visit with my mat and pat. He succeeded in distracting me with our handcuff game, and I didn't even realize how much I truly needed that distraction until this moment.

But it came from an enemy.

I smiled. Laughed. Played. Tail flicked. At the *enemy*.

Not good.

Suddenly self-conscious and not knowing how to act, I clear my throat and look down at my lap. "Thanks for the distraction," I mutter.

"Anytime."

My eyes snap up, drawn to the huskiness in his voice. His *anytime* was definitely insinuating a distraction of the sexual variety. My tail wags inside my pocket, and I slap my hand over it. Rook smirks and then turns to leave.

"Hey!" I say, shooting to my feet and racing over to the bars. "Aren't you forgetting something?"

"Oh, right." Walking backward, he digs into his own

pocket and then tosses me all three packets of Pop Rocks. Cherry flavor. My favorite.

I smile at the bags lovingly. "I've missed you."

I hear Rook's low chuckle echo down the corridor as he walks away. I drown out the sound with Pop Rocks candy explosions and tell myself that there's no chance in hell that I'm falling for the enemy.

It's not my style.

Nope.

Not in a million years.

6

"I'll give you five cup-a-noodles, ten assorted king-sized candy bars, and free pruno for a month," a witch offers to my left.

The small crowd around me starts to grumble as they assess their offerings or complain about the bid being upped.

"Oh, that's a good one," I observe. "But you lost me at pruno. That stuff gives me serious heartburn, and I don't like feeling like a Drake," I tell the witch, while simultaneously mock-spitting on the ground to curse the Drake name. Dragons are the worst.

Her face falls slightly and then immediately brightens again when she thinks about something else. "How about shower head for a week instead?" she offers, and I choke on air at her words.

I perk up. *No one's offered me sexual favors yet.* Totally taking that as a compliment.

I clear my throat and try not to ruin my rep by staring at her wide-eyed like a newb. I'm two months into my twelve month sentence, and I have quite the thing going for myself here. Okay, fine. *Zen* has quite the thing going on here, but I go through daily prison life with a Zen umbrella over my head, and you'll hear no complaints from me about it.

Rook still hasn't made his move and tried to break me out yet, but he *is* making other sorts of moves. As in, his head. He's become more and more head wobbly with each week that passes. He's even had to resort to tying his tail down to keep it from shimmying and flashing all his pretty tail feathers for me. I still smile and feel all kinds of giddy when I see him with his tail tied to his leg. Maybe his attraction to me is holding him back from taking up Alpha Bowen's offer to break me out of this place. I know that my own tail is constantly being shoved in my pocket. Whatever his intentions are, I can't deny that we're ridiculously drawn to one another.

Meanwhile, my shank business is booming.

"Do we have any other bids?" Zen calls out, saving me from having to address the whole shower oral sex thing.

I mean, the witch is cute. And what's that saying? When in Rome, do the Romans?

"A case of large Jolly Ranchers!" a wiry male shifter calls out, pulling me from my thoughts of sexy Romans doing the dirty Roman Candle. "Plus six cans of Coke, a dozen sugar cookies with the pink frosting and sprinkles, and four packages of Pop Rocks."

My head snaps to him, my eyes filled with interest at the mention of Pop Rocks. How does he know my weakness? I eye the shifter cautiously.

Can't seem too eager. I point at the item up for grabs. "This is a sturdy piece made out of lunch tray, mystery adhesive that would glue your ass to a rocket and have you up in space with no trouble, and gneiss. You're telling me that four packages of Pop Rocks is the best that you can do?" I question, my gaze hard.

The male shifter looks confused for a beat. "What's gneiss?"

I gasp. Blasphemy. These inmates need some serious rock tutelage. "*What's gneiss?*" I repeat, shaking my head at his ignorance. "It's only the best striped metamorphic rock formed from high pressure and temperature alone. This little beauty will stand the test of time, and I've made it as sharp as Wolverine's blade," I explain as I hold up the shank.

"How the hell do you know that?" Sophie asks on a snort.

"I'm a cockatrice; we have a thing for rocks." I shrug. I thought this was common knowledge. Just like dragons like hoarding golden treasure and useless shiny things—so stupid—cockatrices like to collect rocks.

"That's what she said," Sophie cackles, punching one of the water fae in the shoulder and raising her eyebrows like, *get it?*

Zen shakes her head. "You're better than that, Sophie."

I laugh at the dig.

"Fine. *Ten* packets of Pop Rocks, a case of Jolly Ranchers, six Cokes, but no sugar cookies," the skinny male shifter calls out.

"Done!" I shout back with a smile.

Several groans and curses ring out as people get up, pissed at having lost, but I couldn't be happier. I made out like a bandit.

"The item you've purchased will be delivered when Sinclair has received payment," Zen calls out, and the male shifter nods his head and disperses with the rest of the group that's breaking off.

"I call dibs on a Jolly Rancher," Sophie declares beside me.

"Sorry, Soph, I have plans for those, but you and the crew can have the Cokes," I offer instead.

"Fine. But they better not be diet," she grumbles, and I smile and give her a pat on the back. I don't blame her. Diet soda is nasty.

"Alright, Joe, you ready for another epic treasure hunt?" I ask the giant troll, my tone the high-pitched saccharine kind that's usually reserved for talking to baby animals. I just can't help myself with the big guy. He's just too adorable with his grunts and his big ass self, and since he doesn't talk, he's the best secret keeper ever.

Joe grunts happily—or at least I think it's a happy grunt, they all basically sound the same—and follows me as I go full Shawshank and scour the yard for any more pretty rocks that either need to be added to my collection or molded into their true shank-tastic form. Everything else, I give to Joe for a snack.

"Ohhh, amphibolite!" I shout out after about twenty minutes of treasure hunting.

I hurry to pick up the rock and bound over to my troll, who's currently gnawing on some concrete pieces. We've come to an understanding that he doesn't eat rocks until he shows them to me first so I can give him the all-clear. I once caught him chewing on a beautiful sliver of obsidian, and I about lost my mind.

"Now, Joe, you may be thinking to yourself, didn't she just sell a shank with a similar rock? And that's where you'd be wrong. See the speckled pattern? It's different than the stripes of the gneiss," I explain, turning the rock around in front of us. "They have similar coloration though, which is mind-blowing, because the gneiss is derived from granite, whereas the amphibolite isn't! Can you believe that?" I ask him excitedly.

Joe grunts. Excitedly.

I nod. "You're absolutely right, Joe! I'll use a blue lunch tray for this one instead of the red, it'll really complement the speckles. Such a good suggestion." I hug Joe's meaty thigh, since I can't reach his midsection, but yelling pulls my attention away from the big troll teddy bear.

Some shouts sound out, and I look over at the football game going on just in time to see a male vamp throw a football right in the face of an ogre. The ogre's nose smashes even flatter against his face, and black blood immediately starts gushing out. He bellows in pain, and the vamp just barely misses getting splattered with ogre blood. Yuck. That shit smells like cat piss, and once it touches you, it takes *weeks* to get the scent out.

The yard breaks out into chaos, like someone just flipped a war switch into the *on* position. I clap with glee. I was hoping my fight with the wolf shifter in the cafeteria during my first day was going to be a prison brawl, but he got collared too fast for it to really count. I love running with Zen, but the downside is no one includes me in their fights. That'd be fine if I hadn't already written *prison brawl* on my bucket list, but everyone knows once something is on the list, it can't come off until it's been accomplished.

"Oh my gosh, Joe, look how fun!"

I point at the massive fight that's growing by the second and start hurrying right into the heart of it. I take note of where the ogres are battling and arc away from it because...no thank you cat-piss blood. A kitsune snarls at me as I join the fun, but I just boop it on the nose before introducing it to my right hook. I coo as the split tail fox shifter gets all wobbly and goes down embarrassingly fast.

I shake my head and tsk at it. "Not the hot shit you thought you were, huh? I like your tails though," I tell the unconscious shifter as I dart off.

Someone plucks a fairy out of the air and throws it at

me. I catch him before he can slam into an ice wall that someone has conjured. "There you go, little Tinkerbell," I tell him sweetly as I help him straighten up and get his bearings.

"Shove that Tinkerbell shit up your ass, you dirty cunt!" the fairy yells at me. Out of nowhere, it conjures up a toothpick-sized sword and slashes at me.

"What the fuck?" I exclaim as I jump back, just barely avoiding an eye-gouging.

"I'll fuck your nostrils with my fairy cock and have you sneezing my cum for weeks," he threatens, and I reel at the little shit's nastiness—that's a visual I really could have done without.

My hand flies up to my nose to protect my vulnerable nostrils. I start dodging toothpick sword attacks, all while the fairy hurls insults and threats at me with each parry. I'm not sure if I want to laugh, run screaming, or take notes at the foul shit coming out of the little guy's mouth.

"Did your Cheeto dad fuck a lemon? Is that why your hair is so ugly? Or is the yellow just making a run for it so it can escape your dumb bitch brain?" he sneers, flying in front of my face as he tries to stab my hand.

"Hey!" I yell at the winged pest, drawing the line. "It's fucking citrus ombré, you ignorant twat, and you wish your hair was this hot!"

With that, I shift my hand into talons and flick the little mosquito from hell away. The fairy gives a very un-tough girl scream as he goes flying through the air and smashes into a wall. The sound restores my good mood.

Who knew fairies were such angry little assholes? Tiny dick syndrome is in full effect with that one.

The shouting and fighting from the other inmates all over the yard snaps me back to attention, but I get knocked sideways when someone slams into me. Righting myself, I turn with renewed excitement, ready to join the fray.

Guards are starting to gather just as a fireball goes screaming through the crowd, and people leap and dive out of the way. It explodes against the outside wall of the prison and singes the concrete as it dies out. Another fireball gets thrown, and I look over to find a fae duo blowing them out like bubbles at a kid's party. Looks like the fae came to play!

I turn back around just in time to watch a big meaty fist come right for my face.

Well, this isn't going to feel good.

I take the hit, releasing a small grunt as the fist knocks into my cheek. Serves me right for taking my eyes off the fight all around me just to watch the fire. In my defense, cockatrices can't ignore pretty colors like that. It's science.

Reaching up, I catch the second fist before the dude can hit me again. I look up into the man's growling face and find none other than Beast—the wolf shifter from the cafeteria. He's finally back to settle the score.

I give him a beaming smile, which only serves to piss him off even more. I'm still clutching his fist, and we both wrestle for control over it. I laugh. I've always *loved* the game tug-of-war. Wolfy growls and swipes at me with his other hand, but I catch that too.

"What else you got, little fella?" I chirp excitedly, loving the look on his face that tells me he didn't think I was this strong.

Pain suddenly rips up my back, and I gasp from the shock of it and push the wolf shifter away from me. I turn to find *another* wolf, this one fully shifted, his claw-tipped paw extended. I can already feel blood dripping down my back where he swiped those razor-sharp nails down the length of my spine. He snaps his teeth at me.

Oh, so that's how it's going to be? Just going to chuck *fair fight* right out the window and go for someone's back? I thought my family was bad, but at least we always fight face-to-face. I mean, what's the point of winning if you can't do it the right way?

With a blink, I pull my beast forward. My cockatrice is simultaneously pissed and excited at the lesson we're about to teach these two dishonorable shifters.

I feel armored scales rip out of my skin, covering my torso and legs as I grow ten-times the size of my human height. My arms extend, and sharp spurs shoot out of my wrists. Thick bat like wings spill out of my arms, ribs, and middle back, and colorful feathers in every shade of red, orange, and yellow sprout down my spine. The tip of my tail has spikes that join the plume of tail feathers there to be battle-ready.

"It's a dragon!" someone screams, as I flash from woman to beast in seconds.

I reach out and catch the attacking wolf with a taloned hand and throw him across the field like he weighs nothing. He slams into the surrounding fence, and it sends jolts of electricity painfully into him before he crumples to the ground in a cloud of dirt. I let out an eardrum-rupturing screech.

Not a dragon.

I mock-spit on the ground at the thought.

I'm a motherfucking cockatrice, bitches!

I spin, accidentally whacking into and knocking down a bunch of fighting inmates with my tail.

Oopsie. It always takes me a few minutes to adjust to my large size when I shift.

Walk it off, folks.

I lock my bright yellow snake eyes on Wolfy and snap my bird's beak at him. He stares at me, mouth open, and I stretch out to my full height so he can truly appreciate how badass I am.

He just stands staring up at me, stunned.

I know, right! I think cockily.

He's clearly too enraptured by my beauty and powerful prowess to move. I roll my eyes and then bitch slap him lightly with the non-pointy underside of my tail, reminding him to get his head in the game.

Unlike *some* people, I like a fair fight.

The slap up the back of his head seems to do the trick, and Wolfy starts to shake like a wet dog as he moves to shift.

An alarm starts ringing in the background of all the chaos and noise, but I ignore it as I wait for Wolfy to be ready. This bitch is going down.

My tail goes full golden retriever and starts wagging excitedly, forcing me to knock more unsuspecting fighters over.

"Crap. My bad," I squawk unintelligibly at them over my scaled and spiked shoulder.

Come on, tail, don't embarrass us.

But then I see the reason for its wagging. Rook, in all his prison guard glory, is stalking my way.

I get stuck watching him for a moment, because it's like one of those slow-mo moves in action movies where the dude walks away from an explosion or some shit. Fire blazes behind him, fights seem to magically part as he walks toward me, and his muscles are bulging with every step and swing of his arms.

My tail starts thumping so fast, it's like the bunny's foot from *Bambi*.

"Watch it!"

I look back and see that my tail almost took out Medusa. Her snakes hiss at me reproachfully. "Sorry," I tell her, except I say it in cockatrish, so it comes out like, *goroshhhh-hahissssss.*

She flips me off and then jumps back into the fight, just as Wolfy uses my momentary distraction and attacks me. Fully shifted now, his wolf is a big, ugly motherfucker. He could seriously use a trip to the groomers. Baring his teeth, he launches at me, earning impressive height as he arcs and lands right on me, his teeth latching onto my neck.

Fucking ouch!

My cockatrice roars in pain, shaking her head back and forth to try and dislodge him from our throat. But the wolf's teeth dig in harder, despite the fact that his body is being flung back and forth.

I try to bend my long neck down to peck at him, but the angle is wrong and I can't get to him. My arms are now wings, and they're great for flying but not so much for flexible bending. I'm basically like a hotter, feathered T. rex.

Since my arms are useless for snatching him off, I take to the air instead. With a powerful sweep, my wings lift me off the ground, and I shoot up like a rocket, hoping the move will catch him off guard enough to let go.

I fly higher and higher, as fast as I can, feeling the wolf whine against my throat. But just before I can reach the clouds, I slam into an invisible barrier that crackles on contact, and I start falling, dazed from the electrified impact.

Wolfy's whines intensify, but after a couple of seconds of free-falling, I manage to shake the stupor off and flap my wings, righting myself in the air.

Fuck. This prison's magical barrier is no joke.

Despite my awesome flying moves, the wolf still hasn't let up. If anything, he's just holding on tighter. The pain in my neck is almost to the point of being unbearable. Wolfy tries to partially shift, turning just his front two legs back into his human arms so that he can grab hold of me and not fall, but all he ends up doing is losing his fur there and getting stuck in this weird and gangly half-leg, half-arm stage.

Fed up with him, I start doing barrel rolls in the air. His leg-arms scrabble for purchase, but my neck is too big around for him to get a good hold. When he starts frantically grabbing me and plucks out a couple of feathers, that's when I get really pissed. *No one* messes with my feathers.

I dive.

The air whips at us so strongly that Wolfy's teeth *finally* start to loosen on my neck. The ground rushes up at us faster and faster, but I don't slow down. It's me against him, and Wolfy just entered a game of chicken with a goddamn cockatrice. You can't win chicken against a half chicken. This dude has no hope.

We're a hundred feet from the ground. Fifty. Thirty. Twenty. Ten.

He starts to full-on panic as the ground gets closer and closer.

He screams and squeals in a wolf-human way, and *just* as we're about to hit, I pull up my wings parallel to the ground and shoot forward, my underbelly barely missing the dirt. Wolfy isn't so lucky. I purposely drag his body against the ground, giving him the worst road rash in history.

With a yelp, his jaw unhinges off my throat, and he lets go, his body flipping to a stop in a heap. I circle back around, slowing my momentum as I go, and land right over his bloody, panting body.

I snap my beak at him, clucking at him aggressively, my beast ready to tear into him. Wolfy has the good sense to tuck tail, which, in shifter's language, is waving a white flag.

But my cockatrice isn't satisfied. Our throat is throbbing, blood pouring from the deep wound he left with his teeth, and she wants to get even.

She lunges for him.

The wolf barks, eyes wide with terror, because he *knows* that he's about to get pecked to hell like a bag of seeds. But right before I can turn him into minced wolf meat, Rook suddenly steps between us.

My cockatrice jerks back in surprise. Holding my eyes, he shakes his head. "That's enough, Sinclair. It's over."

I look around and see that the fight has indeed been broken up. Most of the inmates are already kneeling in the dirt and are either being gathered up because they're in major trouble or taken away for medical attention.

But Wolfy growls behind Rook, like he's suddenly all tough guy again now that he has a barrier in front of him. I snap my beak at him and cluck angrily, my wings coming out in a move of intimidation.

Rook spreads his arms out on either side of him to regain my attention, mirroring my movements so that I can't get to the bastard. I make a growly noise at Rook for interfering and narrow my eyes at him. My cockatrice is not impressed right now.

Rook smirks, and then slowly, so as not to alarm my beast: reaches into one of the pouches at his belt, pulls out a fist-sized rock, and holds it up to me.

Holy shit. It's so pretty!

I stand corrected. My cockatrice is super impressed right now.

I step forward, but Rook moves his body and begins to walk backward, away from Wolfy. A total diversion tactic, and it's working.

"Come on, this way," he coos, dangling the greenish rock in front of me like a carrot on a stick. My cockatrice lumbers after him, talons digging into the dirt yard with every step.

When Rook is satisfied that we're far enough from

Wolfy, he smiles. "Good girl. Now shift back, and I'll let you have this," he says, shaking the rock enticingly.

My cockatrice doesn't want to shift back though. Instead, she starts clucking again, but this time, it's like a feminine, throaty, come-hither cluck. Rook's smirk widens, and his own tail tries to come out to play with mine.

I'm distracted when I see a group of more prison guards heading our way, including the Warden. *Shit.* He looks super pissed as shadows hover around him and shift in a very disconcerting way. When the guards keep walking closer and closer, my beast grows nervous. A pissed off screech comes tearing from my mouth, and my cockatrice rears up, spreading its wings in warning.

Rook tries and fails to regain my attention, but the rock is all but forgotten as the guards pull out weapons and aim them at me.

Oh, so that's how it's gonna be?

With a ferocious roar, I swing my scaled, feathery tail and swipe it at the guards. Only the Warden is able to dodge it, like his shadows make him untouchable. The rest of the guards go flying back, bowled over like pins, their shouts and grunts ringing out through the air.

They all jump back to their feet as quickly as they can, and my eyes narrow. They should've just stayed down, because now they're just asking to be pecked to death.

"Wait—" Rook's call gets cut off when the Warden nods, and the guards suddenly open fire at me.

Huge barbs shoot out of their black tasers, loaded with both electricity and magic. I manage to dodge some of them, but even through my tough hide, a few of them hit me on my chest and back, the barbs digging into my skin and sticking with brutal accuracy.

Letting out a ferocious and pained shriek, I shake side-to-side, but without proper arms or hands, I can't get the barbs off of me. Electricity and magic course over my body and dig through my skin like splinters of lightning glass. I bend my neck down, my beak snapping and trying to rip out the small darts. While I'm distracted, the Warden comes up and snaps a collar around my leg.

I feel it the moment the cold magic activates. It *hurts*. It hurts so fucking bad.

Snapping into place, the collar grips my shifter power like a dentist yanking out a tooth. One minute, I'm a giant cockatrice, and the next, I'm naked on the ground in my human form, with five tasers still stuck to my skin.

"You muddder fuhhkr..." I slur, as I try and fail to curse out the Warden who's staring down at me with a sinister grin. My mouth won't work right, and my vision is blacking out, but I manage to shoot him the middle finger right before I pass out.

7

"I'm hungry!"

My voice echoes down the dark labyrinth of the corridor as I clutch onto the rectangular peephole in the thick iron door. My eyes strain to the right as I try to stare down the endless length of the hallway, but despite my heightened shifter senses, there's absolutely nothing to see down there.

I woke up yesterday in this dark, dank cell room that smells like vinegar and sweat. At least, I think it was yesterday. I'm underground without any guards, other inmates, or even the sky to be able to tell for sure.

I got myself landed in solitary confinement. I guess the guards here at Nightmare Penitentiary aren't too fond of being tail swiped by a fifteen-foot cockatrice.

At least the collar was already removed by the time I woke up, and the wound at my throat from Wolfy thankfully healed too. But I still have marks all over my body from where the magical taser guns hit my flesh. All my injuries aside from the taser burns have healed without a mark, so those magic-laced electric barbs pack a serious fucking punch.

This entire cell is made of iron. The walls, the ceiling, even the damn toilet and sink. A sink which gives off water that tastes like toilet water and, you guessed it—iron. Yummy.

There's nothing else in this six-by-six iron cell aside from a cot and a lone pillow that's more case than filling, and the gray uniform on my body that's about three sizes too big. I rolled up the waist, legs, and sleeves and tied the midriff together to try to cinch it a bit, but I'm still swimming in it. I've changed the color to starbursts of tie-dye orange, yellow, and red, and it practically glows beneath the lone lightbulb hanging above me.

This place is seriously boring, so I've been playing around with changing the colors of my clothes and taking a lot of naps, but I'm all napped out right now. Luckily for me, I've always been a self-starter, so I know how to occupy myself. Chalk it up to the many, many times my mat grounded me when I was a kid.

Sighing, I grumble a curse at the shadows and go slump on my flat pillow again. Digging into my pocket, I grab the piece of iron pipe that I managed to break off the sink, and get back to work in the corner of the room.

Hours later, I'm so engrossed in my task and singing "Oops!... I Did it Again" that I don't hear anyone approaching until my door suddenly clinks open, and I turn to look over my shoulder at Rook stepping inside.

His bright turquoise eyes land on me, and damn, he looks good in the dim lighting. His hair looks like it's almost glowing in greens and blues. His mouth is open like he was going to say one thing, only for him to close it and frown. He cocks his head as he takes me in. "What are you doing?"

"I'm digging a tunnel out of my cell like Andy Dufresne. *Obviously*," I say, because duh.

Instead of getting pissed or running off to tell on me like

a prison guard probably should, Rook smirks. "I thought you didn't want to get out of here."

"I don't," I say, shrugging. "But tunnel-digging is a good way to pass the time."

He snorts and then tosses me a burlap sack. I manage to drop the pipe and catch the sack before it hits my face. I open it and peer inside. I find a blanket, a change of uniform, some apples, water bottles, packaged snacks, and even some candy.

"Cellwarming gift?" I quip.

"Pretty much. The guards upstairs are pissed at you. They all voted to let you starve down here."

Geez, it was just a little tail swipe. I grab one of the packages of crackers and dig in, eating all six in rapid succession. Thank goodness. If they left me down here much longer, I would've seriously started to worry about how hungry I've become. I have no doubt that this prison would gladly starve some of its inmates.

"But not you?" I ask, my mouth full of food and dry crackers flying out as my cheeks bulge like a chipmunk.

He shrugs and sits down against my closed door, hiking a knee up to rest his forearm on it. The move looks way too sexy for my food-starved brain to ignore.

My stupid tail goes a-thumping.

I quickly shove it in my pocket and turn back to my tunnel. Well...it's more like a divot. I've only managed to dig about an inch down through the weakened wall in the corner where the iron cracked and split open, revealing crumbling rock behind it.

"Is that a tail in your pocket, or are you just happy to see me?" Rook teases.

"Ew," I say quickly, digging through the rock harder than necessary.

"Ew?" he repeats. "What does that mean?"

"It means come up with better lines," I reply.

"Your tail doesn't mind my lines," he says with a teasing glint in his eye. "It's happy to see me."

I scoff. "My tail couldn't possibly be happy to see you. It just...likes cellwarming gifts. That's all." I lie, trying to keep my voice incredulous despite my cheeks starting to flush.

"I think your cockatrice likes me."

I shoot him a glare over my shoulder and drop my pipe, flexing my sore hands. Picking up the satchel again, I pull out one of the apples—*bright green, my favorite*—and bite into it.

"Pshhhh...you wobbled at me first. That means *your* cockatrice likes me," I say around my bite.

"Didn't your mother ever teach you not to talk with your mouth full?"

"Yeah. All the time," I say as I chew. "That's why I still do it."

He chuckles, the shadows curling into the clefts of his dimpled cheeks. "You don't get along with her, huh?"

I swallow the sour apple down. "She sold me off to a power-hungry, psychopathic rival alpha without even consulting me or telling me until it was done. What do you think?" I deadpan.

Rook considers me. "So that's why you're hiding out in here?"

"Why? You wanna break me out for some money? Prison guard salary not cutting it for you?" I snark.

"I do alright for myself," he says, not really answering my question.

"Hmm," I say, taking another big bite of apple.

"If you don't want the match, why don't you just tell the male that?" Rook asks me, like it's all just that easy.

I give him the *come the fuck on* side-eye. "Because it's

Alpha Bowen," I answer, knowing the name alone will explain all the reasons why his question is ridiculous.

I watch Rook and wait for the telltale recognition and concern to enter his eyes, but he just looks at me blankly.

My mouth drops open in shock. "Are you seriously telling me that you don't know who that is?" I demand, studying him for any hint that this is all some kind of ruse.

"Should I know who that is?" he questions.

I shake my head at him. "Uhhh...he's only one of the most powerful cockatrice alphas in the world. Of course you should fucking know who that is! Did you grow up in a cave?"

Rook snorts. "No, but my lounge travelled a lot. We stayed out of the useless conflicts and the gossip."

I pause and take a moment to try and imagine what it would be like to grow up in a lounge like that. But...I can't. I've never heard of a lounge that wasn't into power plays and politics.

"Must've been nice," I tell him around another bite of apple.

"Sometimes it was. Sometimes it was lonely," he admits, and I'm taken aback by the confession.

I study his face, and he lets me. There's no hardened mask or defensive posture. He's relaxed, enjoying himself even. Here, in this really uncomfortable room. How...strange.

The solitude and quiet of my cell wraps around us tightly, and it feels oddly intimate and safe in this moment. I wonder what would've happened if we'd met under different circumstances.

"My lounge was always up in all the shit...and it was still lonely," I tell him, suddenly wanting him to understand that the grass wasn't greener on my side either.

"I guess we have that in common then," he says,

surprising me. Our eyes lock, and there's a moment that passes between us. It's not just attraction. It's nothing close to wariness. There's a palpable link between the two of us that makes my heart rate quicken in my chest. We have...things in common. I'm suddenly seeing him as a person—as a fellow cockatrice. As someone who might've been just as lonely as me.

Shaking my head at myself, I try to sever the connection that feels like it's trying to snap into place. Although I can tell that he feels it too. But instead of trying to ignore it like me, he's just watching me steadily, drinking my every movement and expression in like he thirsts for it. Maybe I was wrong in my assumption. Maybe he isn't the one that Zen was hinting at.

I clear my throat, needing to break this emotionally-charged silence between us. "Alpha Bowen is known as the king of destroyed lounges. He takes what he wants and doesn't care about the destruction or ruin left in his wake."

"You've seen this?" Rook asks, his eyes going wide with shock and worry.

I pause. "Well, no...not exactly, but everyone knows what he's about."

Rook raises an eyebrow in question, his stunning tropical water gaze glimmering with disbelief and reproach.

"Don't start that devil's advocate bullshit with me, okay?" I warn. "Alpha Bowen tried to claim me as repayment for a debt. He didn't bother to ask me what I thought of the whole thing, just like my mat and pat. That's all I need to know. Someone who can do that could never care about me, and I'll fucking rot in this prison before I live under someone's boot for the rest of my long, feather-blessed life."

Rook raises his hands in surrender, and I bite into my apple, chewing and stewing on anger, hurt, and frustration.

"I get it. I wouldn't want that life either," he admits, and my seething softens ever so slightly. "So when you're not getting yourself locked up in prison, what sort of stuff are you into?" he asks, and I'm thrown off by the question.

I groan and shake my head.

"What?" Rook demands with a smile so gorgeous that it almost has my breath hitching.

Look away, Sinclair. Do not stare directly into that megawatt smile, or you'll go blind. The safe eclipse viewing advice feels strangely applicable here, so I'm going with it.

I turn away and stare at what I think are claw marks in the wall behind Rook's head instead.

"I hate the *what do you like to do* question," I explain, refusing to make eye contact.

He waits for me to elaborate.

"I do a ton of shit, but do you think I can remember any of it when I'm asked like that? It's like the question itself is some kind of mind wipe. All I can ever think of is the three *F*s all cockatrice love, but honestly, I'm over one of the *F*s, so that answer is one-third a lie."

Rook chuckles. "The three *F*s?" he queries.

"Man, you weren't kidding about your lounge keeping to themselves, were you? Everyone knows the three *F*s: flying, fighting, and fucking."

"And which *F* is the one you're not a fan of anymore?" he teases.

"Fucking," I chirp.

Rook pauses for a minute, like he's not sure what to say to that. He scratches the back of his neck like he's uncomfortable.

I laugh. "Fighting, you idiot. I remembered during the prison yard fight that that shit hurts." I narrow my eyes on him. "But why do males always think they win in the libido department? If you guys only knew how horny most females are on the daily, you'd cover your dicks and run, screaming out, 'Save yourself!' to every male you scurried past."

He snorts. "I would never run, let alone scurry away from a willing female," he counters with a wicked smile.

This playful banter is making my stomach do flips. I look him up and down assessingly. "I knew you had fucked up standards. You're just ready and waiting to pounce on any ol' willing female, huh?" I tease.

He gives me *the look*. "I assure you, I have high standards, Sinclair." He says my name with the hint of a purr that makes my clit sit up and take notice like a dog ready for a treat. "You should really talk to someone about that low self-esteem, though. You shouldn't be classifying yourself as just any ol' willing female. You should think more highly of yourself."

I roll my eyes and try to erase the blush from creeping up my neck and into my cheeks. Did he just admit that he's into me? I have to stop myself from giggling and batting my lashes at him.

Get it together, Sinclair.

Despite my efforts to rein it in, heat and desire fills the space between us until it almost feels like I can wrap my hands around it. I find myself picturing me and him together, of me straddling his lap while I run my tongue over the seam of his mouth. I imagine how he'd feel, all hard and stable beneath me, getting up close and personal with his masculine beauty and those entrancing eyes of his.

But...what the hell am I doing? Regardless if he's working on a plan to sell me out to Alpha Bowen or not, he's a prison guard.

When the silence stretches between us, both of us endure this pull and tug between us until Rook finally gets to his feet, severing it. "I better go. If the other guards find out I'm down here, they'll give me shit."

"Okay. Tell the Warden I said hi."

He snorts. "Definitely not gonna do that."

I snicker. "Scaredy cat."

"Hell yeah. Everyone is scared of that fucker."

"I heard that he slinks around in the shadows at night and sucks on people's souls while they sleep."

"Guess you're safe," Rook teases.

I throw my apple core at him. "Hey! I'll have you know that my soul is awesome, and he'd probably really love the taste of me."

Whoops, badly worded. At the mention of my *taste*, Rook's eyes take on such an intense heated look, that I'm forced to glance away.

"Behave, Sinclair," he says roughly as he opens the iron door with a loud creak. "I'll be back tomorrow."

I nod and follow him, pressing my face up against the rectangular peephole as he closes the door behind him and locks up. "How long are they making me stay in here?"

"One day for every guard you gave the smack-down to."

I groan. "Geez, you swipe your tail one time and everyone loses their minds."

He smirks. "Good luck with your tunnel."

"Yeah, yeah," I say, wriggling my fingers at him as he turns and walks down the dark corridor. I watch until I can't see him anymore, and then I slump onto my flat pillow and dump out the satchel, intending to use the rest of the contents to do a little bit of interior decorating in this place. It needs all the color it can get.

The second the contents are on the floor at my feet, my eyes home in on the green rock he left for me—the same one he held up to me in the rec yard when I was in my beast form.

A smile crosses my lips as I pick it up and turn it over in my fingers, admiring the color and texture. My tail slithers out to rub on it like a cat, and I realize with a little bit of dread that I already miss the asshole, and he's only been gone for five seconds.

I'm in so much trouble.

Rook is hanging out with me in my solitary cell again, just like he's visited me every day for the past three days. His visits are the only thing I can look forward to, because solitary is...well, solitary. It's lonely. Boring. Time drags like a dog's ass on the carpet. But the moment my ears perk up at the sound of footsteps coming down the corridor, I know it's him, and my heart goes full flutter. It's fucking annoying.

He usually shows up just when my stomach starts to growl and I've gone through all my food, like magic. And despite all the warnings I tell myself, despite the fact that I know I shouldn't, I've formed a friendship with him already. I've learned how funny he can be, how easy to talk to, and that we have things in common. Plus, he's very easy on the eyes, and he always brings me a satchel full of goodies. What's not to like?

Today, he smuggled me in an entire hot plate of dinner. I nearly moaned when I saw the steam. After days of tepid water and packaged food, eating a bowl of hot chili and fresh cornbread was like heaven. He also brought me another rock. It's sitting against the wall with the other one, and I'm not too proud to admit that they're the best things in the room.

"I'm just saying, you're not a very good prison guard, that's all," I tell Rook as we sit across the small room, our outstretched feet touching every so often when we move.

He has a big bag of chips that he's been chomping on for the past ten minutes, and he lifts his fingers into his mouth every once in a while to lick off the salt. My mouth waters every time. I find myself wanting to snatch his hand and suck those fingers into my mouth instead, and it's not because of the sodium craving.

"Fuck that noise, I'm an awesome guard," he tells me.

"You tried to talk my cockatrice down instead of tasing me like the others," I point out, mostly because I'm curious as to why he did that. I've been thinking about it for days.

"Why would I tase you?"

"Did you see me? I was ferocious."

He laughs and licks his fingers again before he runs his tongue over his pillowy bottom lip. I find myself mimicking him, and the corner of his mouth kicks up a notch. "You were adorable."

Immediately, I rear back and frown at him. "*Adorable*?" I say, affronted. "I was not adorable. I was vicious and bloodthirsty! Did you see the barrel rolls I did in the air?"

"I saw," he says, clearly trying not to smile. "Really good flying."

"Thank you," I say pertly.

"Personally, I wanted you to do more barrel rolls and throw the wolf fucker off you. I was this close to fucking him up that day."

His words catch me off guard. "Why?"

Rook shrugs and buries his eyes and hand in the chip bag, like he's avoiding looking at me. "Because. I didn't like to see you hurt."

Aww.

My cockatrice perks up inside me, and the hair on my head turns a deep, beating heart red, right along with the plume of feathers at the end of my tail.

"Oh," I say awkwardly.

"I should've let you fuck him up," he goes on, swallowing

his mouthful. "And I wouldn't mind tasing some of those guards, either."

"See?" I say, pointing at his face. "Terrible prison guard. You definitely have fucked up standards."

"Fucked up standards?"

"Mm-hmm. Why else would you be hanging out in solitary confinement with a convict?" I challenge.

Rook chuckles and finally sets aside his bag of chips. I'm half-relieved, half-disappointed that I won't see any more finger-tongue action. "Come on, now. I saw what you were found guilty of. You'll have to forgive me if I don't lose sleep at night over talking to someone who took an ice cream truck and went all Robin Hood with the contents. If the police hadn't forced you to crash, you'd have had to pay a fine for the ice cream and gas and that would've been it. You're not exactly a hardened criminal."

I wrinkle my nose. "Am so! I set off a glitter bomb in the cop's car, and it went off right in his face," I tell him, urging him to be impressed with my unlawful prowess. "Plus, I have my shank business to prove it," I argue.

He starts laughing, and I watch as he grabs his stomach, his whole body rocking with amusement. It would almost be contagious if it weren't at my expense.

Rude.

"Do you really think the guards around here would let you make actual weapons?" he questions, his laugh getting a little higher in pitch as he wipes a laugh-tear from his eye.

I look at him incredulously. "What do you mean *actual weapons*?" I demand.

"Pieces of comb stuck in tooth paste?" he offers, like it proves something.

"Hey, The Minty Hedgehog is lethal as fuck!" I defend, and Rook completely loses his shit at the name.

He starts laugh-squealing like a ticklish little girl while

mouthing *The Minty Hedgehog* over and over again. I watch his breakdown with a lot of judgement in my green eyes, not appreciating his lack of appreciation at all. He slaps his knee with one hand like that will help him get over the giggles faster.

I have to bite my bottom lip to keep it from poking out to reveal the pout I feel. I'm tempted to throw something at him.

"Well, the joke's on you, because people are buying them. They clearly see the potential my work has in aiding their vendettas," I argue, crossing my arms over my chest. "They're super dangerous. You could totally shank-kill someone with one of them."

Rook stops laughing long enough to shake his head and reply. "They're buying them to get on Zen's good side. Word on the block is that she's got something in the works for a break out. They all want to be taken with her," he tells me, and my mouth drops open.

Well, shit. He just might be right.

"Word on the block, huh? More like, word from Alpha Bowen, your puppet master," I accuse.

"Why would I be working for Alpha Bowen?" Rook asks.

"You tell me."

He shakes his head, and I go quiet as I try to think through other business opportunities I could do. I can't believe no one really likes my shanks. I thought they were awesome. I have to make money somehow though, or I'll go crazy without being able to make deals for necessities and snacks.

I guess I could keep selling them, regardless of whether or not the other inmates actually find them useful or not, since I'm still turning a profit. I try to think about what else I could procure or fashion into a must-need item here in Nightmare Penitentiary.

Rook smiles as he watches me think, and I'm momentarily distracted by his dimples again.

I want to lick them.

I shake away that thought and grab the rest of my cornbread, shoving it into my mouth in a massive bite. Maybe if I keep my mouth full, I can convince it not to do all the naughty things that are currently streaming through my head.

Rook watches as I chew, his eyes darting down to trace the movement of my tongue as I lick up the crumb spilling over my bottom lip. His green eyes darken slightly, and then his hair, which I thought was just glowing from the trick of the light earlier, actually starts to *glow* glow.

I choke on my bite until I can swallow it down and then shoot up to my feet. "Holy shit. You can glow?" I ask, pointing at his head.

It's super rare for cockatrices to be able to shift colors like I can with my feathers and hair and whatever touches my skin, but it's even more rare for a cockatrice to be able to illuminate all its pretty colors.

I'm suddenly like Ariel, my eyes hypnotized and reflecting Ursula's glowing contract. I can't stop staring at his luminescent green and blue hair. The end of my tail thrashes out of my pocket before I can stop it, and it starts flicking around like it wants to twerk its way into his pants. Oh hell, how am I supposed to resist him *now*? This is bad.

We stare at each other, eyes wide, breath caught, and some major sexual tension spreads between us and sticks us together like glue.

Fuck, he's hot.

Muscles. Dimples. Glowy hair. *Gah! I can't stop looking at the glowy hair!*

I'm suddenly wet and hot between my thighs, and he's growing himself a snake in his pants.

"Stop glowing!" I snap, well...I try to snap at him. It comes out like a *really* embarrassing moan. I bite on my bottom lip hard enough to split it.

"I *can't*," he says through clenched teeth. Even his fists are clenched at his sides. His entire body has gone rigid, and his eyes are stuck on the movements of my tail, as my feathers bounce from yellow to orange to red and back again. Show-off.

I need to turn around. I need to stop looking, and he needs to leave before I do something I'll regret. *He's probably the enemy,* I remind myself. My cockatrice rolls her eyes at me. If she had fingers, she'd flip me off, because she doesn't give a fuck. She just *wants* to fuck.

"Rook..." I warn.

But instead of hightailing it out of my solitary confinement cell like he should, he seems to lose just as much control as me, because his hair starts glowing even brighter, and then his goddamn neck wobbles.

I'm only so strong, dammit.

"Fuck."

We both move at the same time.

In an instant, we're slapping against each other like pancakes on a skillet.

His mouth crashes onto my mine, my hands sink into his hair, and our pelvises grind against each other while my tail enters a goddamn flicking frenzy.

I need him to fuck me right now, or I'm going to explode from need.

"Let me fuck you," he growls into my ear, like me trying to maul him with my mouth *and* vagina wasn't permission enough.

"Yeah, duh. Hurry up!" I snap before I start climbing him like Mt. Everest. I need him in me ASAP.

He slams my back against the iron wall, and my adrenaline hikes up along with my shirt as he delves a hand beneath the fabric to squeeze my breast. *Ohmygawd* his hand is so hot on my flesh, and he's squeezing with just the right amount of force.

"Grab my cock," he orders.

"Then get it out for me, asshole!"

He chuckles, and I feel his hand go between us and land on his belt. He has a whole prison guard buckle situation going on down there that I don't have the time or the patience for, quite frankly.

My open mouth trails over his neck, my teeth grazing his pulse as he undoes his belt, buttons, zippers and hell knows what else. When I finally feel his pants drop around his ankles, I slap his hand away so that I can grind against him.

"Fuck, Sunrise. Slow down."

Aww, he's using my nickname during sexy times. That's cute, but... "No."

Wrapping my hand around him, I get the full experience of his girth. He's thick. And heavy. And his skin is so damn soft, yet his cock is so hard, it makes my mouth water.

"You better know how to use this thing," I tell him.

He nips my neck, scattering goosebumps over my flesh. "I know how to use it. You better know how to take it."

Fuck, now I'm drenched.

As if he can scent it, his hand comes down to the waistband of my pants and slips inside, his thick, hot fingers skimming over my panties. My very unsexy, way too big, white cotton, prison-issued granny panties. No way in hell am I letting him see these suckers. I reach down and push my pants and underwear down at the same time just so that he doesn't get a chance to spy what they look like.

"Eager thing, aren't you?" he purrs.

I rip my shirt over my head, so that all I have on now is a white sports bra. I rip that off too, letting my girls hang free.

I sigh at the feeling of them heavy with need, my nipples aching.

Rook's hands come up to cup them, his fingers pinching against my pink nipples. "You're fucking gorgeous, you know that?"

I'm pretty sure I don't look gorgeous right now, seeing as I still have taser marks on my skin and some major bedhead, but I'm not complaining.

"Shirt off," I order him.

He holds my gaze, his fingers still plucking at my nipples hard enough to make me groan. "I give the orders when we're fucking, Sunrise."

"Yeah, good luck with that," I snort. "I'm—"

My words choke off when Rook suddenly whips off his shirt because, *holy fuck*, he is ripped. I mean, I knew he worked out. I could tell from his biceps. But I didn't expect his tanned, beautiful body to look like *this*. His abs could form their own ice cubes.

"Come to mama," I say, dropping down so I can lick my tongue up the groove of his stomach.

His skin lurches beneath my touch, and he growls as I lick my way up to his nipple. "If you're gonna be on your knees in front of me, then you're taking my cock in that unstoppable mouth of yours."

I smirk up at him. Why is he so dominant and perfect? He's like everything I've always wanted in a male. "You mean like this?" I tease before leaning down and licking up the length of him.

His hands come up to grip my hair. "Fuck yes."

I swirl my tongue around his tip, tasting him and loving the way he moans and thrusts his hips toward me, his body begging for more. I wrap my lips around the sensitive end of him and hollow out my cheeks. Rook throws his head back, and that's when I make my move. I pop off his dick and stand up, pulling him toward me as I lean my naked back against the cold iron of the cell wall.

"What the hell?" he asks, all sullen like some kid who just had his favorite toy stolen from him.

I giggle inside.

"I just decided you haven't earned one of my epic blow jobs yet," I tell him, and his disbelieving eyes flash with fire as I throw down some unspoken gauntlet. "In fact, I don't know if you've even earned this pussy yet," I add.

He may think he can be all bossy when it comes to the fuckery, but he's got another thing coming, because I want it *all*. I want to boss *and* be bossed, and not every male can handle that. Nothing gets me going like a tug-of-war. I like to play. I like to see who can win. And I want to see what Rook is about before I ride his dick. I want to know if he can handle me the way I need to be handled. I've had way too many disappointments in the past, and I don't want to be disappointed again.

We stare at each other for a beat. My vagina screams, *somebody play with me!* And when I see his lips curl, I know he just flashed a *challenge accepted* my way.

Alright. Let's see what you're made of, Rookie.

8

"You want me to *what*?" Rook asks.

His face is incredulous, his pants are still around his ankles, and his dick is bopping like a Hanson brother.

I don't know whether I feel more amusement in this moment or arousal. I'd say it's fifty-fifty.

"It's no big deal. Just some sex games so I know you're worthy. We'll call it *Minute to Dick It*."

He scowls at me. "No, we won't."

"Fine," I say breezily as I push away from him and pick up my shirt and start to pull it back on. I make sure to let my girls bounce extra nicely and arch my back as I tug the fabric over my head.

"Wait," he rushes to say, and my movements pause.

I look over at him past the sleeves. "Yes?"

He grinds his pretty white teeth. "What sort of sex games?"

I suppress my grin as I pull the shirt back on all the way. I leave my pants and panties on the floor, though, so my shirt hits me mid-thigh.

His eyes scan the length of me. "Fuck, you look like every inmate fantasy I've ever had, but better."

I beam at him and grab the pipe from the floor. "Look at you, already earning a point!" I say excitedly before walking over to the wall and scraping the pipe down it. With a loud screech, I scratch a tick mark onto it to keep track of his points. "You're doing so good already."

Eyes still lit up with hunger, he brings a hand down to his cock and strokes himself once. Twice. Three times. "Yeah? Just how good, Sunrise?"

I swallow hard, my eyes flicking back up to his face from the erotic show that's going on down south. "Don't try to distract me."

He just smirks.

"Can I borrow your watch?"

Taking his hand off his stiff member, he undoes the clasp on his wrist and tosses it over to me. I catch it and press the buttons, setting the timer. "Okay, *Minute to Dick It*. You have sixty seconds to put a chip on the end of your dick and shoot the chip into your mouth."

Rook stares at me openmouthed. "What? I'm not doing that." When I don't reply, he huffs. "What the fuck is the point of that?"

"Lots of reasons," I reply, holding up my fingers to tick them off. "Shows me you have good eye-dick coordination. It also shows off how hard your dick is. And it'll also make your cock salty, which is good for me if I end up licking it some more."

He chokes on my words and then snatches up the bag, grumbling under his breath. "Fucking crazy ass cockatrice chick."

"Tick tock, your timer starts now."

Digging into the bag, he puts a chip on the end of his

dick, a finger on the head, and then *ping!* He flicks it down, and his cock springs up, making the chip fly.

Unfortunately, it hits him in the chest.

"Bummer, man. Try again."

He does. Again and again and again, until I'm laughing so hard that tears are threatening to run down my cheeks.

"Stop laughing!" he says, flustered.

"Sorry, sorry," I quickly say, biting on my lips to keep my giggles from slipping out. "You just need to adjust your projectile angle. You're doing great though. It hit your cheek that time. You're so close."

"This is ridiculous. I can't stay hard for this shit."

"No chip dick, no licky-lick."

His cock bobs. I smile. "Looks like you're staying hard just fine."

"I am going to fuck you raw for this."

Please, yes.

"Then you better stop screwing up. Ten seconds left!"

With another string of curses, he digs into the bag. "Shit, I only have one chip left!" he exclaims, all flustered.

"Make it count, boo."

He scowls. "God, this is humiliating."

"Don't worry, you look hot. And savory," I chortle.

His mouth curls, and despite his best efforts not to enjoy himself, he totally is.

With the last chip on his dick, he concentrates. Five...four...three...two...

Launch!

Mouth gaping, cock springing, neck tilting, the chip goes flying straight onto his tongue.

"Score!" I yell, clapping as I jump up and down in excitement.

He raises his arms in the air, ready to take a victory lap as the timer beeps.

"Well done, Glow Worm."

He cocks a brow and drops his arms. "Glow Worm?"

"Yeah," I say, nodding at his hair that's still glowing. "That nickname is sticking."

"Hmm," he grunts. "Well? Do I get a reward for winning?" he challenges.

I run my gaze over his six pack, his strong thighs, the way the shadows wrap around every muscle and indent. Damn, he's perfect.

"You do," I say, drawing another tick on the wall before dropping the pipe and stepping toward him. He watches me as I come forward, ready to make out with him and taste that salty cock catapult of his, but I stop myself just in time. "No, no, no," I chastise and push away from him, shaking my head at myself for almost buckling and ending the game early.

My vagina threatens to mutiny, but she should know better than anybody how important these tests really are.

"You've only passed one test. There's more."

"More?" he asks, his voice radiating exasperation. "How much more are we talking about?"

"Well, I would typically make you do a hundred pushups in a minute to test your endurance, but you've been hard this whole time, so I think the question of endurance has already been answered," I tell him, ticking off a finger. "I could blindfold you and see if you can track me, but with the cell being so small, I think that'd be too easy. So really all that's left is…" I run through the various tests I've administered in the past and try to figure out what would work best in this case. "Ah, got it," I announce with the snap of my fingers. Then I whip off my shirt and reach for his dark blue uniform shirt which has been abandoned in the corner.

"Wait, why are you getting dressed in my clothes?"

"Because mine would have been *way* too easy. Yours have buttons, clasps, and zippers, which is just what I need.

Rook huffs and runs a hand through his colorful hair. "Why do I feel like you're trying really hard to *not* fuck me?" he asks, shaking his head and watching me as I grab his pants from the floor and put them on next.

I give him a look that says, *oh please*. "Why do I get the impression that you're not trying hard enough *to* fuck me?" I fire back. "Did you think I'd be easy just because I'm a naughty little convict and you're a big strong guard?"

I lace my voice with desire and run a finger down the buttons of his shirt while my eyes bank with heat. Rook licks his lips, and his cock bounces with sudden excitement. If he had a chip on that thing, it would've launched high enough that I could have caught it in *my* mouth instead. We'll have to play that game later.

"Is this some kind of role play?" Rook asks hopefully.

I giggle. "Nope. But if you can get all my clothes off, you can fuck me any way you want to, and I'll be a good little cockatrice and do exactly as I'm told."

All traces of exasperation and irritation are gone, and his face turns carnal. "Finally," Rook sighs before stepping toward me, his movements desperate and his eyes bleeding desire.

When I hop back a step, he narrows his eyes at me.

"Hold up, Glow Worm, you haven't heard the rules yet," I declare. "I need you to show your skill set to me. So you have to undress me...without using your hands."

He studies me for a beat. "And if I can..."

"Then I'm yours."

The words spill out of my lips before I can stop them. Rook's eyes flash with something I can't identify, and then he's closing the distance between us before I can elaborate and explain that I only meant that I'm his for a sex-sesh, not that I would be his...for, like...ever.

He stops centimeters away from me, and his gaze bounces back and forth between my eyes. Determination sets his features, and he stares down at the buttons on his uniform shirt like he's trying to solve a puzzle. The way he looks over every button and zipper and clasp on my body...it's intense. Calculating. I can feel the charge in the air from the sexual challenge I've given him. His inner beast likes it.

A thrill works its way up my body, and I suddenly find myself wanting to say fuck the game and just tackle him instead. But then he bends over and wraps his teeth around a button, and my brain stutters to a stop. Suddenly, all I can focus on is his face pressed against my sternum, his lips closing around the navy blue button, and how fucking good he smells.

I wait a second for him to pull some crazy move and unbutton the shirt with his tongue. I can picture him tying cherry stems in his mouth for practice when he was younger or unwrapping Starbursts with only his tongue in preparation for a day like today. But instead of figuring out a way to finesse the situation, he grinds the threads securing the button to the fabric with his teeth and pulls back away from me until the button rips right off.

Well, that's one way to do it.

I gasp as the shirt falls open ever so slightly at my chest, and he bends down and tears off the next button with his teeth. Fuck cherry stems and Starburst wrappers, this is how to get shit done!

And damn, it's hot.

He snaps more threads, another button goes flying, and my pussy clenches with excited anticipation.

See, told you this was a good idea, I tell my lady bits smugly. My clit just shrugs me off.

A slight whimper escapes my lips as he pops off another button, and Rook looks up at me from under his ridiculously long lashes. His eyes say *I know*, and I'm tempted to silently communicate back *you don't know me*, but the only problem with that is it seems like he does.

With his hands folded behind his back, he looks like he's ready to take an evening stroll instead of participating in sexcapades. His deliciously defined back muscles bunch as he goes to work biting the shirt open, and I just want to run my hands over every perfect inch of him. I've never been so attracted to a male before, which makes this situation all the more ridiculous.

Rip.

Another button loses its fight to stay attached, and the uniform shirt is now gaping to my navel. He rubs the scratchy skin of his cheeks against the exposed soft skin of my stomach, and all I can think about is what it will feel like to have those scratchy cheeks between my thighs.

I try to focus on the here and now and not the useless thoughts that are running through my head, demanding that I figure out what all of this means or accept that this is ultimately doomed to go nowhere between us. It's just sex, I tell myself. Rook is like a gift wrapped up in cockatrice feathers, so why shouldn't I enjoy a little fun?

If anyone finds out, we could get in a shit ton of trouble. But somehow...that only makes this hotter. Forbidden fucking with my prison guard? Yes, please!

Two buttons to go. The fabric is hanging off my hardened nipples, just a breath away from being exposed. I feel like I'm one of those taut threads he keeps pulling, ready to snap. My breath is coming on quicker, my skin flush. This moment seems like it's about to change something, which I don't get. I've had meaningless hook-ups before, and I've never been all worried or overemotional about them. So why does this hook-up seem different? Seem like...more?

One button left.

I try not to squee with nerves as I watch him free the last button and spit it out onto the floor with a clack. The shirt and I both just sit there waiting to see what he'll do next. He straightens up, his gaze molten as he stares at me for a moment.

I swear, he eye-fucks me so hard I can practically *feel* it. I can read the heated promises in his eyes, and somehow it chases my nerves away. I suddenly don't care if I'm an inmate and he's a guard. I don't care that this could never work outside of this cell. Here and now is more than fine by me. And I seriously want it right fucking now.

I reach down and unclasp my pants, dropping the zipper down. The large pants drop right off me, and Rook looks at me, confused. "Did I lose?"

"No, you fucking won."

I push his buttonless shirt off my shoulders and attack him like he's the pool and I'm competing in a belly flop contest. It's not pretty, but I couldn't give a fuck. He grunts from the body tackle I just executed, but his arms reach out and support my weight as I wrap myself around him. His warm skin against mine is like the best feeling ever, and I moan as I claim his mouth.

I tease his tongue with mine, and we're both suddenly all hands and tightening arms like we're hanging off a cliff and trying to find the best handhold to take us to the top. The train of colorful feathers on his tail shoots up, spreading and shaking as we eliminate any space between our bodies. I chuckle into his mouth at the sight and turn to look at the impressive display. Like a male peacock, his tail feathers fan out, the iridescent blue and green colors glinting proudly.

"Nice," I murmur.

"Just ignore it," Rook groans against my mouth as he nips at my lower lip.

I smile and capture his tongue to suck on it after he flicks it out to tease my kiss-swollen lips. "My tail has a mind of its own too," I explain, and I try not to giggle even harder when his tail feathers start to sway and writhe hypnotically.

Fuck, that's pretty.

Fulfilling my promise, I drop down to my knees and lick him from base to tip, letting my tongue swirl over the head and suck up every hint of salty goodness. He grunts, my name spilling from his lips as I lap at him, giving him just a taste before I pop off, my tongue darting out to lick up the bead of precum gathering, and look up to gauge his reaction. "Yum," I say.

His eyes are hooded with lust. "Fuck. I want to taste you," he tells me as he pulls me up. His hands are holding my ass to support me, and he spreads my cheeks slightly and leans in, sucking on my bottom lip.

"Later," I promise, because if I don't get this dick inside me in less than two point five seconds, I'm going to spontaneously combust.

Rook opens his mouth to say something, but whatever it was turns into a groan of pure ecstasy as I align the head of his cock with my soaked pussy and drop down on him slowly and smoothly. I throw my head back and close my eyes, so all of my senses can focus on the way he feels as he fills me up inch by inch.

We couldn't fit any more perfectly.

The wet curls between my spread thighs meet the hair at his base, and I grind against him, leaving a stamp of desire before I lift up until he almost pops out. I drop down on him harder, my hands on his shoulders for leverage, and this time, I open my eyes so I can watch his face. His eyes are closed, and he sucks in air between clenched teeth, a deep moan escaping on his exhale while our tails twist around each other. Seeing him like this...tense with desire and going crazy with lust because of *me*...it makes me feel powerful.

Like Rook can feel my eyes on him, his lids slide open. Flaming desire smashes into me as our gazes connect. I feel completely consumed by his blazing hot look, and his grip on my ass tightens. He walks our connected bodies toward a wall and presses the feverish skin of my back against the iron barrier. I hiss at the shock of cold against my back, and then my hiss morphs into a gasp as Rook pins me in place and starts fucking me. Hard.

Oh. My. God.

He works in and out of me so roughly that I can't even think. He feels so good. So beyond anything I've ever experienced before, that my whole body just up and decides that Rook is now classified as a god, and we will devotedly worship him for the rest of our days.

I come so fucking hard and fast that I can't even scream. It's like the pleasure steals the air in my lungs as it shoots through me. I'm forced to shove my face against where his neck meets his shoulder and just do this really weird gurgle thing. I'd be embarrassed if I weren't riding the best damn high my body has ever experienced. I didn't even know it was possible to come that fast, and from nothing other than his cock. I always have to have other stimulation going on either with my boobs or clit in order to come, so this is completely new territory for me.

"That's right, Sunrise, ride it out. You feel so fucking good," Rook says into my ear as he slows his pace slightly and grinds against me more with each thrust. The new rhythm does all kinds of things for me, and just when I expect my orgasm to slip away, he works to make it lap steadily against my insides instead.

Holy shit, that's good.

I giggle, completely lust-drunk, and he smiles and kisses me slowly. I can taste languid appreciation on his skilled tongue, and I can't decide which I like better, the hard fucking or the sensual fucking that he's doing right now.

I feel his tail ripple at the same pace as his thrusts, and I'm so captivated by it all that it almost feels otherworldly. Who knew it could be like this? I've been getting subpar sex for years. He's going to ruin me for all other males in the future, I just know it.

I kiss Rook back with passion, memorizing the feel of his tongue, his teeth, his lips. I revel in the way he makes me feel. My orgasm finally tapers off, my pussy fluttering over his thick cock one last time. I twine my fingers in his glowing hair and own his mouth like he's owning my pussy. You'd think I'd be all tired and rubbery after such an intense orgasm, but now that I know what he can do, I want more.

Like Rook can read my body, his pace slowly picks back up. He thrusts his cock into me deeper, my body being smashed roughly between the wall and him. I break away from his mouth, needing to pant and moan and tell him all the ways that he's incredible and how good he feels. I love being taken like this. I love that he's dominant enough to do it, while still pliant enough to let me be the boss too, like with the games.

I nip at his earlobe. "Again," I say. He chuckles, and then he does exactly as he's told.

If I thought he was fast before, I'm now learning that was only Rook's medium-fast sex setting. I call out his name over and over again, and it's simultaneously a prayer, a plea, and a warning not to set my vagina on fire with the current speed and friction. This is clearly not his first rodeo, and I'm not even mad at that. Just give me all the orgasms, and I couldn't care less about anything else.

"Hold your knees and spread for me," Rook orders, and for a moment, I question how the fuck that's going to work, but then I remember that I now worship him as a sex god, so I do exactly as instructed.

I unwrap my legs from around his waist and drop my hands from his neck to support under my knees instead. His one hand on my ass supports most of my weight, and his chest presses hard against mine, keeping me pinned to the wall.

His other hand comes up and buries in my hair, and he tugs lightly at the strands. I groan in approval at the tender sting of pain. Now that I'm spread obscenely for him, the current position lets Rook hit all kinds of new things inside of me. He gets to work again, and I'm a mewling, begging, complimentary mess in no time.

"Are you ready?" Rook asks me, his lips caressing the shell of my ear.

I have no idea what he's asking me, but Rook could tell me to ignore a real-life Baby Yoda right now in this moment and I'd do it. He's *that* fucking good.

I moan, and Rook must take that as a yes because the next thing I know, his train of feathers are compressing together, and his tail flips up between his legs and slips between us. It caresses the base of my filled pussy, and my breath hitches when it grazes over my clit.

I can feel the soft feathers first, and then I get the firm, smooth scales as he applies pressure, the end of his tail pressing down on me in a weirdly perfect way and making me jolt. The new sensations take everything to a whole new level, and I start to wonder how I'll ever be the same after this.

He's going to turn me into some sex-crazed puddle of blissed out mush, I just know it.

Meh, there are worse ways to go.

He never slows his pace, as his tail works to tease me, the perfect combination of firm and soft, flicking and pressing. He fucks me like lightning striking down against the earth, so fast that the thunder of my moans has to chase it to catch up.

Rook pulls my hair lightly, just enough to have me tilting my head back so he can nip and suck on my neck. His tail moves again, gliding from my clit to wrap behind me, and then it starts to slowly circle my asshole. *Oh, fuck.*

The movement matches up with the circles his tongue is creating on my skin before he nips at a spot and then sucks it into his mouth. He tilts my hips, his hand squeezing my ass tight enough to leave a bruise, and this new angle hits a perfect spot inside of me while my clit is being stimulated with every drag of his cock. When his tail presses *just* inside my back entrance, I'm a goner.

My sudden orgasm is thunderous as it booms through me, and I'm completely lost to sensation. I feel like I'm slowly breaking apart into a million atoms that are just exploding out into the room, and then I'm suddenly snapping back into place, screaming out his name.

"Yes!" Rook roars victoriously, like my current state is all he's ever needed in life. I feel his pleasure jet inside of me as he climaxes, filling me up with the red-hot cum that all male cockatrices have.

Rook's release feels more scorching than anything I've ever felt before, but that doesn't surprise me. Female cockatrices are built to withstand any level of heat, so it doesn't burn so much as warms my insides in a way that makes me feel like I'll be able to glow too. It's like he's coating me from the inside out, bathing me in our mutual bliss. It's an incredible feeling. I've never felt so satisfied, safe, or cherished as I do right now.

Thrusting up, he buries himself deeply one last time, like he wants to ensure every last drop hits its mark. His actions almost feel like they're sitting on the cusp of a claiming, but I dismiss that thought and chalk it up to just the most epic sex. Ever.

I open my mouth to say something, but nothing comes out. I've officially been fucked speechless. I couldn't even talk if I wanted to. My brain refuses to form words, so I just end up mumbling gibberish and then sighing in contentment as the last of my orgasm ripples away.

Chuckling, Rook untangles his hand from my hair and drops his hold back to my ass where his tail is wrapped around me possessively, the feathers petting the curve of my butt cheeks. I pull my hands from my knees and wrap my arms around his neck again.

We just stand there, tangled against each other, breathing it all in. Rook nuzzles my neck, and I lean into it like some lovesick teenager. I feel shattered, but in the best possible way.

How have I gone my whole life without knowing that this is how it can be between two people? I get it now. I get why people call sex intimate. It was never that way for me before. Fun, pleasurable, disappointing—but never intimate.

I realize that my tail has gotten in on the petting action too, and my tail feathers are currently running up the outside of his thigh and back down again.

"That was..." Rook starts.

"A-muh-zen," I slur at the same time he exhales, "Perfect."

Can orgasms make you high? I feel so fucking floaty right now.

I pat him on the back like I'm wordlessly saying *well done*, and Rook chuffs out a laugh. I can only imagine the blissed out smile that must be stretched across my face, but I can't actually feel my face to tell for sure, so whatevs.

As if he's not ready to let me go yet, Rook keeps me in his arms as he picks me up off the wall and carries me to the iron cot that's been built to hang out of the wall. He sits down on the flat mattress, keeping me straddled in his lap.

My knees hit the cool metal of the bed frame, and I wonder how long he's going to stay inside of me...not that I'm complaining. He could probably announce that we're going to now stay like this forever, and I'd bump knuckles with him and be cool with it. I side-eye myself at that realization. *Get a grip, Sinclair. No dick should have that much power.*

His tail runs its feathers up my spine in a soothing caress, and Rook pushes my hair back from my face. It wasn't really in my face to begin with, so I get all giddy at the thought that he just did it because he wanted to touch me. I mean, I *am* pretty amazing, so I don't blame him, but it's good that he agrees.

With expertise, he sucks my bottom lip into his mouth and then kisses me slowly. My brows shoot up with surprise even as my eyes close as he sweeps his tongue inside my mouth with tender reverence. I've never had a guy want to makeout *after* sex.

Holding his arms, I cling to him as I kiss him back, suddenly nervous. Rook has me feeling like I'm some kind of blushing virgin, when the reality is that I'm anything but. Apparently, I need to re-evaluate my expectations though, because holy sex god, my eyes have now been opened, and my vagina is forever changed.

After a few minutes of the sweetest makeout session ever, Rook pulls away from my lips, and a whimper of protest leaves me. He laughs softly. "What are you thinking, Sunrise?" he asks softly, his turquoise eyes flicking over my face.

"That my vagina wants to worship you," I reply breathily. When I realize what I've said, I slam a hand over my mouth.

Really, brain? First we can't talk and then you let that loose? Keep that shit inside!

Rook's soft laugh turns into more of a bark, and he runs his hands through my hair again. I sit smugly in his lap, because I can tell that he's *really* drawn to my colors.

"Did you know your hair color flashes when you come hard?"

"It does?" I ask, partly surprised and a little bit embarrassed.

I look at my ombré locks like they've betrayed my confidence.

"Mmm-hmm," he purrs as he plays with the ends of my hair. "It might be one of my favorite things. Right after being inside of you and hearing you scream my name."

I blush, and a giggle escapes me that's really high-pitched even to my own ears.

Fucking hell, Sinclair, are you capable of playing it cool?

"So I've made your favorite things list already?" I tease, all too aware that he's *still* inside of me.

Once again, our back and forth is taking on a level of intimacy that I'm not sure how to navigate. He touches me so affectionately; it's like he thinks I'm the one that should be worshipped. He's relaxed beneath me, his hair glowing softly, radiating pure contentment. The fucked up thing is...I feel the same way.

It's bad enough that I just shit where I eat, or rather, fucked where I need to hide out, but if anyone finds out about this, that could cause serious issues. The other guards didn't like me hurting one of their own, so I seriously doubt fucking one is going to go over any better.

Rook leans in and nips at my shoulder, his hips rocking slightly. *Is he seriously getting hard already? How is that even possible?*

I'm about to start riding him so I can test out just how hard he is—you know, for science—when static crackles to life in the cell, and a male voice rings out. "Rook, are you still here?"

Rook and I both jump as the sound intrudes on our moment and slams us both back to reality.

More static. "I thought you left a while ago, but someone said your truck is still in the lot. We could use some help if you're still around," the voice blasts from the speaker of Rook's walkie-talkie.

He quickly lifts me off him and scrambles for the radio clipped to his utility belt. He takes a deep breath like he's trying to compose himself and then presses down on a button on the side of the radio. "Yeah, Mac, I'm still here. I was getting my laundry done. What's up?"

Static crackles. "Can you come to Block Black? You'll know what's up when you get here."

"On my way," Rook calls out casually, and then the radio goes silent. "Shit," he curses as he starts looking around the cell for all of his clothes.

I get up and hand him his underwear and pants. He gives me a grateful smile and starts pulling everything on.

"I'm sorry," he offers as he takes his shirt from my outstretched hands.

"It's fine," I reassure him.

I wonder for a moment if *getting my laundry done* is some kind of code. Do the guards fuck inmates often? Or do they really just have inmates do their laundry for them? I want to ask, but Rook is clearly in a hurry.

"How are you going to explain the no button thing?" I ask, as I watch him pull on his shirt that now gapes down the middle and shows off his muscular chest and abs, every single button long gone.

"It's fine. Weird shit happens all the time when you work in a supernatural prison. Your cell block is nothing. The deeper levels and the other buildings for the serious criminals...shit is crazy over there," he replies, and once again, I wonder what that means exactly.

He's in such a rush that he hasn't noticed that I've swapped his name tag again as a surprise and snatched the plain one again. He unknowingly brought me all the supplies I need on his last visit, and his name right now is surrounded by dick shaped jewels. The dicks glimmer under the bad lighting above us, and I wish I could see his face when he discovers them. I have to put a hand over my mouth to hide my smile.

I watch him wrap his belt around his waist and start buckling it into place. I stand there awkwardly, feeling his cooled and drying cum on my thigh, and all I suddenly want to do is take a hot shower. I love having sex bareback, but it's messy. At least my shifter birth control is getting put to use. I was in quite the dry spell before this.

"Hey, can one of the perks of fucking a guard be after-sex showers?" I ask casually as he checks himself over to make sure he has everything that he's supposed to.

He closes the distance between us in two strides and pecks me on the lips before turning toward the door. "I'll make sure you get cleaned...tomorrow."

"*Tomorrow*?" I bark out, irritated.

"Yeah, I like the idea of my cum dripping down your thighs, and your body covered in my marks and scent," the arrogant asshole says with a possessive smirk. "Don't worry, we'll get you *all* kinds of cleaned up tomorrow."

His tone indicates that *getting all cleaned up* really means a whole lot of dirty shit. A chill of eager anticipation breezes over me so that I can't even continue to be irritated about him making me wait.

"See you tomorrow, Sunrise." With that, the door to my cell creaks open, and he walks out, shutting it solidly behind him.

I watch the empty space where he just was for a beat, and then something he said registers.

Wait. Marks?

Did that fucker *mark me*?

I quickly replay everything we just did in my head. Did he bite me or something and I didn't notice because the orgasms were that good? I walk over to pick up the broken iron pipe that I've been digging with. All of the scraping I've done to it has created a shiny spot. I hold it in front of me like it's a mirror and try to see through the really bad, convoluted metallic reflection, hoping to discover just what in the hell Rook meant by *marks*.

I run it all over my neck and face, and then I spot it. I wipe the pipe and then the base of my neck to make sure it's not dirt or something, but nope, this motherfucker has given me a fucking necklace of hickeys.

I'm going to kill him.

After I fuck him one more time though, because why not take advantage of all of those skills?

But after that, he's definitely going down...on me...and then for sure he's a dead man.

9

The asshole cockatrice has been gone for days.

I know this, because he left his damn watch behind. It's been three goddamn days that I've been sitting in this fucking solitary cell, with only a rusted water fountain to try to clean up with. That thing barely trickles out, and the water is browner than a cockatrice's shit stain.

I've been steeping in my own spite, every irritant like an abrasive gash against my temper.

I'm crusty. I still reek of sex. I've nearly run out of all my snacks. I'm *still* stuck in solitary confinement. And Rook. Hasn't. Come. Back.

He visited me every day, staying hours upon hours at a time. He made me feel like we were friends. Like he cared. Like we had a connection. Then we fucked, and it was the hottest sex I've ever had in my entire life. And then he just...bailed.

Was that walkie-talkie thing totally contrived?

I just imagine all his prison guard buddies with a system in place, where they give a false alarm to each other so that they can leave after sex. Is that what he did? Hit it and quit it?

Every hour that I'm left to stew alone with some of his cum still crusted on my skin that I can't get off without an adequate shower, I feel angrier and angrier. I'm also hurt, and that pisses me off even more.

I don't want to have hurt feelings over that asshole. He left me after fucking me, so what? He tricked me with his tender kisses and soft caresses and attentive words, but why should I care? I'm not going to, I tell myself. I *order* myself not to. I refuse to go all heartbroken girl over him. I'm tougher than that.

The moment I get out of this cell, I will let him have it, and then I'll find a different guard to fuck, just to prove to myself *and* him that Rook doesn't mean anything to me either.

That'll teach him.

Stupid hair-glowing, head-wobbling, feather-fanning cockatrice!

"Wow. It reeks like sex in there. Is that how you're passing the time?"

I jump at the voice on the other side of my cell door and bolt to my feet. I stare at the unfamiliar female through the now open slot on the door, and I'm immediately drawn to her. I find my feet moving closer before I even note that I've walked across the room to meet her. There's a prison guard with her, wearing a blue uniform with a hood covering his face, but he's quiet as he stays in the shadows, his posture decidedly bored despite me not being able to see him.

Looking through the small opening in the door, I see that the female is dressed in a red uniform much like my gray one. She has dark hair at the roots that changes to an awesome electric teal color that I instantly appreciate, and she has an equally beautiful face. She's leaning against a silver cart filled with food, and my stomach grumbles.

"UberEats?" I quip. "I placed my order ages ago. Not a good way to earn a tip."

The girl smiles. "Sorry. You gave me the wrong address," she replies, playing along.

I give myself a mock forehead slap. "Of course! I forgot to put 101 Naughty Corner Solitary Avenue."

"Happens all the time," she says before motioning down to the tray. "What'll it be?"

I stand on my tiptoes so I can see the array of food options she has through the door's window. "I guess...the plastic-wrapped sandwich, a bruised banana, the bag of crushed chips, the stale cookies, and some room-temp bottled water. Except multiply that order by five," I tell her. "Solitary makes me hungry."

With a soft laugh, she starts passing me things through the slot on the door clearly meant for food—which in my case is an assumption, because until now, no one has delivered food to me other than Rook. I take the items one after the other. "What did you do to end up in here?" she asks. "You seem...not terrible. Not like some of the others I meet down here, anyway."

"I just joined in on a prison yard fight, turned into my beast, and knocked over some guards," I tell her with a shrug as I place my goods on the floor. "What about you? How'd you get put on food duty?"

"Just lucky I guess," she smirks.

"What are you?" I ask before I can stop myself. I'm drawn to her in this really strange way, and yet I have no idea what she is.

"Late," she answers, sidestepping my question. "I gotta go back to the other level and deliver more food. See you around."

"Wait, what's your name?" I ask, watching as she turns to wheel the cart back the way she came.

"Selena. You?"

"Sinclair."

Her scent finally hits me, and a smile crosses my face. "*Ooh*," I exclaim, surprised. "I see what you are now." Damn. No wonder I was drawn to her. She's a *siren*. Her very nature draws people in and drives them crazy. "Work it, girl," I say, fanning myself and tossing her a sultry smile and a wink. "It's getting hot in here."

She laughs, the sound melodic. "Nice to meet you, Sinclair. Don't eat all that in one sitting."

I shrug. "No promises," I tell her. "Oh, and I'm a huge fan of Pop Rocks candy. If you see any, do a girl a favor," I add, and she nods with a smile before disappearing into the shadows with her escort.

As soon as she's gone, I change my uniform into the same red color that she was wearing, wishing I could be put on food duty too. Think of all the snacks I could nab!

Oh well, at least the prison decided to feed me today. That's something.

Sitting down on my cot, I bust out some of the food she gave me and have myself a prison picnic for one. The food is delicious. The company kinda sucks though.

I'm sleeping heavily, dreaming about fucking multiple men at one time, all of them faceless, and none of them with a lick of cockatrice to them. Boring brown hair and no tails to speak of, they're giving me mediocre sex and subpar orgasms, and they're nothing at all like that asshole prison guard of whom I now no longer speak.

"Sunrise."

I frown in my sleep as one of the Average Joes stops thrusting into me as he says that word.

"Sunrise," he says again, but his moving lips don't line up with the voice, so it's like a bad Japanese voice-over movie.

"Stop talking," I grumble, my jaw feeling heavy, though it has nothing to do with the dream-threesome I just had, unfortunately.

"Sunrise."

Great, now it's the other faceless dude saying it. What, are they stuck on repeat?

"There is no damn sunrise! I know that, because you can't see the goddamn sun in this goddamn dark, depressing cell!" I tell them, hoping they'll all just shut up and let me get back to the unexceptional fornication.

"Sunrise!"

"Fuck! *What*?" I jolt awake at my own yelling and blink wide-eyed at Rook who's standing over me. The haziness of the dream exits the recesses of my memory as I take in the stupid prison guard who's finally deemed me worthy enough to grace me with his appearance in my cell.

Narrowing my eyes, I turn over on my cot, giving him the cold shoulder. Literally. My shoulder is freaking freezing in this dank cell because I refused to use the blanket he brought me. A stupid refusal in hindsight, because this place is super drafty, but I was feeling prickly.

I feel his weight settle on the cot behind me and the iron frame creaks. "Hey," he says, settling a hand on my hip. My blood boils at the contact, and my tail testily slaps his hand and then flicks it away from my body. "Are you okay?"

"I'm dandy," I reply, monotone. "Now go away. I'm sleeping."

I hear him sigh. "Look, I'm sorry it took me a bit to come back here. Things have been crazy."

My blood pressure rises faster than a sixty-something Texan with an affinity for red meat and arguments. "A bit?" I repeat, turning back around and then fluidly sitting up so I can scoot back and face him head-on. "It hasn't been a *bit*," I mock. "You've been gone for five fucking days!"

My screech is so loud and unexpected that Rook cringes back slightly. He has the audacity to look all hot and scruffy, his hair messy and somehow still perfect. He tries to reach for me. "I'm sorry, Sunrise."

"Don't *Sunrise* me!" I snap, getting to my feet to put some much needed distance between us. I don't want him to touch me. I can't trust my body not to react if he touches me, and I don't want that.

I cross my arms in front of myself. "Do all your conquests get a shower? Or was that just a way to appease me?"

He frowns, getting to his feet. I try not to notice how sexy he looks or the fact that he switched out his name tag back to his regular one. He ruined the game between us by being such an ass.

"Conquests?" he repeats.

"Mm-hmm. Let me see your belt."

The line between his brows deepens. "What?"

"Your belt. I wanna see if you have a new notch in it."

His confusion turns to anger in a flash. "What the fuck is your problem? I told you I was sorry. I couldn't get back here!" he shouts, his rumbling voice knocking against the small space of the room. "You're not some fucking conquest, Sinclair."

"Sure," I say calmly, my face derisive. "Can I get a shower or not? Preferably before your little guard friends call you for another bullshit Operation Black Block."

Irritation traces the edges of his hardened face, and he

stalks toward me. I don't move, because I won't give him the satisfaction of cowering or running from him.

"You think real highly of me, don't you?" he asks, his face a mask of anger.

"That would imply that I think of you at all. I don't," I reply with a cutting whip. "You were a good fuck; I'll give you that. But now that's over, which you clearly demonstrated by leaving me down here to rot in your crusty cum and silent absence. Thank fuck the prison fed me, or I would've run out of food."

His eyes flash with remorse, but I ignore it.

"Did you and all your guard buddies laugh your asses off?"

His face grows stormy as his mouth tightens. "Stop saying this shit, Sinclair. It wasn't like that. *I'm* not fucking like that."

I shrug. "Whatever. I don't care," I say dismissively. "Now, unless you're giving me food or taking me to the shower, get out."

Rook runs a hand down his face and glances around, like he's looking for a way to make it out of this mess. "Look, Sunrise—"

"Don't call me that."

He clenches his teeth. "I can't get you into the showers today, but I'll come back tomorrow, and—"

"Save it," I snap, interrupting him. "I've heard your *I'll come back tomorrow* bullshit."

"It wasn't bullshit," he seethes.

"Mm-hmm," I say, keeping my tone unaffected and bored as I walk around him and head back to the corner of the room. I pick up my pipe and start digging again, just to give myself an excuse not to look at him.

"Sinclair."

I ignore him, scraping the pipe along the rock, making

dust and rubble fall at my feet like the crumbles of my stupid heart.

"Sinclair," he tries again, but I just dig harder, making the screech of the pipe drown out his stupid, rumbly voice. "Just... Fuck," he curses, before he turns and storms out of my cell, slamming the door behind him.

I keep digging long after he's gone, my movements jerky and irritated. "Andy Dufresne never had to deal with this shit," I mumble to myself, hating the heat I feel in my eyes. Nope. I will absolutely not have any emotion whatsoever about what just happened. I will not, under any circumstances, feel sad.

Fuck him.

And fuck me too for falling for it.

I growl, pissed off and needing to purge it as I slam the pipe down hard into the divot I've created in the wall. I use way too much force and must hit something super hard because the tip of the pipe skips away and somehow arcs over and slices deeply into my thigh. It hurts, and I grit my teeth against the pain. Blood immediately pools and quickly spills over my thigh. I try to pant through the stinging sensation and the tears that well up in my eyes.

"Fuck!" I shout, angrily chucking the pipe across the room. It bounces off the wall with a clang and then comes flying back at me.

Shit!

I dive to avoid getting impaled, and glare at the pipe as it clatters to the floor and rolls to the corner for a time out.

"I made you what you are today, and this is how you repay me?" I yell at it.

I hobble over to the blanket and press it against the cut on my leg. Like me, the blanket isn't the nicest smelling thing anymore, but I scoff and shake my head. Who cares? I probably just got tetanus or fucking Ebola from the pipe. What's a little blanket bacteria to add to the mix?

Blood soaks through the folds of the blanket quicker than I'd like, and I pack more against the wound and apply harder pressure. *Fuck, that hurts.*

I sit, angry, frustrated, and stewing in pain of the emotional and physical variety. What if I bleed to death in here? Iron isn't good for shifters. It fucks with our natural healing properties, so who knows how much this thing will bleed?

I wonder how long it would take for anyone to find me if I did bleed out? Maybe my new food delivery friend, Selena, will be by to bring me some more stale cookies and find me in a puddle of my own rusted blood. Knowing me, my death-sprawl will probably be really embarrassing. I won't be a pretty corpse, I just know it. I'll be the cadaver with the drool hanging out of her mouth and a piss stain on her pants.

Sigh.

Continuing to dramatically think of my imminent death-by-plumbing-pipe, I stare up at the blinking fluorescent light, wishing I could just see outside. I need to feel fresh air on my face and smell things besides rotten desire and BO. At first, solitary confinement didn't bother me, but I'm starting to go stir crazy now.

Lifting the blood-soaked blanket, I look at the cut on my thigh, noting that it sort of looks like the bleeding might be slowing down. Or maybe that's just wishful thinking. I quickly tear long strips from the blanket of assholish origin —which is what I will now call it—and wrap the strips against my wound, tying it off tightly. I do that a couple more times until it feels pretty secure, and then I pull a knee up. I rest my elbow and forehead on my knee, and I just let my mind wander. It lands on Rook, but I flick the spinner away, trying to land on something else. Something pleasant. But my mat and pat come up next, so I flick them away angrily, only to land on Alpha Bowen next. Fuck you, mind spinner. Those are all terrible topics.

I need to get out of this cell.

I must doze off sometime between *not* thinking about one shitty person or another, because the next thing I know, a loud clang jerks me awake.

I pull my head up, alarmed, and swipe stringy orange hair away from my face. The door to my cell opens, and it takes my eyes a second to wake up and blur together who it is. I huff and look away from Rook, wiping the drool from my cheek and chin.

My head hurts, my body is sore from the weird ass position I fell asleep in, and I just know that there's an embarrassing red mark on my face from where my head was pillowed against my arm. I blink, ready to steel myself with irritation that he woke me up and found me like this, but...I feel weird. I open my mouth to tell him to *fuck off*, but it's so dry that I can't seem to make my tongue work, and I'm a little dizzy.

"I said I would come back today, and I did. Sinclair, please don't be—" He pauses, stopping in his tracks. "What the hell? Why are you bleeding?" he demands, his nose flaring as he takes in the scene.

A bag of something drops to the ground, and suddenly Rook is down on the hard floor next to me, his hands cupping my face. "What happened?"

He looks down at my leg, and I follow his gaze. The bandages that I wrapped around my cut are soaked in crimson, and there's a drying puddle of my blood next to my leg.

Did he say today? Damn, how long did I pass out for?

"Did *you* do this?" Rook asks, and I have just enough wherewithal to roll my eyes at him.

I close my mouth and open it again to speak, but it's as dry as the Sahara, and I croak more than talk. "You clearly think a little too highly of yourself," I tell him, my voice all sand and gravel. "It was a tunnel-digging accident," I explain, oddly out of breath.

What the hell is wrong with me?

His lips press into a thin line. "Come on, we need to get you looked at. Everything in this fucking prison is toxic, and you've lost way too much blood." Rook scoops me up off the floor with minimal effort, and I'm impressed and pissed at the same time. I gather all the waning strength that I have and try to push out of his arms. I don't budge an inch.

"You are not taking me back to that doctor. She's a fucking psycho, Rook. Promise me you won't take me there." The words feel like glass in my throat as I utter them, but my eyes plead for him to listen.

He studies me for a second, and I can see the debate in his gaze. I shake my head *no*, and he exhales a defeated breath. "Fine. I won't take you there, Sun—" he starts, but I glare at him, not wanting to hear the nickname that's now tainted with disappointment and loneliness. "Sinclair," he corrects. "But you need help, which means I'm going to have to patch you up. Can you stop hating me long enough for me to do that?"

I tilt my head yes, and then despite myself, rest my head against his shoulder as he starts to carry me out of the cell. He moves so fast that I almost feel like I have motion sickness. I close my eyes to help combat it, but that just makes it feel worse. My leg throbs angrily, and I have a serious crick in my neck from sleeping on my elbow and knee for so long. I meant to take a little rest, not lose a whole day.

When I open my eyes again, Rook is carrying me into a large, clean, white-tiled bathroom, with several private shower stalls. It's too nice to be a block bathroom, but I can't imagine he would have taken me to the guards' locker room either.

Rook looks down at me, and he must see the questions in my eyes. "It's a new addition to Nightmare Penitentiary. It's going to house more criminals of the white collar variety," he explains in answer to my unvoiced question.

I look around again with that new information rolling around my mind. Figures. If you're white collar, then you're used to certain perks and privileges. Why should prison be any different? I suddenly want to smear ogre blood all over it. Let them bathe privately in the smell of cat piss while their lawyers get them out on technicalities and they laugh smugly together about all the shit they get away with.

Rook sets me down on a cool tiled bench, and he pulls his support away slowly, like he's expecting me to fall. Psh, I'm not some weak ass. I totally don't need his help to—whoops! That ground sure is tilting funny.

Rook catches me before I can face-plant, and he sets me upright again. I roll my eyes at the worried look in his gaze. I obviously would've stopped myself from falling...or the floor would have caught me. Either way, it would've been fine. He's overreacting.

When he watches me for several seconds and I don't tip over again, Rook disappears into a stall and turns on the water. He's back in a flash, kneeling in front of me, and I wonder if I just blacked out again or if he really moved that quickly. He carefully unties the knots in the makeshift bandages around my leg and unwraps the torn pieces of the dirty blanket of assholish origin. The fabric sticks to the cut like it tried to meld together and become one. He pulls the strips of fabric away, making me hiss in pain, and the edges of my cut come up too, like they're trying to keep the fabric from leaving. It's like watching two lovers being torn apart; hurts like it too.

As soon as he gets the bandages off, my leg immediately starts to bleed again. I watch the tracks of blood slip down my thigh, and I can't help but feel like it's mourning the loss of the bandages. I stare at it for another beat before fingers snap in my line of sight, and I'm pulled from my weird ass thoughts.

The snapping fingers lead back to Rook, and I focus on him. "I need to go get some things for your leg. That iron must've been laced with something. It's fucking up your healing. I think you're hypothermic too, Sun—I mean, Sinclair, so I'm going to sit you in the hot water, and you should start to feel better in just a couple minutes. Our cockatrices bounce back pretty quickly, but I don't know how long you've been like this..." Rook trails off, and I can see anger and frustration etched in his expression as he speaks.

"Just sit and get warmed up, okay? I'll be right back," he stares at me for a moment, but I don't react. My thoughts are muddy and thick.

With a troubled exhale, he pulls my oversized gray shirt over my head and picks me up before carrying me into the steam soaked stall. The hot water hits my bare skin, and I hiss and shy away from the heat.

Rook tenderly shushes me as I whimper. "You need this, Sinclair. I know it feels too hot right now, but just give it a couple minutes, and then it won't feel hot enough, I promise."

He sets me down on the warm tiles, and a waterfall of heat envelops me. I rest my head back against the tile, and Rook watches me to make sure I'm okay for a minute before running out. I can hear his boots squeaking against the pristine white tile, and then all I hear is the water falling from the showerhead to patter against the floor and flow down the drain.

After a couple minutes of the scorching water raining down on me, I realize that my body stops trembling. I didn't even know I'd been shaking. Slowly, the hot deluge brings me back to life like some magical potion. My brain slowly feels like it's clearing up, and the scorching water rinses out the gash in my leg, helping to clean out whatever iron-rusted muck was in there. A steady stream of red swirls down the drain, but it's no longer dirty, and it already looks and feels better. Things around me start to seem more in focus.

Just like Rook said, the hot water soon doesn't feel like it's burning me alive anymore. As my temperature regulates, I find that I need it to be even hotter. I look down at my cut and the water flushing it out. I reach up and turn the dial all the way to red. The water instantly gets hotter, and I sigh at how good it feels.

Cockatrices can have trouble regulating their temperatures sometimes. It's not an issue really when it comes to the heat, but when it comes to the cold, we can catch hypothermia very quickly. I can't believe I didn't notice the signs. Stupid, cold-ass, lizard-killing solitary confinement cell.

I scoot more directly under the shower spray and moan.

Fuck, that feels good.

The sound of my satisfaction echoes around the tiled bathroom, and I feel wrapped up and cocooned by it. I feel like me again, washed clear of my injury and sex session.

As I start to rinse out my tangled hair, the sound of squeaky boots on tile bounces off the walls, alerting me that Rook is back with whatever he left to get. I suddenly feel unsure and vulnerable. I don't know how I feel about him being here, taking care of me.

I'm grateful that he found me and knew how to help without taking me back to the creepy Dr. Brina, but it doesn't excuse his abandoning me for the last five days...or six.

Dark blue pants appear to the left of the wall, and Rook moves closer. When he turns the corner and sees me, a flash of relief moves over his features. "Oh good, you turned up the heat. How are you feeling?"

"Better," I answer as he kneels down to get closer to eye-level with me. "It got weird there for a second. My cut and bandages were having a full Romeo and Juliet moment, but I'm normal again."

Rook snorts. "Normal? I don't know if I'd go that far," he teases, and then he puts his hands under my armpits and picks me up like I'm a toddler.

He sets me gently on my feet, water spraying on his clothes, adding darkened droplets wherever it lands. We both stand there beneath the swirling steam and just stare at each other. His turquoise eyes look sad today, but I blink away any concern I might have about it. His sad eyes are his problem.

Like he can see my hardening thoughts, Rook clears his throat and steps back from me before grabbing a bottle of shampoo from a niche in the wall. He must have set all of this up before, because there's a rainbow-colored washcloth, body wash, and shampoo and conditioner just waiting to be used. I sigh. If he thinks a rainbow washcloth will ease the sting of five days of stewing in abandonment, he's an idiot.

My eyes scoot over to the washcloth. It *is* pretty, though. So bright and colorful and—*dammit, Sinclair, don't let him distract you with bright colors!*

Rook pours the shampoo in his hands and puts the bottle back with the others. He rubs his hands together and then spreads shampoo all over my orange and yellow tresses. He threads his fingers through my hair and starts to scrub and massage my scalp.

I should stop him.

I definitely *will* stop him...in just a sec.

It's just that—to be safe, of course, because I'm still a little weak—it might be good to just let him keep doing what he's doing.

I mean, he's oddly good at it, like he took a scalp massage class or went to *How to Wash a Girl's Hair Until She Orgasms* school. Either way, he's clearly *very* passionate about hair care, and who am I to deny him that happiness? I'm a boss at compartmentalizing. I can hate him and still get a scalp massage.

The more he tends to me, the more I find myself leaning into his strong hands. When I realize what I'm doing, I immediately straighten up and put my game face back on.

Oh no you don't, Rookie. I see your game, and it's not going to work on me.

I step away from his magically relaxing fingers and rinse my hair, putting some needed distance between us. I feel Rook's resigned huff, but I don't look at him as I wash all the suds away until my hair squeaks. Man, it feels so good to not be covered in grime and bad memories. I grab for the conditioner, but Rook beats me to it. I narrow my eyes at him and put my palm out expectantly.

He searches my eyes for something. "Sinclair, I know you're—"

"Don't, Rook," I warn, cutting him off. "I want to get clean, and then I need to sleep and heal. I'm not going to play your games, and I won't be asking you to play any more of mine either," I add, my meaning clear.

With a tic in his jaw, Rook hands me the bottle of conditioner. I feel victorious yet strangely sad when he does. I squeeze a massive amount in my hands and start working it through my long layers and tangles.

"Why are you in here in your uniform?" I ask, as I take him in while finger combing knots out of my hair.

He gives an unamused snort. "I didn't think you'd be very receptive to my being naked in here with you, and I was in a hurry." He shrugs, and his shoulders slump with defeat.

An electric jolt of sympathy strikes through my chest, but that just annoys me. Why do I care if he's upset or bummed? What in the hell did he think I was going through when he didn't come back for days? Did he even think about how that would feel or look to me?

With renewed justified anger, I rinse my hair again and reach for the washcloth and body wash. This time, he doesn't intercept me. I lather the washcloth and get to work, ridding myself of dirt, his scent, our cum, and all the regret that sits like a layer of grime on my skin. I look at him as I scrub away what we did, but instead of tracking my motions with the washcloth over my naked and wet body, he stares right into my eyes.

I can almost read the apology and sorrow in his stare, but I'm just so...pissed. And I'm embarrassed. He affected me—hurt me—and I let him. I don't like feeling vulnerable like that. I don't like someone else having that sort of power over me.

Not paying attention to where I'm dragging the washcloth, I accidentally rub over the cut on my leg. I hiss out a curse of pain.

"It looks better already," Rook observes.

"Yeah. I didn't realize I was being so affected by the cold and whatever rusted grossness was in the iron. It was stupid to get weak like that," I admit, and Rook's sad eyes turn even more contrite. "I won't let it happen again," I declare, but I don't know if I'm talking about the hypothermia and the wound...or us.

We're quiet for a minute, and I step back into the spray,

letting the rest of the suds rinse off. The heat once again wraps around me, and I wonder how long I could stand under the molten stream before it started to turn cold. The white collar criminals are going to be getting way more hot water usage than what the rest of us prisoners get. Lucky pricks.

"Thank you," I finally say, breaking the silence. I may not like him, but I'm not an asshole.

"It was nothing," he starts dismissively.

"No, it wasn't nothing," I insist stubbornly. "I was in bad shape, so thank you."

Rook searches my face again, and I've never felt more grateful to have water pouring down on me, because it hides the tears that start sneaking out of my eyes.

"Sunrise, please just let me explain. If you won't hear me out, then at least let me make it up to you. I'm begging here. What can I do to make this better?"

"Nothing," I say quickly with the shake of my head, but my resolve wavers when another tear falls out. "I don't know... No, definitely nothing," I say again, wavering and pissed at my traitorous mouth for not being firmer.

Why is being mad so hard to maintain? I spent five days working myself up into a frenzy. Then he showed up and I let him have it, exactly like I should have. But he takes care of one little booboo and a case of the shivers, and suddenly his sad eyes are killing me? Why am I being such a sucker?

I fold my arms over my chest and look around the shower stall. "So what was your plan?" I ask, trying not to be affected by his emotions.

"The plan?" he asks, confused.

"Yeah, the plan. You had this whole shower situation set up before you brought me here, so what was your plan before you walked into my cell and saw the state I was in?"

Understanding dawns in his eyes, and he reaches

behind his neck and palms his nape, like he's suddenly all shy and shit. I'm not fooled.

"Well...I was going to entice you to the shower. Help you get cleaned up. Eat you out until you were wrung out and pliant, and then apologize until you were ready for angry sex," he tells me casually, ticking off a mental list in his head.

I try not to react to anything that he says, but his words open the floodgates on my pussy, and my nipples harden against my will. Good thing my arms are folded over them, and my face is still in angry bitch mode.

Nope, I'm not affected at all, I tell myself over and over again as I shout at the dirty images flashing through my mind to fuck off.

"Well, that was a stupid plan," I tell him primly.

The corner of his mouth does the faintest hitch up. "Is it?"

"Yep," I say, popping the *p* and licking my lips to lap up the water. "I don't do angry sex. When I'm pissed at you, I'm pissed at your dick too. You bring that thing anywhere near me, and I'll be more likely to cut it off than want to ride it."

He lets out a laugh, and it's like his stupid dimples cast out a couple of fishing lines that hook the corners of my lips, forcing me into a smile. I reel that shit in real quick.

"I'll keep that in mind."

"Why bother? You don't need to file away info about me. Like I said, you were a good fuck, but we're not having any kind of a repeat performance."

Rook eats up the space between us the moment those words are out of my mouth until his hips are pressing into me and he's standing all the way beneath the water, his clothes soaking through immediately. But does he look like a ridiculous wet dog? No, of course not. He looks like a wet dream, and his hair starts to glow again. My breath comes in short pants that have nothing to do with the humid air.

"I'm sorry," he says, water spraying off of him and misting over my face. "Trouble came up, and I was called away. Yesterday was my first shift back. I wanted to get someone to help you, but I don't trust any of the fuckers here. I made sure you got food delivered, though,"

My eyebrows hike up. So *he* made sure Selena stopped by to give me food?

"Where did you go?" I ask, curious about how much information he'll divulge.

"I was called away to my lounge. I came back as soon as I could, I swear."

Maybe it's stupid, but the vehemence in his voice makes me believe him. I grapple with the sodden strings of my anger, trying to keep hold, trying to stay strong.

"And Black Block?" I ask.

"A real call, I promise. They called in all available guards to handle some shit that went down. If it were up to me, I would've stayed all damn night with you and taken you again and again until your throat went hoarse from screaming my name."

I swallow hard at his words. "That's ridiculous. My throat doesn't get hoarse."

He chuckles, and I can feel the sound travel from his body to mine. "It will during our repeat performance," he says, throwing my earlier words back at me. "And trust me, Sunrise, that *will* be happening."

My tail starts whipping around behind me, and he reaches around and splays his hand at the base of it, calming the erratic wagging. "I fucked up. I'm sorry. Let me make it up to you."

"How?" I ask quietly, feeling the last threads of my resolve snapping apart like the buttons on his shirt.

His hand at my tail slowly traces the curve of my scales before he reaches the bottom and curls the feathery end up in his fist, the same way he grabbed my hair while he fucked me. My breath whooshes out of my chest at how erotic that feels.

"First...I'll kiss you," he says huskily, his voice quiet but rough in my ear. "Lick at your lips and own your mouth until I make you wet between your thighs, just to show you how sincere my apology is," he says before his mouth comes on top of mine.

He starts doing exactly what he promised, but I bite down on his tongue the moment it snakes out to demand entry. Blood prickles out of the small wound, and he rears back, running his injured tongue over the fronts of his teeth.

"Whoops. Guess that's my response to your first stage of *making it up to me*," I say scathingly.

"I'll just have to try harder then," he replies, jutting his hips forward on the word *harder* so that I can feel exactly how hard he's talking.

I lean my back against the cool tile, trying to keep my body from reacting to his nearness. *Play it cool, Sinclair.*

"If kisses don't convince you, I think I should just worship your pussy instead," he says before dropping down on his knees in front of me. His hands give my hips a squeeze.

Fuck.

My center heats, and my legs quiver enough that I know he can feel it where he's grabbing me. Seeing him dripping wet and bowing down before me, his blue and green hair casting soft light onto the white tiles, makes me feel powerful and wanted. Exactly the opposite of the way he made me feel those past five days. This is the feeling I want to keep. This is how I want to feel.

I lick my lips again at the desire that won't stop building

between us despite my efforts to chase it away or ignore it. Maybe it's stupid and naive of me, but...I believe him. I believe that something came up, and he tried to come back to me but couldn't. I believe that he's sorry. I just hope he doesn't break my trust again.

"You make a pretty speech, Rookie, but I doubt you're talented enough to follow thr—"

My words cut off with a yelp as his head suddenly dives between my thighs. His tongue takes a slow, rough swipe from my pussy to my clit, a growl coming from his chest when he tastes the cream already gathered there.

He spreads my lips with his thumbs and stares at my pussy like it's some treasure he just found. I watch him lean back in and wrap his full lips around my clit, sucking on it rhythmically until tingles start to move through my body. He pulls off my clit with a pop and starts to mouthfuck me like he's lapping up his favorite dessert. His tongue pierces inside of me like it's ready to pin me in place and lick me dry.

"Psh, you call this pussy-worshipping?" I say breathily. "I've had, like, way better," I lie, my weight turning to jelly on wobbling feet.

He pulls my injured leg up and rests it on his shoulders, spreading me even wider and making it all the easier for him to consume me. He nips at my clit, and I whimper in pleasure, unable to swallow it down fast enough. The sound spurs him on, and with another growl, he doubles down on his efforts.

"Oh!" I cry out, my hands coming up to help support me; one hand lands in his hair and the other at his neck.

His head bobs as he dines on my desire, and I don't fight the urge I have to squeeze his neck. Slipping my hand around him, I feel muscle and tendon beneath my hand as I grip at him, and it's impossible not to appreciate how strong and powerful he is. And yet, he doesn't fight this little show of mine for dominance. I love the sensation of my fingers digging into his windpipe. And surprisingly, my dominant hold on him seems to make him even more vigorous. He pushes against my grip, as if wanting me to squeeze even harder.

I do, and he groans, and then he latches onto my clit and begins to suck with more vigor. I let out a gurgled, choked-off scream, my head tipping back against the wall. My hand tightens around his neck again, before I drag my fingers up, letting my nails scratch him, marking him like he marked me.

Sliding my palms up, I bury both hands in his wet hair and guide the pressure of his face against my pussy. He's giving me control while also giving me pleasure. He's on his knees, taking my small digs of pain, while dishing out nothing but laps of pleasure. So damn sexy.

I orgasm on a withering sigh, one that rumbles up from the base of my tail and echoes out of my open mouth. My entire body shudders, and my knee gives out. My body is lost to pleasure and refusing to hold me up any longer. Rook once again catches me in his arms, and he holds me as I quake and quiver and ride out my orgasm.

Holy climax, that felt good.

Just like that, my anger gives me the peace out sign and walks off bow-legged, done for the day. Rook's lucky he's so good with his mouth.

He stands up with me in his arms and shuts off the shower before stepping out of the stall, our bodies leaving a puddle of water on the floor. Rook wraps me up in a scratchy, overly-bleached towel, his hands reverent and methodical as he sweeps off every bead of moisture collected on my skin.

"You look beautiful when you come, Sunrise," he

murmurs as he squeezes the towel around my dripping hair. "Sit. Let me look at your leg before you get dressed."

I sit down, and we both grow silent as he looks at the cut on my thigh.

"You should be okay, but just in case, I'm going to wrap it and give you an antibiotic that should take care of anything that might have snuck into your system," he explains as he reaches over to a first aid kit.

I don't say anything as he gently spreads ointment on my thigh and carefully wraps a clean white bandage around it. He hands me two oval pills and a bottle of water, and like a good girl, I swallow them down. I wipe water from my mouth, and we both stand up.

"You do pretty good on your knees, Glow Worm," I declare, and we both smile.

"Good, you're calling me Glow Worm again. That means I'm out of the doghouse."

"Barely," I warn him before I move away from him and start dressing into the clean uniform he left for me on the bench. When I'm clothed, I turn around, finding him stripping down and tossing his wet clothing onto the floor with a slap.

"You gonna escort me back to solitary naked?" I ask. "I gotta admit, the view would be good, but things might shrink up from the cold."

He snaps a towel at me, making me squeal and laugh as I jump out of reach. "Your solitary sentence is over, so you're going back to your regular cell now," he tells me. "And you don't have to worry about anything shrinking while you're around," he tells me before moving over to the bench and grabbing a new uniform that he left out for himself.

"Good to know," I tell him, as I brush my fingers through my hair and start braiding it.

I'm doing everything I can to avoid looking at the very

hard, very large dick standing up between his legs. I may have let what happened go for now, but I'm not rewarding his behavior. He's going to have to make it up to me with a few more orgasms and pampering before his cock gets any attention.

When we're both fully clothed, Rook escorts me out of the showers, and we take a long, winding walk from one building to another, until we're back in the building for minor offenders.

Back at my cell, Rook opens the door for me, and I find myself sighing happily at my familiar four walls. "It's good to be home," I joke, falling onto the bed with a bounce. This place is so much better than solitary. I don't even mind the sound of someone urinating down the hallway.

Rook closes the cell door, watching me through the bars. "This isn't your home, Sinclair," he says quietly, and my smile drains away at the seriousness of his tone.

"It is for now."

But he shakes his head, not accepting my answer. "This is a hideout. Not a home."

I narrow my eyes. Dude goes down on me once and gets forgiven, and now he's ready to double down on pissing me off again?

"If you have something to say, say it," I grind out, sitting up straight to look at him.

"Ooh, Sinclair and the PG are fighting!" someone shouts from one of the other cells.

"Shut up!" I call back before getting up and walking over to him. "Say it," I repeat to Rook.

He lets out a breath. "Fine. It was cowardly of you to run instead of facing Alpha Bowen or your matriarch and patriarch. You should've just confronted them and told them your thoughts. Not run away to hide in this shithole."

My back prickles with offense. "Just because you fucked

me once and gave me"—I start to count how many orgasms but give up when I pause for too long—"a bunch of orgasms, doesn't mean you know shit about my life. You have no idea what you're talking about, so you can shove that judgmental tone and your unsolicited advice up your tight ass," I snap. "I'm a problem solver, not a fucking coward."

"No?" he tosses back. "Then prove it. Stop hiding. Don't try to up your sentence. Don't try to stay here. Find another way to solve the problem. Find a way you can face them and take control of your life."

"Easy for you to say," I snap. "You didn't grow up the way I did. You have no clue what I'm up against."

Rook inhales audibly, and I can tell he's about to retort with more shit, but I cut him off. "Just go away before you really piss me off, Rookie," I say, suddenly exhausted. "I don't want to fight again, and you're totally ruining my post-orgasm bliss."

He huffs and runs his fingers through his hair. He watches me for a beat and then breathes a soft laugh out through his nose. "Fine, sorry. I just...I don't like the thought of you wasting your life in here."

"It's not a waste," I say, looking up at him. "I met you, didn't I?"

His breath falters, intensity burning in his eyes at my words.

"Fucking gag me," an inmate groans.

"I'll make you fucking gag on your cock if you don't stop interrupting!" I chirp back sweetly.

Rook chuckles and shakes his head at me. "You have such a filthy mouth."

"You like it," I tell him, and I love the way his eyes flicker with heat.

"I do," he agrees quietly. "Now behave yourself. I won't

see you for a couple of days; I have a rotation in a different part of the prison."

He grabs hold of my chin and pulls my face near his, planting a quick kiss on my lips before pulling away. Leaving me tingling, he gives me one last heated look and then turns and walks away. I shake my head and then smirk. Sucker didn't even notice I switched out his name tag again. Double the dicks as last time. Totally fitting.

10

"You've got a visitor."

I look up from my new business venture that I've been busy with and look at the prison guard. It's Sandbag—the same jackhole who escorted me to see my mat and pat before. "No thanks, I'm all booked up at the moment."

I hear my cell door clang open, and he glowers at me, taser gun in hand. "I wasn't asking."

I frown at him and put down my project, setting it on my bed. Just the sight of the taser makes my skin prickle in all the places I was hit before. Those marks took forever to go away. "Okay, okay. Don't get your spanx in a twist."

Following him out, I psych myself up for round two with my mat and pat, but when I get pushed into the visitor's room and see the person on the other side of the glass, my steps pick up instead of drag. I plop down in the metal chair and practically rip the phone receiver off the wall in my hurry.

"What are you doing here, Dinah?" I ask the female cockatrice who happens to be one of my best friends from my lounge.

Dinah grins back at me from the other side of the plexiglass. Her bright purple pixie cut looks plummy under the bad prison lighting as her deep set hazel eyes take me in. "Damn, Sinclair. Look at you."

I look down at the gray uniform and shrug. "I know, I know. It's not exactly doing my figure any favors, but it's basically like wearing pajamas twenty-four-seven, so it's kinda worth it."

She chuckles, but it's forced, and I can see the tightness around her eyes that immediately sets me on edge. "What's wrong?"

Her smile dims slightly, and a million worst-case scenarios reel through my mind.

"We're in trouble," she tells me stiffly, like the words are climbing out of her mouth despite her efforts to keep them inside.

"Who, you and Tark? Did something happen to Verity?" I demand, picturing Dinah's purple pigtail clad three-year-old and her mate. I'm half crouched over the metal chair I was just sitting in, like if Dinah just says the word, I'm ready to bust out of this place and do anything I can to help her.

"No, Sin. They're fine," she assures me. "Verity's wings are getting so strong and so fast. Tark and I found her almost five inches off the ground the other day in the backyard. Scared us to death. It also made us proud as hell," she tells me, beaming.

I smile at the thought, both of us lost in the beauty of her feisty little girl for a second.

Dinah shakes her head and blows out a breath. "It's the lounge, Sin. Matriarch is pretending like everything is fine. But I don't think it is. You know Stur, Cena and Mack's son?" she asks, and I nod. "He went missing last week."

My brows dip with concern. Stur's mom, Cena, is pretty

frail, and he helps take care of her. He's not the type to just run off.

"When his parents reported it to Matriarch Denali, she didn't seem surprised by the news. She also didn't seem like she was in a hurry to figure out what happened to him. She just kept saying that she was sure he'd turn up."

I sit back down in my chair and try to think through why my mat would have reacted so out of character. She doesn't allow anyone to fuck with her lounge. Not out of a sense of love or devotion, but because it makes her look weak, and that's something she won't tolerate.

"Right after the meeting with Cena and Mack, Matriarch Denali was seen on the phone yelling at someone. Then she just hopped in a car and disappeared for the rest of the day. Stur showed up two days later looking exhausted. He told everyone that he met a girl, but no one believes him."

I shake my head, not believing that story either. Stur is the nicest, most responsible kid I've ever met. He wouldn't just run off to go chase tail and leave his mom to worry.

"Cena called me a couple days ago," Dinah goes on. "She asked me to make him a sleeping draught. When I asked why, she started crying and told me in confidence that Stur had been taken by Alpha Fitz's lounge and held for ransom. There was no girl."

My eyes widen in shock, terror and worry pumping through me as the pieces of the puzzle slip into place.

"Stur told his mom that the Fitz lounge claimed that *our* lounge owed them money. They're going to keep taking members of our lounge and hurting them until we pay what's owed. Stur told his parents that Matriarch and Patriarch Denali made him swear he wouldn't say anything, or risk him and his family being kicked out of the lounge."

I stare at her, openmouthed. *How the fuck could my mat and pat be so cruel and selfish?* I mean, I've always had my problems with them, but I never knew them to be bad alpha leaders of our lounge.

"Stur has been having nightmares since he got back, and Cena was hoping I could help him get some rest. He looked bad, Sin," Dinah says, shaking her head. "Cena swore me to secrecy, but I have an awful feeling that what happened might not be over. I knew I had to come talk to you. Do you know what's going on?"

I run a tired hand over my face and try to rein in my anger. I'm not sure what exactly to tell her. I'm still waiting for Zen's guy to get me all the details, but I have the overwhelming urge to warn Dinah, especially if the lounge is in danger. Mat and pat are clearly trying to keep everything quiet, but that's putting the lounge at even more risk. They can't protect themselves if they don't know what's going on.

I blow out a breath. "You know how I thought getting locked up in here would void the contract my mat and pat signed with Alpha Bowen?"

Dinah nods, leaning in toward the streaked glass as I get ready to drop all kinds of information bombs on her.

"Well, unfortunately, I discovered that there was another aspect of that deal, which no one told me about. It seems my mat and pat got the lounge mixed up with some debt. Alpha Bowen was settling it as part of the agreement he made for me."

Dinah brings up a hand to cover her mouth as her face morphs into shock and then confusion. "So it's true. Our lounge does owe money. But how?" she asks, just as puzzled by this information as I was.

I shake my head, at a loss. "I'm still piecing that together. It's a bit difficult from here, but I should know all the details soon. I'm not sure how it happened or even how much, but my mat and pat both confirmed it when they came to visit. It seems that Alpha Bowen isn't going to uphold his end of the contract until my mat and pat uphold theirs."

I pause, and the next words I have to say feel like a hot coal searing my throat. "Dinah...I don't think the lounge is safe right now. I was hoping to get the details and then figure out a plan, but if another lounge is taking people..." I trail off, but my meaning is clear. No one is safe.

"I have to tell the lounge," Dinah announces hollowly.

"Yes, but you also need to be careful about who you tell and how," I warn her. "My mat clearly wants this whole thing to be kept under wraps. If someone tries to call her out, she's going to exile them and scramble around to shut people up. You guys can't afford to have forces attacking you from the outside while also dealing with attacks from my mat within. You know what she's capable of," I tell Dinah, and her gaze grows dark as she nods her head.

Dinah's parents were kicked out when she was young. She was raised by an aunt and uncle still in the lounge, and we all grew up being told her parents were bad and we should hate them. Dinah and I learned when we were teenagers that the story we had been told when we were little wasn't true. Dinah's mat was going to challenge mine, but my mat exiled her before she could.

We didn't tell anyone, too afraid to suffer the same fate, but we've always wondered how many stories out there like Dinah's exist because of my mat's underhanded and power-hungry ways.

"How are they doing?" I ask softly, not liking the pain and anger in my friend's features.

"Mom and dad are good," she says with a smile. "Maybe Tark, Verity, and I will take an impromptu vacation out to visit them until our lounge is safe again," she tells me.

"That's a good idea."

I'm so glad that Dinah was able to track her parents

down and that they have an amazing relationship. I'm glad that she can go somewhere and be safe with her family, but her words haunt me.

Until the lounge is safe again.

The sentence runs through my mind on a loop, and I have no idea when it will happen or how to make it possible. If I had known my lounge was at risk, I would have never left. I would have tried to find another solution, but I'm in Nightmare Pen now, and I have to figure out a way to do something from here. I need to find Zen.

"How are you doing in here?" Dinah asks, pulling me from the plans I'm putting together in my mind.

"Good," I shrug. "Food's amazing. My squad is fierce. I have a successful shank business, and I'm about to launch something new that I think is going to be a huge hit," I tell her. "There's also a superhot prison guard."

Dinah giggles and shakes her head at me. "Only you, Sinclair Denali, would thrive in a place like this."

"I'm totally taking that as a compliment."

"You should, Sin. You most definitely should."

"Okay, go on. Get out of this place, go take your kid and your mate somewhere safe," I tell her. "Wyve, Pya, Tracy, Hank and Forrest are who I would go to before you leave. They all know how to keep their mouths shut while looking out for others. They can spread the news quietly while you head out to see your parents."

She puts her hand up against the plexiglass, and my throat gets tight as I do the same.

"Miss you, Sin," Dinah tells me, her voice cracking with emotion.

I smile at her, but it feels sad. Forced. "Miss you too, Di. Only nine more months to go," I tell her, and she nods and wipes a tear off her cheek. "You tell Verity that I have a year of tickles and tummy raspberries to make up for."

Dinah laughs and pulls her hand away. I feel the loss of it immensely, even though the thick barrier keeps me from truly connecting or feeling the physical comfort I'm suddenly missing. I need to figure out a way to keep Dinah and her family safe. I need to figure out a way to save all of them.

We throw out tear-filled *I love you*s and then crack up when I accuse Dinah of fucking with my rep and making me look all soft. My heart lurches as we hang up our phones. I watch her leave, calling out blessings of protection to the heavens and promising any listening deity my eternal devotion if they'll watch her back.

I release a heavy, stress-filled exhale and wipe my eyes before standing up. I walk to the door and bang on it to let the guard know I'm ready to go. I silently hope it will be Rook that steps forward on the other side. He's annoying, but I'm in the mood to be annoyed. I need the same kind of distraction he gave me last time.

Disappointment wafts through me when the sliding peephole on the door opens and I see that it's Sandbag still standing there. I bite down my groan. Anxiousness crawls up from my stomach to roost in my chest. Let's hope he can get me back to my cell without "accidentally" tasing me.

His dead eyes look behind me, checking to see that my visitor has left, and then they snap back to me with a glare. You're not done yet," he grumps, and the peephole on the door slams shut.

"What the hell?" I call out. "I spoke to my visitor. She left!" I shout at him, turning around to motion to the empty visitor table.

Except I freeze when I realize that there's someone sitting in the chair that Dinah just vacated. I stare at him with confusion, no recognition sparking in my brain. I stand at the door for a moment, unsure of what to do. Is this dude lost?

He picks up the receiver of the phone and motions with his head for me to do the same. The silver-feathered tail wagging behind the man is enough to get my hackles up. The expensive suit and briefcase he's toting leads me to suspect that he's here on official business. The question is, whose?

I sit down and pick up the receiver again, holding it up to my ear as I study him. He looks to be in his thirties, with a short silver beard and hair and darkly tanned skin. His eyes are so dark they're nearly black, and despite how intense he looks, he flashes me a friendly smile. My heart pounds in my chest, but I try to remain impassive-looking.

"Sinclair Denali?"

"Who are you?" I ask.

"I'm Trex. Beta of the Bowen Lounge."

Fuck. *Alpha Bowen's second-in-command?* This can't be good.

"What do you want?" I ask warily.

"I hope you're being treated well, Miss Denali," he says, instead of answering me.

A stupid blush creeps up my cheeks. Oh, if he only knew exactly how *well* one of the guards is treating me...

"It's fine," I say after clearing my throat awkwardly.

"Glad to hear that," he says with another warm smile. I notice for the first time that his left incisor is capped silver. Either he lost it in some kind of fight or it's a fashion statement. With this male, it could be either option, really.

"Miss Sinclair, I'm here today on official business from Alpha Bowen. He sent me to make sure you're...taken care of."

I snort. "I'll just bet he did."

"I can assure you, Alpha Bowen wants nothing but your

wellbeing," he tells me. "Which is why he was so confused as to why you would evade his attempts at freeing you from unjust persecution."

Fuck, this guy either has balls the size of Mars or he knows that this room isn't tapped.

"I wasn't interested in being broken out," I say. "And I have nothing to do with Alpha Bowen, so he's not my concern."

"I thought you might say something to that effect." He grabs the clasps on his briefcase and flicks them open. Shuffling through it, he brings out a stack of bound papers. "I brought the contract that was made on your behalf, as proof that you do, in fact, have everything to do with Alpha Bowen."

He holds it up to the glass, and I see the blood signatures the contract is bound with and my name on it, right there before my eyes. I feel sick.

My angry green gaze flicks back up to the beta's face. I shrug. "Like you said, it was made on my behalf. I never agreed to anything."

The beta sighs and puts the contract away, like I'm being a difficult child. "Miss Sinclair, the contract is binding. When you're released from this penitentiary, you will go to Alpha Bowen and become his mate."

Fury heats up my body until my palm starts sweating where I grip the phone. "Guess it's too bad my sentence just got prolonged then," I lie, smirking over at him. "Alpha Bowen is gonna be waiting a long, *long* time."

He narrows his eyes. "I see."

"Do you?" I challenge. "Because from where I'm sitting, you and your alpha don't know when to catch a hint. I don't want him, and I sure as fuck don't want to be his mate because of some contractual obligation that my *fucked up matriarch* drew up for her sole benefit."

We stare at each other through the glass for a beat, and I let him see every inch of the righteous anger on my face. Fuck him. Fuck his alpha too for sending this male over to lecture me.

After a moment, he nods. "Alright, Miss Sinclair. I can see you need more time to adjust to the idea."

"No, I don't," I quickly say, watching as he puts his things away and re-latches the briefcase. "I don't need time. My decision has been made. I'm not going to him."

The beta's mouth stretches into a slow, arrogant smile. "Oh, you will, Miss Sinclair. You will."

My beast's instincts immediately rear up. *Is he fucking threatening me?*

He stands, and I stand up too, both of us still holding the phones. "Alpha Bowen has added unlimited funds into your prisoner's account to ensure that you're comfortable while you're here," he says, shocking the hell out of me. "He's also arranged for you to have some luxuries added to your cell. He hopes you enjoy them."

I gape at him. "He can't fucking bribe me."

The beta shrugs, unconcerned. "You get more privileges, fitting of an alpha leader's mate."

"I'm not his mate!" I hiss.

"Have a pleasant day, Miss Sinclair."

"Suck on a shit-covered rock," I fire back.

His silver-tipped tail flicks as he hangs up the phone and smoothly walks away.

I sit back down in a rush, my knees practically giving out as the adrenaline from our verbal contest drains out of me. I hang up the phone and rest my head in my hands. Fucking Alpha Bowen and his fucking arrogance and barely-there threats. Why the hell can't I get away from this dude? You'd think a girl getting herself thrown into prison would be a big enough hint for him.

The door behind me opens, and I swing around to find Sandbag ready and waiting. I guess that means I'm done with the visits for today.

"Come," he barks at me like I'm a dog, and I'm tempted to rip the phone receiver off the wall and junk punch him with it.

Instead, I do as I'm told. The memory of magical tasers keeps me in line. Well, that and the fact that I *really* don't want to go back into solitary. My shop is officially opening for business tomorrow, and with all the work I've been putting in, I can't wait to see the other inmates go mental trying to get their hands on the kickass shit that I've got. I need to be smart, no matter how much this guard pisses me off.

Sandbag pushes me to walk in front of him. It's a favorite game he likes to play where you have to guess where you're supposed to be going and if you guess wrong, he punishes you. Usually, an inmate will earn a well-placed kick to the knee or a slap to the back of the head. It's just enough to piss you off and rob you of your power, but not enough to leave any lasting marks that could be used as evidence in the event that an inmate tried to report him.

One of the few things I look forward to when I *do* get out of here is tracking this fucker down and letting my cockatrice play with him.

The smell of food reaches me just before the hallways converge, leading to either the cafeteria or my cell block. I let my nose lead the way, and I'm surprised when no smacks or jabs come at me. Sandbag pushes me to join the line for food and then leaves. Relief washes through me when he disappears around a corner. The dude pisses me off and gives me the fucking creeps.

I grab a lunch tray and wait patiently for my turn to get a bologna sandwich, mac 'n cheese, and some cinnamon apples scooped onto my tray. The chatter and noise of socializing inmates enjoying their meals helps lift my spirits, and I try to not let myself be too weighed down by the problem with my lounge and the problem with Alpha Bowen. I'll find a way to fix it all. I know I will. I won't be a coward and hide away like Rook accused me of doing. I'll figure out a way to solve all of this.

Sophie the wolf shifter scoots over for me as I slide into my usual spot with the crew. Zen smiles at me around a mouthful of gooey baked cinnamon apples, and I giggle at the blissed-out look on her face. I've never seen Zen go gaga for the food here like I always do. Maybe I'm rubbing off on her.

"Where have you been?" Sophie asks me.

"I had visitors," I answer and then turn back to Zen. "Have you heard back from your guy about that thing I asked him to look into?" I inquire hopefully.

She swallows her bite, and her face falls when she looks down at her tray and sees that her plate is empty. She looks so sad that I push my tray toward her.

"You can have my apples, Zen," I offer, and I swear, you'd think I just handed her a winning lottery ticket.

She doesn't say anything, just digs into them while I dig into my mac 'n cheese. She finishes faster than me and wipes her mouth before pulling out a phone. Pausing with a spork in my mouth, I stare at her and at the phone, shocked. I look around, prepared to see guards scrambling our way to confiscate it and haul her off to solitary, but everyone just pretends not to see it.

"Hey. Yeah, I'm checking in about that info on that lounge I asked about. Anything yet?" she asks as she picks at non-existent dirt under her nails.

She makes a sound and then holds the phone out to me. I stare at it and then at her, unsure what I should do. It's one thing for untouchable Zen to whip out a phone in the middle of lunch and use it with no consequences, but I doubt I'd be that lucky.

"Go on," Zen encourages, and I pluck the phone from her extended hand and hold it like the precious and priceless artifact that it is.

"Hel..." I clear my throat. "Hello?" I ask as I press the phone to my ear. It feels so natural and so naughty all at the same time.

"Is this Miss Sinclair Denali?" a smooth feminine voice asks.

"Umm, yes," I reply hesitantly.

"I haven't been able to procure the information you requested about Alpha Bowen. But I did acquire details about your lounge and their financial issues."

I'm shocked that Zen's info guy is in fact a girl, but I shove that aside so I can focus on what's being said. I hold my breath as she speaks, wondering what she's about to reveal. Have my mat and pat been skimming? Could they be involved in something worse?

"It appears that your lounge acquired another lounge from an Alpha Arin sometime several years ago. When they absorbed that lounge, the Denali's also absorbed a great deal of debt too. They've been slowly paying it off ever since, and even borrowed from other lounges to attempt to pay it off," she tells me. "I must preface this next bit by warning that it's hearsay as I've not been able to confirm anything on the side of Alpha Bowen and the Bowen pack, but it appears that Alpha Bowen claimed all the debt and then claimed you, or at least, that's what I put together when I was able to get a brief look at the contract."

I nod my head and then remember that she can't see me. "Okay, thank you," I tell her, my mind reeling with what she just told me.

"Rest assured, I will continue to work to get the rest of the information you wanted."

I thank her again and then hand the phone back to Zen. Zen proceeds to start chatting away with whoever that female is, catching up with no worries about her surroundings and the rules. The guards don't even blink in her direction. I'm in awe, but what else is new?

I pick at my sandwich and try to think through what all of this means. The info about Alpha Bowen and trading me for the debt relief is nothing new, but where the debt comes from is blowing my mind.

When I was younger, Alpha Arin pissed my mat off somehow. I think he called her a name at a cockatrice gathering—probably something that was true—and it enraged her. She declared war on his lounge, and a couple years later, she got what she wanted and Alpha Arin was dead. She wasn't keen on having to take responsibility over his people, revenge was all she cared about. Apparently, she didn't care that she took on a mountain of debt to acquire that lounge. She just did it to prove a point. Now, it's caught up to her.

I shake my head, frustrated. She's too damn prideful. She couldn't let his slight go and, because of that, the Denali lounge now finds itself in the position that it's in. I mean, for fuck's sake, she *sold me* to help keep her mistake quiet. There's no way of knowing how many cockatrices have suffered or been punished to stay silent in order to cover her messy tracks.

I'm so disgusted by all of it that I don't even know what to do or think. I suppose on one hand, it's good to find out that no one in my lounge is stealing or messing shit up that way, but the fact of the matter is, my mat's pride is too destructive to be ignored anymore.

I sigh, suddenly tired. I know the *how* of it all, but I still don't see a way to fix it. Not one that doesn't involve my ownership or having to challenge my mother. I scoff at that thought. She's so damn slippery I don't even know if I'd be able to get a formal challenge in. She's exiled or killed everyone who's ever tried before, and I'm not confident I could force her hand. The lounge needs solutions now before my mat gets everyone hurt.

I have to find another way to fix this. If I can't, then...maybe I need to start thinking about mate life. From the minute I was told that I belonged to Alpha Bowen, I rejected it. I fought it and ended up here, but if I had known then what I know now, I wouldn't have chosen prison. I'm not selfish enough to let my lounge suffer when I could fix it. And as much as I hate the thought, I might just end up at Alpha Bowen's feet with my tail tucked between my legs. It might be the only way I can settle the debt to save my lounge.

I get up from the concrete bench and take my tray and stack it with the others, determined to find a solution that doesn't end up with me throwing my life away to a stranger.

If there is one, I'm going to fucking find it. I just have to do it soon.

11

"Inmate 11764. Get up and put your back against the wall."

I groan, my awareness coming in like a bad radio signal. Licking my dry lips, I yank the thin blanket over my head and ignore Sandbag's voice.

"Inmate!"

"Ungh," I groan. "What?"

"Get your ass up and put your back against the wall."

It's too early for this shit.

I flop the blanket over to the side as I hear the cell door open, but then I accidentally fall back asleep. I was up way too late last night, working on my products to get ready for market day today.

Suddenly, my mattress is being ripped off the bed frame —with me still on it—and tossed to the floor. I go sliding, the back of my head slamming into the wall. I sit up and glare at the guards. I open my mouth to curse at Sandbag and ask what the fuck is going on, but I stop short when I see what they're doing.

A brand new, triple-thick mattress is being put down where the old prison-issued mattress and I just were. I stare at it in shock as two guards put it down while another one tosses down a package of brand new sheets.

I watch, mouth gaping like a fish, as more guards file in, one after the other, dropping stuff off into my cell. Blankets. Pillows. A small, battery operated TV and DVD player. A battery-operated mini-fridge. Even a blue and green tie-dye beanbag chair. *Pretty.*

I scramble to my feet, standing on top of the stained, rail-thin mattress that's slumped on the floor. "What is all this?"

"*Luxuries*," Sandbag replies with a sneer. "Your fucking cock boyfriend set it up for you to have all of this shit."

I stare at him for a moment, confused as to why Rook would get me all of this stuff and wondering how he convinced the guards to set it all up. Then the sleep sluffs off my brain, and it all clicks. Ah. Alpha Bowen's bribes have arrived.

The guards file out of my cell, taking my old mattress with them, and Sandbag shakes his head at all my newly added goodies and then storms out, slamming the door behind him.

I look around in awe.

I walk over to the new mattress and whistle at how plush and thick it is. The sheets are bright blue to match my new beanbag chair, and they're silky soft. And pillows! So many pillows.

When Beta Trex told me that Alpha Bowen was going to give me *luxuries*, I was ready to be an ornery martyr about it and not use a single thing. But damn. Scratch that idea. I'm going to enjoy every damn perk that just got delivered because the thread count on these sheets is through the roof.

Besides, despite what Alpha Bowen might think, sitting in a beanbag chair that he paid for does not equate to accepting a marriage proposal or agreeing to his claim of ownership over me. So there.

I quickly make up the bed, and then I test out all my new stuff. I collapse into my beanbag throne, letting the bright colors wrap around me. My mini-fridge is stocked full of soda, water, sandwiches, yogurt, and candy bars. My TV has a stack of brand new DVDs beside it, and my eyes run over the titles.

Pride and Prejudice. 10 Things I Hate About You. The Proposal. How to Lose a Guy in 10 Days. Overboard. The Ugly Truth.

There's a shit ton more, and every single one of them is an Enemies-to-Lovers romance.

I grit my teeth. Alpha Bowen thinks he's so fucking funny and clever. I'd like to let my cockatrice peck his ass. If he thinks he's gonna go from enemy to lover status, he's sorely mistaken.

I'm still gonna watch all of those, though. Not because I'm falling for his shit, but because I have serious TV withdrawals, and I've always been a sucker for Mr. Darcy.

"Right there, Joe, that's perfect," I tell my troll BFF as he drops down another chunk of broken concrete.

It's very handy to have a dude around with so many muscles. He shoves the block up against the others that he's gathered so that I have a broken hodgepodge surface that somewhat functions as a table. I needed something to display what I'm selling today.

I walk around the surface laid out on the ground of the rec yard, eyeing the patchwork concrete. "Hmm," I say, going to the left where I see one of the clumps has a sharp edge poking out. "Can you take care of that, big guy?" I ask, pointing at the piece of concrete that's jutting out.

Joe clomps over, grabs the heavy slab, and takes a bite right out of it. Now that he's chewed off the jagged part, he sets it back down, and I have a much smoother edge for my "table."

I beam at him. "Perfect. You did such a good job!" I say, giving him my best encouraging voice as I pat him on the side.

With a table to work with, I'm ready now. Let's hope everyone likes these more than the shanks.

I put my fingers in my mouth and let out an ear splitting whistle, calling attention to everyone in the rec yard. The forty or so inmates around look over, and I know it's go-time.

"Hey!" I wave excitedly.

No one waves back.

"Tough crowd," I mumble to Joe. He picks up another piece of concrete and starts eating it.

The inmates go back to doing whatever they were doing, and the guards continue to stand around the perimeter, talking shit and doing their best to look intimidating.

Alright, guess I'm gonna need more than just my shining personality to draw people in. Time to pull out the merchandise.

Since we aren't allowed to actually bring anything outside with us, I had to stuff everything into my pockets. I start pulling the pieces of fabric out one by one and laying them on my concrete table, smoothing the wrinkles out.

The moment I start laying the pieces out, people start to take notice. By the time I put down the last one, I have an audience. Bingo.

"What's this?" Zen asks, coming to the front of the gathering crowd.

"My new store," I tell her proudly.

Everyone's eyes are riveted on the fifteen pairs of underwear I've displayed like a Victoria's Secret employee putting out the BOGO sale on V-day.

Zen picks one up by the corner. "How the hell did you make these?" she asks, staring at what once was a pair of standard, prison-issued, white granny panties and is now a super fun thong, complete with pink rhinestones in the shape of an ice cream cone on the front. "Lick me until ice cream," she reads, and I beam at my ingenuity of stitching that on.

I nod and pluck them from her fingers to hold up for everyone to see. "I'm tackling an injustice here, people," I tell my fellow lawbreakers. "We are self-respecting females, and we deserve better underwear than the bleached butt bloomers we've been forced to endure," I say with complete seriousness. "No more," I declare, passionate enough to be giving a women's rights speech. "Our asses deserve better than these," I say, holding up one of the plain pairs of underwear that we're all issued to prove my point. "These are sad, and I'm here to make sure no one has to go through panty shame ever again."

The females in the crowd nod emphatically. A few of the males do too.

"I'll be taking bids today," I announce, letting them look their fill at all the pairs I have to offer. I set the pretty panties in my hand back down, as well as the granny panties to remind them of what they'll be doomed to wear if they miss out. "Make sure you offer up something good. These bad boys are gonna go fast," I say with complete confidence.

"How did you dye the fabric to be different colors?" someone asks, holding up a pair that I managed to dye light pink.

"Stolen kitchen items mostly."

Instead of looking grossed out, she nods like I just really

impressed her. She probably wouldn't be so impressed looking if she knew that one in her hand was colored from an entire bottle of ketchup, but...trade secrets and all that.

"Is this one decorated with Pop Rocks?" my broken-eyed Medusa squad member asks, staring at the pair in the very middle. It's my crowning glory.

I smirk. "Yep," I say, stepping forward. "The Pop Rocks panties are my masterpieces."

Somebody snorts, but I toss them a glare over my shoulder, shutting them up instantly. Putting my attention back on the panties, I admire the three Pop Rocks pairs that I made. They look downright high fashion.

I'm still in awe over the pretty bow I made on the back of one, and the lavender color I managed to dye the other. But all three have a nice Pop Rocks collection glued on the fronts to make them look like they're covered in gemstones. Total masterpiece stuff right there. It also took a hell of a lot of willpower to glue those candies on instead of eating them.

Someone else picks up a pair that I made to look like camouflage. It's very sexy G.I. Joe. "Ah, don't wear that one if you've got a peanut allergy," I warn. "Oh, and wash at your own risk," I add. "I can't guarantee they'll hold up for multiple wear, but I *can* guarantee that I'll have more to buy every Friday. And all sales are final, so don't try to return any. That's just nasty."

I clap my hands. "Let's start this panty pride parade, yeah? Just think, no more embarrassing granny panties when that sexy guard you've had your eye on feels you up in the hallway or that hot asshole inmate talks dirty to you from the vent. Now you can drop your pants for them with confidence," I say with a nod. "Alright! I'm accepting bids starting...now."

For a moment, nobody says anything.

I look around, my confident smile superglued on but my morale starting to deflate nervously. Fuck. This is gonna be embarrassing.

But just before I totally slip into mortification mode, it's like everyone takes a collective breath before they all start shouting at once. Suddenly, the gathered females are shoving, spitting, cursing, hell, even a fist fight breaks out.

I sell all fifteen pairs in five minutes flat, and I come away that much richer. Snacks, dibs on the front of the lunch line, an extra shower rotation, and even some sexual favors that I definitely won't be cashing in, but it's still flattering.

Smiling as the last of my customers walk away, I glance at the rest of the females who missed out. "Don't worry, I'll have more for sale next week."

A few of them grumble as they move on, while more start cursing and talking shit about the ones who managed to snag some pairs. One of the female vampires vows that she's "never talking to that skank Marla again" all because Marla outbid her. I grin. Market day is the best.

"Well done," Zen says with a smirk.

"Better than the shanks?"

"Much," she replies before walking away.

"Here you go, Joe," I say, tossing him a nice piece of quartzite I found. "Thanks for your help."

He munches on it happily and trails away.

"I thought I told you to behave while I was gone."

My lips tilt up at the sound of Rook's voice, but I sweep it away again before turning around to face him.

"Oh. Hey, Rookie," I say coolly. I'm not gonna let him think I've forgotten about the last time we talked. I'm still mad at him for calling me a coward.

He gives me a look. "I've been reverted back to Rookie again, huh?" he asks, put out.

"Mm-hmm. It's deserved."

He moves to get closer to me, then pauses. In the middle of the rec yard, we don't have any amount of privacy, and he seems to come to that same realization the moment I do. "Come on," he says before turning to walk away.

I debate about not following him for a moment, but I missed him, dammit. I haven't seen him for a couple of days, and despite the fact that I'm still pissy over what he said, I find myself trailing after him.

Rook goes to the end of the yard to the locked gate, where another guard stands watch on the other side. "I'm taking her in early. She was caught selling in the rec yard."

The PG snorts. "I heard," he says, casting eerily yellow eyes at me. "Where'd you get all that extra underwear?"

"No comment," I say, because it's probably not a good idea to tell a prison guard that I stole it off the laundry cart.

Following behind Rook, he leads me back inside the building. I'm intensely aware of his body as we walk, my eyes tracking every movement.

Neither of us say a word, but if anything, it just adds to the sexual tension between us. As I watch, his strong arms swing at his sides, and I'm reminded of how they held me pinned against the wall. His steps remind me of the way he prowled closer to me. His bright hair keeps me riveted, like I'm expecting it to glow any second, and his tail swishes behind him, curling toward me like it wants to reach out and wrap around my leg. I'd like it to reach out and wrap around my ass again instead.

"Need a bathroom break before I take you to your cell?" he asks, pulling me from my dirty thoughts.

"What? Oh. No, thanks. I'm good."

Rook tosses a pointed look at me. I blink at him and shrug, like, *what?*

He sighs. "Okay. I'll take you back to your cell. To your *monitored* cell."

"Oh. *Oh!*" I say, realization dawning. He totally wants *unmonitored* dirty time with me. "Right. Uh. Bathroom break. Definitely need a bathroom break first."

"Good choice," he murmurs before turning down a different hallway and leading me to the bathrooms.

My tail flicks impatiently, ready to capitalize on the hungry rumble of his voice.

"Go ahead," he says, opening the door for me. He leads me to the bathroom that's blessedly empty, since the rest of the block is either in the cells, in the rec yard, or in the cafeteria.

"Hmm, I think someone clogged the toilet, Mr. Prison Guard, sir," I lie. "Can you check it out?"

With a smirk, he comes in, and as soon as the door swings shut, he's on me. Mouth on mine, he swallows up the surprised sound and grinds his hips into me.

"I fucking missed you," he breathes before running his mouth against my sensitive neck. "And you're also due for a punishment."

I yelp when his hand smacks against my ass. "Ouch!" I snap.

"That's what you get for changing my name tag again. *I love cock?* Really? I don't know how you made so many damn bejeweled penises, but it's good to know that you didn't run out of those the first time you framed my name tag with them."

I snort out a laugh. "I thought it was a good touch. And you can't be mad. I was simply declaring your love for your own people, you are a cock...atrice," I say with a wry smile.

Fast as a snake strike, I reach down and lightly backhand Rook's balls. He *oomphs* and slightly folds over, bringing a hand up to plug his nostrils, like that's gonna block out his pain. He looks like a kid who's about to cannon ball and doesn't want to get water up his nose.

I start to laugh, which earns me a plugged nose glare. I tilt my head and adopt an *awww poor baby* mien.

"What the hell?" Rook grinds out.

I shrug. "Punishment."

"For what?" he demands, slowly straightening up.

"Would hitting a prison guard in the balls be something a *coward* does?" I ask chirpily.

Rook huffs out an exasperated breath. "Sunrise, I don't think you're a coward. I said the wrong thing, and I'm sorry. I don't like seeing you in a place like this, that's all. Yes, you have people watching your back right now, but there are very dangerous people in here that are always looking for chinks in the armor. It's not safe."

Rook steps into me, his large, hard body suddenly flush with mine. He cups my face, and his thumbs caress my cheeks as he looks down at me, his turquoise gaze intense.

"I care about you. I know that might seem weird because of where we are, but our surroundings don't change anything for me. I care, and I don't want anything to happen to you."

I stare up at him, my eyes soaking up his earnest gaze and my mind soaking up his words. *He cares for me.*

I fidget, not sure what to say or do. It's not that I don't feel those words on the tip of my tongue too. It's that I don't know exactly what to think about the taste.

On one hand, I'm not sure if I should trust whatever is going on between us. And on the other hand, I can't deny my attraction or the pull I feel whenever he's around and sometimes, even when he's not. I think about him maybe a little too much, and that's probably not a good thing, considering my circumstances.

But instead of saying any of that jumbled, complicated

mess...I just kiss him. I pull his full lips down to mine and kiss him with everything I can't bring myself to say.

I tease his tongue with mine and twine them together in the same way it seems fate has twined us. You're not supposed to find the person you've always been looking for in prison. It makes answering innocent questions like *how'd you meet* really fucking awkward.

Aww, how'd you two lovebirds get together? Don't worry about how we met, Patty, worry about yourself.

See? Awkward. I don't want to have to scream that at little ol' Patty from the grocery store. And it'll only be natural for her to ask, because she saw this totally adorable couple, aka us, and just *had* to know where I snagged such a specimen. I can picture Patty's face when I politely say *prison* just before she asks me if I want to purchase reusable bags.

The only problem is, this feels so fucking right. Every time I'm with him, my beast settles into him. *I* settle into him. We just...fit.

And I realize that's what I've been looking for my whole life. As I ran away, as I hid out. I was looking for somewhere where I fit. Somewhere that I could be happy. And now that I found it...it's heartbreaking to think that I probably won't be able to keep it.

As Rook threads his hands in my hair and kisses me passionately, all of those worries and troubled thoughts fall away. I can see myself being happy with Rook, and not just as a passing, fleeting fling, but as a long-term commitment, and that's something I've never felt before. I want to pretend, just for a moment, that a future like that is possible.

We trade longing hunger and unspoken promises with our lips, and I can feel exactly how deep his *I care for you* goes, and I know he can feel the same from me. I don't know what's going to happen between us, but I want to soak up every moment with him that I can.

Throwing caution to the wind, I reach for the buckle on his utility belt. We can fuck the unknown out of each other for all I care at this point. I just know I want him in a way that's consuming and terrifying, and I'm learning to be okay with that.

Rook sucks on my lip and pulls back while he reaches down to stop my hands. I give a tiny grumble of protest, and he chuckles. "I can't, Sunrise. Fuck, I want to—you have no idea how badly I want to—but I'm supposed to be on duty out in the tower. They're going to send someone to look for me if I'm not back soon."

My brow dips with consternation, and I suddenly understand why toddlers throw fits the way they do. If they feel anything like this, then I get why a tiny person would toss themselves on the ground and test the strength of their lungs. "Glow Worm," I whine as I try to lean in for more kisses.

He pulls back like the tease that he is, and I end up looking like a fish going for food that was just sprinkled at the top of the water. I'd feel embarrassed by it—and will probably relive this moment every night when my brain plays a reel of every embarrassing or awkward thing I've ever done in my whole damn life—but I'm too fucking strung out on Rook and turned on to care.

"Just a quick fuck," I plead. "Ooh, let's do the *I dropped the soap* bit in the shower!" I say excitedly. "You can have your way with me as I bend over *real* slowly...while I'm handcuffed," I say with a suggestive eyebrow wag. Prison has really good kinky sex scenarios.

Rook growls hungrily, leaning in and nipping at my lip before he pushes away from me like I'm a flaring flame. He holds his hands up, either surrendering, or because he's afraid to touch me, I'm not sure which. I'm going to go with the latter, because if he were surrendering to me, he'd have his cock buried balls deep inside me and I'd be gasping his name in his ear in between begging for more and telling him *yes, right there!*

"Don't give me that look, Sunrise," he sexily scolds while running his fingers through his bright hair with frustration. His scalp has started to pulse with a sharp glow. "I want you so bad, you have no idea, but I *have* to get back to work. I've already been gone too long."

His eyes plead with me to understand, and I give up on a sigh and nod my head. "Fine," I capitulate.

Relief fills his features, and he reaches for my hand. "I'll walk you back real quick," he offers, but I shake my head no.

"I'll stay here for a minute and then find my own way back. You go before you get in trouble or something," I tell him.

"If you have to pee, I can wait for a second," he declares, like it makes him some knight in shining armor.

I chuckle and shake my head. Poor, innocent Rook. "I don't need to pee, Rookie. I need to shove my hand down my pants and play with myself. If I can't wring out at least two orgasms, I'm not going to be able to function for the rest of the day."

Rook looks at me, dumbfounded.

I raise my eyebrows at him. "What? You only have yourself to blame. You can't get a girl all hot and bothered and think it doesn't need to be dealt with."

I drop my hands to the ties of my scrub pants and start to untie the bow. Rook just watches me like he doesn't understand what I'm saying. I shove my hand inside my pants and underwear, and I'm so fucking wet I don't even need to lubricate my clit—it's plenty juicy already.

I manage about half a circle before Rook growls, "Fuck it," and starts to unbuckle his belt.

Hooray!

My insides explode with a cheer like my body is a stadium and the home team just scored a touchdown. Rook gets his pants down quickly and then sits down on a wood-topped bench that the inmates use when they're waiting for their turn to shower.

I kick off my shoes and have my pants and underwear off by the time his ass is hitting the bench. I push him back from where he's leaning over to untie his boots and crawl into his lap instead. I reach into his open pants and pull out my vagina's best friend, stroking it for good luck. Then I line myself up and sink down over him, and we both moan out in relief, like suddenly, all is right in the world again.

He pulls up my shirt and pops my boob out over the top of my sports bra as I rise up on his thick cock and drop myself back down. He brings my other breast out to play with too and pinches the nipple as his mouth closes around the other hard tip. I moan quietly and then start riding him, like he's the bull of the year and I need these next eight seconds to change my life.

Rook moans and nips at my nipple while pinching the other even tighter, and a flash of sensation moves from my needy tits down to my clit. The sound of flesh slapping against flesh fills the bathroom, and the base of his cock gets wetter and wetter with every downstroke of my pussy.

It's a race to the finish line for both of us. We're carnal and animalistic in our fight for what we need as I bounce on his dick. I'm bucking up and down over his cock like he's a bounce house and I'm trying to catch enough air to do a backflip.

Finally, we're both getting a taste of what we've been craving since the last time he was deep inside of me. It's not enough. I just can't seem to get enough of this male.

I grab the back of his head as he switches nipples and flicks the hard tip with his tongue before sucking it into his mouth. I encourage what he's doing as I grind on him and lean down to whisper in his ear. "You feel so fucking good," I purr. "Do you feel how wet you make me, Glow Worm? Do you feel my pussy fluttering around your cock as you go deeper and deeper?"

Rook moans and pops off my nipple. "Fucking hell, female."

He pulls my lips to his and kisses me stupid, while lifting us up and switching our positions. My back touches the wood of the bench, and I spread wide for him. Rook starts to fuck me like he's drowning and can only breathe once I'm screaming his name. He holds my shoulders so I don't scoot up the bench while he drives into me over and over again. I try to bite back the screams of ecstasy, not wanting to give us away, but it's so fucking hard. And the fact that we could be caught any second...it's a dangerous, titillating turn on.

My body fills with tingles that are steadily collecting at my core. "Yes," I encourage, throwing my head back to revel in the building orgasm. "Just like that."

"Look at me," Rook demands. "I want to see your eyes when I make you come all over my cock."

My lids snap open at his dirty words, and I stare up at him as pleasure builds to its peak. I can tell by his face that he's right there on the cusp with me. I've never come at the same time as someone else, and I'm suddenly super into watching him as he orgasms and fills me up.

I start chanting his name every time our hips connect, and then seconds later, we both explode into nothing but a culmination of passion, desire, pleasure, and rapture.

Rook and I watch each other orgasm, but it's not weird like it has the potential to be, it's intimate in a way I didn't understand before. His eyes drink in my pleasure, and I can almost feel it add to his own.

We both pant as we come down, and then he bends to

kiss me sweetly. "You were way too loud," he says before pinching a nipple and pulling out of me to get cleaned up. I watch him from my back, legs spread, boobs out, shirt pushed up, and he watches me right back like a lion planning his next hunt.

"You made me," I retort as he buckles his utility belt back into place and caresses every inch of my body with a still-hungry stare.

"Damn right."

I thought that a quick fuck would take the edge off my need for him, but I was wrong. I could spend every second of the day with his cock buried deep in my pussy, and I still don't think I could get enough.

That's when realization hits me like another orgasm. It's not just the sex I crave, it's *him*. All of him. This self-assured, funny, thoughtful asshole has wormed his way into my heart. It doesn't matter how rational I try to be about it all. I'm falling for him.

Rook looks at me like the cat that's got the cream, and all I want to do is stay here for the next day and give him plenty more for him to lap up. I can see in his eyes that he wants the same thing, but reality is a bitch of a cockblock.

"I'm going to think about you just like this for the rest of the day," he tells me as he prowls over and leans down to claim my lips one more time.

His hand runs down my arm, and I do my best to convince him with my lips that we should spend the rest of the day seeing how many orgasms a female cockatrice body can take, but he straightens up. He lifts my hand in his and slowly brings my fingers to his face before picking out my pointer finger and putting it in his mouth. His lips close around it and he sucks, his tongue swirling.

At first I'm irritated, because he's getting me all riled up again just before he's about to leave, but then I remember that's the finger I dipped between my lips and circled my clit with when I was teasing him by playing with myself.

He moans as he pulls my finger out of his mouth. "Now I'll get to taste you for the rest of the day too."

With that, he backs up, his heated gaze drinking me in one last time before he turns and disappears out of the door. I sigh and sit up. What the hell am I supposed to do about him?

I shove the thought aside and remove my bra and shirt as I stand up, rolling my eyes at the thrill of glee that moves through me at the very wet and sticky situation going on between my thighs. Well, at least I won't have to worry about getting cleaned up this time. I chuckle and get into the shower as I think about all the different places that Rook and I could christen in this prison.

I wonder if the Warden has a desk in his office?

12

It's meatloaf day.

The day I've been waiting for ever since I got here. The shining jewel of all cafeteria food. Juicy, savory, delicious meatloaf. I can't wait.

Except some stupid fuck decided to go on a vampiric rampage or some shit, so now our entire block is on lock down. I'm so pissed I can't even enjoy watching any of my DVDs.

But when I hear a familiar rolling cart heading my way, I perk up and jump over to my cell door just in time to see Selena the siren coming my way. "Please tell me you're delivering my meatloaf," I beg, not even caring that it sounded like a dirty innuendo.

Selena cringes and passes me a covered tray through the food slot, and I eagerly take it and open it up. As soon as I do, I cringe at the sight of a rotted apple, moldy bread, and a decayed piece of meat that in no way resembles delicious, juicy meatloaf. And—*is that a worm?*

"What the fuck?" I say, offended, before tossing the food back out through the slot so it clatters on the floor.

"Sorry," she says guiltily before she turns and hurries away like her ass is on fire.

I glower at the place she disappeared from. Fucking management is punishing us with rotten food now? That's just wrong. And that's pretty fucked up for Selena to do it. Although, she *did* sneak over and deliver me some Pop Rocks a while ago, so I guess I can't be too mad at her. I imagine the rest of the prisoners will give her enough shit about this delivery, she doesn't need me to add to the pile.

But I better get some goddamn meatloaf soon.

No one is allowed out of their cell until the next day, and it's like there's an electric charge in the air as I make my way down the hall. At first, I chalk it up to everyone just having a ton of pent-up energy from being stuck in our cells for hours on end, but I realize it's for a very different reason when I'm cornered in the cafeteria by a crowd of females. I note that everyone who bought one of the pairs of underwear I made is now circling me...plus, like, a shit ton of other females too.

"Uhh...what's up?" I ask nervously. *Am I about to get shanked for customer dissatisfaction?* "Look, I told you, no returns or refunds. I included all the proper fine print. If you tried to wash it and your bedazzles fell off or something, that's not my fault."

Broken-Eyed Medusa shoves her way forward, and I bring my fists up in front of me in a defensive move, ready to block fists that come flying my way. She might be in my squad, but she barely tolerates me because of Zen's influence. Ever since I asked to pet her snakes, all she usually does is hiss at me. What is it with gorgons not letting their snake hair get any love? I don't doubt that she'd knock me on my ass in a second.

But instead of pulling my hair to kick off a cat fight, she grabs me by the shoulders. "We need more Pop Rocks panties."

Stunned, it takes me a few seconds to gather her words and process them. "Huh?"

"The Pop Rocks panties," someone else repeats—the other female who purchased a pair.

I look at everyone warily. "Uhh, why?"

A very burly, thickly muscled chick shoves her way forward. "Those Pop Rocks...popped."

My brow furrows at her earnest expression. "*Ookay*..."

Broken-Eyed Medusa—who I now will call Bem—gives me a pointed look. "A few of us were getting hot and heavy with some prison buddies, if you know what I mean," she explains. "And well...what happens when you put Pop Rocks into your wet mouth?"

My mind puts it together and... "Oh—*ohhh!*" I look around at everyone. "Are you telling me that my Pop Rocks candies got you guys off?"

"Best damn orgasm I've had in three years," Burly says.

I...I don't know how to feel about this development. I sure hope they washed afterward, or their downstairs ovens could turn into little slices of angry yeast bread.

"Umm. Cool?" I offer, not knowing what else to say.

"Are you taking preorders?" someone else in the crowd asks.

"Uh..."

"When they started going off, it was like little pieces of hail popping down on my clit," Burly says dreamily.

Females start shouting out offers to me, and I quickly hold up my hands to try to regain control before they all go berserk and hold me hostage until I give them more orgasm-inducing candy panties.

"Okay, okay!" I shout. "I'll take orders, just...be cool and back up a little. Give a girl some room to breathe."

The next twenty minutes is basically me corralling and appeasing a cluster of females all vying for me to give them panties with Pop Rocks glued all over them. They're all offering me the moon on a platter. Bem even let me finally pet her hair snakes. *Finally!* It's awesome, too. They're super soft, and one of them even licks me.

But damn, it's exhausting being a star. So much attention is making me a little twitchy.

By the time I see Joe's tall ass walk into the room, I want to jump up and down in relief. I quickly wave to get his attention. The females are still chatting away about how popping orgasms are the new *thing*, but seriously, there's only so much I can say on the subject other than *you're welcome*, so I'm hoping Zen sent Joe here to rescue me.

Joe spots me and makes a noise, and even though I can't hear it over the clamor, I can see from the rise and fall of his chest that it's definitely a grunt like, *there you are*. He waves me over, and I hold up my hand to say one minute and start trying to extract myself.

"Sorry, my friend is here. He needs me, but I'll get to work on more orders," I shout over the din, and then I have no choice but to throw some elbows and start hip checking people so I can get the fuck out of here.

Damn, these Pop Rocks panties really caught on fast. And I gotta say, I'm very curious. I've always loved how the candy feels in my mouth...I just might have to try them out myself.

I'm breathless and tousled by the time I maneuver my way over to Joe's side.

"Thanks for the assist there, big guy," I snark, but Joe just does what he always does. He grunts.

Dipping his head, he heads out of the doorway, and I follow him. I keep checking over my shoulder for the first couple of minutes or so, worried inmates will follow me. When we round several corners and there's still no one on our tail, I let out a relieved breath. "That was crazy, Joe! I mean, I just used the Pop Rocks so I could get the colors I wanted, but if I had known...I would've charged *way* more," I say.

We pass a guard standing at a corner, and he nods at us. I give him a wave.

"I wonder if they feel good for guys too? You wanna try some on?" I ask, and then I shake my head. "Hmm, they'll be way too small. Don't worry, Joe, I'll make some that are troll-size and a couple others for some of the guys to test out."

He grunts again as I follow him down another hallway, around a bend, and then through another empty corridor, and a weird little hallway that seems to be half as wide as the others before widening out again.

"It might take a little while, because I need to meet the female demand first, but don't worry, I'll hook you up."

The lighting in these tunnels looks dimmer, and I realize suddenly that I have no idea where I am. I've just been following my giant prison bestie and jabbering away.

"Are we going to meet up with Zen and the others?" I ask, recalling how I didn't see them earlier.

Joe grunts again, and I relax. "These hallways are very echoey. You grunt, and then I suddenly feel like I'm surrounded by a ton of Joes instead of just one," I observe, but Joe doesn't grunt to that.

"Speaking of, I'm excited for Sloppy Joes later—did you see it on the menu? Those things are good. When I was a kid, I always wanted them, but no one in my lounge was allowed to make them for me. I had to get incarcerated to finally be able to try one, but *fuck*, I've been missing out! Like, I don't even know what they put in that sauce, but I'm telling you, if I could bathe in it, I would."

A scoffing sort of grunt echoes all around me, and I laugh. "Don't judge me Joe, I've noticed the way you put down the beef stroganoff in this place. I bet if there was a pool of beef stroganoff, your big ass would be in there swimming around too," I tease.

The long hallway that we're in winds around to the right, and I suddenly feel like we're walking uphill, or maybe I'm just out of shape and that's why I'm suddenly winded.

"Damn, where are Zen and the crew hiding?" I ask, a little breathless and completely lost. "I know Nightmare Penitentiary is big and has a shit ton of different levels and buildings, but I feel like we're walking a long way. Is there some secret room back here where all the cool kids hang out in or something?" I ask. "Or, *ooh*, are they throwing me a secret surprise party in honor of my Pop Rocks panties?"

This time, Joe snorts, and I find myself suddenly squealing. "That's it, isn't it? Holy shit, I just got so excited, Joe! Is there cake? Oh, please tell me there's going to be cake!" I start clapping, and there's a distinct spring in my step.

"Will you shut the fuck up? You're going to give us away if you keep doing that." A male voice snips, and I freeze and look all around me for the source.

What the hell?

I do a complete circle of the still empty, unfamiliar hallway, before my eyes land back on Joe. I move closer to him. "Did you hear that, Joe?" I whisper as I stare at the shadows all around us, suddenly feeling very uneasy.

"I not only heard it, I fucking said it," Joe announces as he looks down at me, his gaze filled with irritation.

My eyes nearly pop out of my head as I stare up at him, completely dumbfounded. My brain can't process what it means for Joe's lips to be moving and forming words. He's never spoken. Not once. Not to anyone.

"I thought you couldn't talk!" I say, totally flabbergasted.

"Well, you obviously thought wrong," he replies, his voice much higher pitched than I would've imagined.

I frown at him as he starts walking again. "But...you *never* speak. All the times I've talked to you..." My mind drifts off to all our little chats, and my cheeks immediately turn cherry red. "Goddammit, Joe! I told you super embarrassing things!"

He gives me a pointed look, his granite-speckled face looking darker in this shadowed part of the prison. It somewhat resembles the dim corridors that lead to solitary, except I can tell this part of the prison is older. Much older.

"Yeah. I really wished you wouldn't have told me about the time in high school when you got your period and it bled through your pants on Shine Bright Like a Diamond Day when everyone was wearing white pants."

My lips pinch together before I let out a groan. "Yeah, hindsight, I shouldn't have told you that. But really, you only have yourself to blame. If I had known you could repeat my deepest darkest secrets, I wouldn't have told you any of them." I pause and run my fingers through my hair with exasperation. "Shit, Joe, what am I going to do now? You were so easy to talk to!"

"Because you're the only one talking," he replies dryly.

"I don't see your point."

He shakes his head. "Come on. We're almost there."

"Almost *where*?" I ask, looking around much more warily. Two minutes ago, I thought I was following my prison bestie to a celebration. Now, I don't know who this dude is and where he might be taking me.

In answer, Joe stops in front of an iron door that's being propped open with a brick. He pushes it open, and I see an eerie set of stairs leading up. "This way."

"Damn, our prison squad needs to find a less creepy

hang out place," I announce in an attempt to calm my sudden nerves.

I'm somewhat fishing for a reaction from Joe so I can gauge if I need to panic or just chill the fuck out. This is Joe, my buddy. So what if he's chattier than I originally thought? He's still my big, lovable teddy bear. I hope.

My thighs burn as I follow him up the steep steps, my shoes clapping over the uneven stone. "I don't think this staircase is to code, Joe," I pant, as the steepness of the steps never ends. The lighting is terrible too, and there's no railing, so I have to steady myself on the cold stone wall beside us. "Fuck, how much farther?"

"You should exercise more," he tosses over his shoulder, his breath not at all ragged. I don't know how a dude that's nine feet tall and looks like he's made of solid rock doesn't get winded from this.

I'm about ready to ask him to carry me when we finally reach the top, where yet another door is being propped open. Joe goes out first and then holds it for me as I follow, my eyes squinting at the windy night air. It's just past dusk, the first of the stars starting to blink to life.

Frowning, I look around. We're on some part of the prison's roof. I can see the backs of gargoyles and spires peeking at the edge, and gravel crunches beneath my shoes as I come to a stop.

"Uh, Joe? Where's everyone else?"

"They're coming."

More prickles of unease begin to creep down my neck, and alarm bells start ringing in my head. I should've made a run for it when he spoke his first word, but I have no idea where I am. I try to talk myself down. This dude mostly grunts and eats rocks. He's in Zen's squad, and Zen wants me for her own plans. There's no way he'd hurt me and risk her wrath.

I slowly turn to face him and mask all of the panic that's surging through my veins. "Where's Zen?"

Joe ignores me, his heavy steps making the roof creak ominously as he walks to the edge and kneels down at the back of the dormer-looking stone wall. Slipping his finger through what I thought was just an eye-hook stuck into the wall, he twists and pulls, and my eyes widen when the small dormer wall swings open.

"About fuckin' time," a deep voice says from the shadows.

My feet back up instinctively as I watch three figures emerge, crawling out of the space before they step onto the roof and straighten up.

All three of them are males I don't recognize, but I *do* recognize their scent. They're sigbins. Like vampires, they drink blood, but sigbins only do it out of vengeance, not a biological need. Their legs are slightly bowed, and when they're hunting, they walk with their head between their legs. Backward.

It's fucking weird.

They have big, floppy ears on the sides of their heads and each has a tail like a leather whip. They also smell like ass.

Sigbins only live in small groups, mostly because they have petty fights where they kill each other a lot. They can be vicious, but they're also dumber than doornails. There's no reasoning with them.

"Fuck," I curse, my back hitting the closed door. My hand closes around on the handle, and my body tenses, getting ready to run for it.

At the sound of my voice, all three of the sigbins look over at me. The one in the front with greasy black hair cocks his head. "This the one Alpha Bowen wants?" he asks, his grotesque fangs hanging out past his bottom lip.

He looks like the offspring of zombie Dobby and a wild boar.

My eyes fly to Joe, and betrayal douses me like I just got hit with a bucket of ice water. So *Joe* is the one that took up Alpha Asshole's bounty offer to steal me? Motherfucker.

While I'm distracted, the door at my back suddenly swings open on me, sending me pitching forward. I nearly eat shit, but I catch myself just in time and turn to look at who just joined us on the roof.

"Zen?"

Anger rises in me. Zen was in on this too? Goddammit, prison squads are supposed to be sacred! I expected much better loyalty than this from my co-criminals. Yeah...okay. In hindsight, that was probably not so smart on my end.

She starts to walk by me, but right as she passes me, she turns her head and speaks so quietly that I almost don't hear her. "Nice night to swap, don't you think?"

What the hell does that mean?

If she's trying to threaten me, it needs work. Frowning, I watch as Zen's dark eyes sweep over the scene, her body relaxed as she walks forward toward Joe.

"Who're you?" the same sigbin asks, this time looking at Zen.

She ignores him and walks right up to the troll. I watch her lotus tattoo beside her eye begin to glimmer. It's subtle, but it casts a greenish glow over her smooth dark skin, and Joe's charcoal eyes latch onto it.

"Ut oh," he grunts, and then his mouth goes slack, and his eyes become glassy.

"Hey, Joe," she says.

His face grooves into a deep frown, he blinks. Once, twice, and then his eyes grow heavy, and the big troll walks over to the edge of the roof and slumps down, crossing his huge arms in front of him as he immediately closes his eyes and falls asleep.

My brow deepens into its furrow as I watch him start to snore.

The sigbins fidget on their feet. "What's he doing?" the one with the beard asks.

"I think he's...thinking?" Sigbin number three guesses.

"Wait...Nah, he ain't thinking. He's fuckin' sleepin'," Greasy Hair says, like this was super difficult logic to work through. "Oy, wake up, you lazy ass!"

Joe just starts snoring even louder.

"Maybe we'll get paid more since he's sleepin' on the job," Three muses.

Mind whirring, my eyes lock onto Zen. When she tosses me a wink, I understand what she just did, knocking Joe out using her ultra-calming zen power, but it takes me another breath to sort through why. *Swap,* she said. She wants to swap.

My mouth opens in an O as I realize that she's here to take my place and help me. I have no idea how she found out what Joe was up to, but I shouldn't be surprised. Zen seems to know everything that goes on in this prison.

Seeing that I've caught up, she gives me a nod, and I give one back to her.

Clearing my throat, I walk forward, putting up a confident, know-it-all front. "Don't worry, he always does that," I lie, motioning toward the sleeping troll. "Big guy needs a lot of naps because of his height to weight ratio and all that. It's fine though, because she's here." I nod toward Zen, and the corner of her lips tilt up.

The sigbins, looking dumb with their heads cocked, begin to clap their ears together so that it sounds like some really awkward applause. "The cock alpha wants *you*?" the one with the shoulder-length hair asks, looking Zen up and down.

"Of course," she says simply. "Now, are you going to get me the fuck out of this hell hole and into my alpha's arms or what?"

The sigbins do their weird ear clapping thing again, but Greasy Hair shakes his head. "Wait. Nah. The one we was supposed to deliver was a shifter. Like the alpha." All three pairs of eerie eyes skim over to me. "Like *you*," he says, pointing.

Oh, shit.

I laugh, despite my spiking worry. "Don't be ridiculous. It's not me he wants. If you don't deliver her, he's going to be very angry at you for fucking this up. You definitely won't get paid."

The other two exchange nervous glances. "Oh, we better take her. I don't wanna get that mean fucker mad, and we need the money," Beard says, his eyes darting around like he's afraid Alpha Bowen is gonna pop out of the shadows.

"Nah. I think she's fuckin' lyin'. Tryin' to trick us."

Beard and Three slowly digest this information. It takes...a while. But finally, after several seconds, they work out what that means and scowl. "You tryin' to trick us, bitch?" Beard asks, stalking forward and grabbing me by the collar of my shirt.

Shit.

"No, fucker. Let me go!"

Sigbins might not be the smartest, but they're strong, and those massive fangs are wicked sharp. Beard leans in, letting the end of his canine scrape threateningly against my throat. My heart pounds nervously. "We don't like it when people try to trick us."

"Yeah, makes us real...*thirsty*," Three says as he and Greasy Hair circle around me.

Dammit, this is going downhill fast.

If I shift, this whole clandestine meeting will *definitely* not continue to go unnoticed. We're lucky with the positions of the guard towers that we aren't visible. But if I change into my fifteen-foot beast? Yeah, that's gonna be visible. I got tased and put into solitary for shifting and smacking into some guards last time. I don't even want to imagine what the Warden will do to me if he finds out I was part of a prison break, regardless of how involuntary that involvement is.

"We don't fuckin' like liars," Greasy Hair says as he closes in on me.

"Let's teach her a lesson," Three adds, his ears clapping at the thought as his fangs start to drip with saliva.

Fuck that.

In a blink, I shift my fingers into my beast's talons and swipe at Beard. He lets go of my shirt, and we both stumble back away from each other. His eyes widen as he takes in the red slash across the back of his hand. "You bitch!"

With the scent of blood in the air, the sigbins all begin to snarl, and fear dive bombs into my belly as aggression crawls up to roost in my chest. My beast starts to respond.

They snarl at me, and I flinch back, arms raised in front of me in anticipation of a full-blown attack that I'll be forced to let my cockatrice deal with, but then Zen is suddenly between us, lotus flower glimmering bright. "Now, now, boys. Let's stay...*calm*."

Zen's voice rings out like a ripple. It hits me at the base of the skull and reverberates up, up, up, until it feels like my soul is being cradled in a goddamn lullaby.

Everyone, me included, lets out a deep breath of relief. The sigbins stop in their tracks, the tenseness of their bodies draining out from fangs to feet. Slumping over slightly, their ears clap sluggishly, and they get a dazed look in their eyes, mouths agape.

Zen shakes her head at them. "Fucking sigbins," she says under her breath with distaste before looking over her shoulder at me. She smirks when she sees my expression. "Sorry, Sinclair. I couldn't hit them without hitting you too."

I nod my head, trying to shake off the effects of her power. It packs a fucking punch. "Damn," I say, licking my lazy lips. "You could make a fortune mellowing out college students during finals."

She chuckles, and I walk up beside her, still feeling drunk, but not nearly as bad off as the sigbins. "Your power is fucking intense," I tell her. "What else can you do?"

She lifts her shoulder into a shrug. "I can bring out any emotion, but I'm strongest with calming. And no one can do shit when they're too calm to care," she says with a smirk. "These bozos will be good for at least a few hours."

"Impressive."

She nods and looks over to the small opening in the dormer. "Well, I guess this is my exit," she says. "You sure you don't want to come?"

I shake my head. "It's tempting, but I need to figure some stuff out before I go out there." I'm under no illusions that I can evade Alpha Bowen on the outside.

"Okay then. I guess this is goodbye," Zen says, holding out her hand. "Thanks for the escape, Sinclair Denali."

I shake her hand with a pump. "You're not, like...an ax murderess that I'm releasing out into the public, right?" I ask before dropping her hand. I'm only half-kidding.

Zen laughs. "Nope. Don't you know? I'm innocent," she says with a wink before turning to the sigbins. "Alright, boys. Lead the way out. But we're going to do something fun and *not* meet up with the Alpha, okay?" she says, nudging Greasy Hair's boot with her foot.

At her direction, they all turn, glassy-eyed, and start trudging toward the doorway.

Before she leaves, I quickly run up and squeeze Zen in a hug. "Thank you," I breathe into her ear. She pats me awkwardly on the back, and I pull away. "Not a hugger?"

She snorts. "No."

"I am," I reply unashamedly.

She gives me a wry smile. "I know. I've heard your vagina has been *hugging* PG Rook's cock."

I shake my head. Of course she knows. "What can I say? When it's good, it's good," I state with a shrug.

"From the sound of things, it must be *very* good," she teases.

"Wait. You're telling me you have super hearing too?" I demand.

She laughs and shakes her head. "Emotions, remember? I can get just about anyone to tell me *everything*. Every. Single. Detail," she says pointedly.

I swallow down my embarrassment at the thought of her getting all the dirty specifics. "Okay. Noted for future reference. In case I ever see you again."

"You won't," she says, shaking her head. "Not if everything goes right, anyway. I'm getting out of here and hiding up on my own private island for the next eighty years with some hot cabana boys."

"Good plan, but you're sure you can deal with the alpha?"

Another wry look comes my way. "I'm sure. Besides, it'll be these dumbasses who have to deal with his wrath, not me. He must be getting desperate to be putting out an open bounty for idiots like this to come and collect you. And besides, if shit hits the fan somehow, I can calm anyone down enough to slip away," she tells me, tapping on her tattoo.

"Handy power."

"Yep," she says, taking a step back. "Don't worry about me. It's *you* he wants to deal with."

I wrinkle my nose. "You make it sound dirty."

She grins. "Take care of the squad while I'm gone. And don't take anyone's shit."

"I won't," I tell her.

"Take care of yourself, Sinclair."

I give her a little wave before she turns and crouches through the dormer doorway, all three sigbins following after her. "Hey," I call to Three. He stops and looks over at me. "Tell Alpha Bowen that Sinclair is really enjoying the thread count of those sheets," I say, knowing that the taunting words will fuck with him once he realizes his cronies broke out the wrong prisoner.

"Huh?" the dumb sigbin says.

I sigh. "Never mind."

His head is so full of holes and calm power that he can't even deliver an immature taunt for me. It's a wonder they managed to break into the prison at all, but that has to be due solely to their excellent tracking skills and their ability to see in the dark.

Once they disappear through the entrance that leads who the fuck knows where, I shove the opening shut by bracing my feet on the roof and pushing with all my strength, heaving my shoulder and arm into it until I manage to slide it into place.

I shake my head at Joe, giving him my best *I'm disappointed in your behavior* look. When he wakes up, he and I are going to have a major discussion about not trying to break out your fellow squad member from prison unless they ask you to. It's just basic manners.

I leave him to sleep on the roof as I walk back to the door. Knowing Zen's amount of power, it'll be hours before he wakes up, and I'm not about to stick around here and give the guards a reason to tase me.

I slip through the exit and make my way back down the steps and into the maze that awaits below. Meeting the bottom of the stairs, I look around with a sigh. I turn in a circle, dread pooling in my stomach at the snarl of dark passageways that I don't recognize in the slightest. I have no idea which one leads me back to my cell.

Fuck.

13

Yeah, I'm lost.

I've been wandering for hours.

The hallways and doors just never fucking end, and I see some really fucked up things down here in this labyrinth of doom.

I know for sure I'm not in the part of Nightmare Penitentiary where I belong with the other minor criminals who are just here for a slap on a wrist and a short sentence. That fact becomes abundantly clear as I pass by some of the corridors.

I see a passageway guarded by hellhounds. I see a barred, pure silver door with someone inside banging so hard it feels like the whole place is gonna collapse around it. I back away from blades swinging from ceilings and spiked floors blocking red-glowing doorways. I spot a weird fucking ghoul-ghost thing haunting a vent, and blood pooling beneath a windowsill.

Nope. Definitely not in my nice, above-level, minor criminal part of the prison.

After wandering around, I try to backtrack and go back to the roof, deciding it's worth the threat of being tased to just wait until Joe wakes up so he can lead me to my cell. Except...I can't fucking find that either. I should've dropped proverbial breadcrumbs to lead my way home like a good little Hansel and Gretel, instead of just blindly walking and hoping for the best.

I start to get worried when my mouth grows dry and my stomach clamps down with hunger. My feet are fucking dead, and my thighs still hurt from those damn stairs. I must've walked for half a day now.

How fucking big is this prison?

I pass an arched entryway that leads to what looks like yet another empty corridor, but just when I walk past, a blood curdling screaming starts up. I jump and release my own scream as fear and the fight or flight instinct pumps through my whole body.

I feel like I'm stuck in the worst possible haunted maze ever. The Warden should use this place as a solid revenue stream every Halloween. People would pay good money to be this scared and traumatized.

My cockatrice unfurls inside of me in response to my panic, and I focus on scurrying away from the screaming and try to calm my beast down. I can't afford to have her exploding out of me and getting us wedged in this hallway of horrors that's way too small to fit her.

I take deep breaths and scurry down a dark corridor that leads the opposite way of the terrifying shrieks. I walk for about five minutes and then pause when I realize that it seems to get darker the further down I move.

Shit on my tail feathers.

At this rate, I'm going to fucking die down here. If something doesn't reach out and eat me, dehydration and starvation will do it. There's also a serious chance I might actually just get scared to death with the shit going on down here. My entire body is trembling, despite the fact that I'm trying to buck myself up and keep a brave face. But seriously, this place is terrifying.

I need to get out of here!

Of course, right in the middle of my panic is when I hear a faint clicking of nails on stone. Horror yanks on the reins of my body. I try to hold my breath and listen, but suddenly, all I can hear is the sound of my frightened pulse pounding in my ears with a very faint background noise of what I'm pretty sure is something moving closer to me.

Oh God. I'm too young to die!

A whimper starts in my chest, but I bite it back down.

Oh no you don't, body! You shut that shit down. There will be no scared noises giving us away and getting us eaten like the secondary character in the opening of a horror flick. Not today.

I breathe through the dread-filled anxiety and just stand there as the noise gets closer. I don't freeze in fear, because freezing in fear is for scaredy cats and dragon shifters. I'm just...protecting myself. Waiting it out all level-headed like, in case the monster lurking down the pitch-black hallway happens to be a T. rex and my movement allows it to pinpoint my location. Yep. That's definitely what I'm doing. I'm saving myself from T. rex eyes, totally not scared stiff and shaking in the middle of the dark hallway of death.

The nails click even louder on the stone, and I know it's close. Any minute now, a horror so bad my mind can't even conjure an image will come scuffling out of the shadows and into the light and kill me right here and now.

Dammit, I should've fucked Rook *so* many more times than I did.

Why did I waste our precious time together being mad at him when I could've been in a myriad of positions, enjoying all of the things he likes to do to my body?

Stupid move, Sinclair.

I should've told him that I like him...a fucking lot. I

should've made it clear that I've never been drawn to someone like I've been drawn to him, and then I should've twerked all over his mouth while showing him the special set of skills I have when it comes to really getting down and dirty and sucking a cock's cock. He has no idea just what my tongue can do, I barely licked him, and it's all my fault.

I'm on the cusp of promising every deity I've ever heard of that I'll build a sweet temple of worship and make whatever sacrifices required if one of them plucks me from this hallway and relocates me directly in front of Rook so I can show him all my tongue tricks and tell him how I feel, when all of a sudden, something comes scampering out of the dark.

I jump back, my warrior cry coming out more like a terrified girl squeal as I plaster myself against the wall, my eyes blinking wide at the terror that rose from the shadows. This is it! This is how it ends.

Except...

That's...that's a mouse.

Breathing hard, I stare at the tiny rodent whose nails are clicking over the stone, confirming that the sound I heard was this little creature and not Bloody Mary coming to drag me to hell.

I snort and sigh in relief.

"Oh fuck," I pant. "You sounded a lot scarier coming from the black abyss," I say, looking down at it while I try to calm my racing heart.

I shake my head at myself and watch as the ginger rust-colored fur ball with its white face skitters past me. It heads in the direction I just came from, and I scoop it up in a flash. "Whoop, I don't think you want to go that way, Rusty. I've seen some shit that way," I say as I hold it up to my face.

There's a distinct look of intelligence in its black eyes, and I take a deep sniff, just to make sure I'm not manhandling a shifter. Smells like a mouse to me. It sits up on its hind legs in the middle of my palm and starts cleaning its front paws. One of them is white, and I watch as it carefully washes itself to keep it as snowy as ever.

"I bet that's a bitch to keep clean in this place," I observe as the little mouse just goes about its bath, while I watch like some creeper.

I give it a little pet in between its ears and then set it down on the ground. Rusty looks at me for a beat and then starts moving in the direction that I just came from again.

"Don't say I didn't warn you," I call after it.

I swear on my tail feathers that the mouse stops, looks back at me, and then motions with its head *and* tail, like, *are you coming or what, bitch?*

Uhh...

I give the little guy the side-eye, because there is no way that just happened. It's official. I've lost my fucking mind. The mouse sighs at me. It fucking *sighs*! Like it's over people always having this kind of reaction to it.

Then, once again, it motions with its head for me to follow it. I debate for exactly three milliseconds and then do exactly that. Fuck Lassie. Rusty's going to lead the way home.

I hope.

Either that, or my delusional ass is walking right into the mouth of a fucking carnivorous swamp monster or something. It'll be asleep, and I'll just walk right into its mouth and be like, *breakfast is served*! All because I followed a mouse with an imaginary head nod to my death.

"No swamp monsters, okay, Rusty?" I tell him, cringing at how my quiet voice seems to echo for ages down the hallways and make it even creepier down here.

The little nugget of orange fur just trots along, taking every corridor like a pro as it veers left, right, and straight down the maze of hallways. I follow behind, taking so many turns that I can't even keep track. Every time it squeaks, I'm convinced it's trying to talk to me. I've never wanted to know what a mouse is saying so badly in my whole life. Occasionally, Rusty's little pink nose scrunches up, and it stands up on its haunches, like it's counting or something before it deems the coast is clear and starts walking again.

Please, don't let this end with me in Swamp Thing's mouth!

I try to keep my breathing even and ignore all the sore muscles in my body that are screaming at me. This wandering life is not for me. I'm more of a five-minute trot around the backyard and then veg out on the couch for the rest of the day kinda girl.

I'm hungry too. So hungry that the little mouse is looking better and better to my cockatrice with every passing minute, but I flick my beast on the nose until it skulks back to the corners of my consciousness. You'd think I've been lost down here for a damn week with the way my body is whining.

A few more squeaks fill the empty hallway we're traveling down, and I have to stop myself from asking, *what is it, Rusty?* I'm so focused on the mouse chatter as we turn a corner, that when I walk into something hard, dark, and warm, it totally takes me off guard, and I yelp as I go flying backward.

Son of a bitch, it's the swamp monster, I just know it!

Two distinct hands clamp down on my shoulders, yanking me up before I can fall, and then I open my eyes and realize I'm staring into the face of a very relieved looking Rook.

"Oh, thank fuck!" I squeal, wrapping my arms around his waist and hugging him for all that I'm worth.

I've never been so happy to see anyone in my entire life. He smells so good, and he feels even better. He must be a gift from the deities I was chanting to earlier. I made a lot of promises in my head.

"I need you to drop your pants so I can show you what I can do with my tongue," I declare as I squeeze his torso.

His arms are wrapped around me just as tightly and a bark of laughter escapes him. "What?" he asks.

"I like you, Rook. I like you so much it scares the shit out of me. I swore if I ever got out of that place, I'd tell you that, and I'm a cockatrice of my word. I also promised to give you oral and show you my tongue tricks. While also pledging to *get* more oral. More sex, too. Basically, I promised a lot of dirty things."

Chuckling, Rook squeezes me even tighter and kisses the top of my head. "What are you doing down here, Sunrise?"

I sigh, still relieved that he found me. I suddenly feel so safe after hours and hours of being scared out of my mind. I'm not quite ready to let him go yet. "Joe tried to sell me to some dumbass sigbins, but I got away. I've been wandering down here lost for what feels like days, until...Rusty?"

I trail off, remembering my mouse friend who led me to my favorite prison guard. I pull away from Rook to look for the little guy so I can say thank you, but the mouse is gone. I search the floor and call out to it, but the little lifesaver disappeared.

"Who's Rusty?" Rook asks as he starts looking around too.

My heart gets all warm and gooey when I notice that he's not looking at me like I'm crazy, but instead helping me look for something when he doesn't even know what it is. I go all doe-eyed, and I just watch him as affection and appreciation tsunami through me. Rook straightens up and looks over at me when he realizes that he's the only one still searching.

"The mouse," I answer, although I'm not thinking about the GPS rodent anymore.

I walk over to Rook with determination and hunger. His body tenses, like he senses my mood change, and the moment I stop in front of him, I reach down and start unbuckling his belt. This male needs a blowjob STAT.

Rook chuckles and pushes my hands away. "Whoa there, Sunrise. As much as I'd *love* for you to show me whatever tongue tricks you're talking about, you've been missing for a couple of hours, and I'm not the only one looking for you."

I cringe. I *really* don't want to get tasered or put into solitary again.

"Why would Joe try to sell you off?" he asks, his tone stiff and his eyes pissed.

"I guess he took up Alpha Bowen's offer for the bounty on me," I explain, and Rook laces his fingers with mine and starts to guide me through more dimly lit tunnels.

"Guards found Joe asleep up on the roof. They still haven't been able to wake him, but I guess this solves the mystery of why he was up there," Rook observes, his hand tightening in mine.

I stop, pulling Rook to a stop too. "Wait, did you say only a couple of hours?" I ask, suddenly confused. "You mean days, right? Because I swear, I've been wandering down here for, like, *ever*."

Rook smiles. "You and the troll turned up missing for the head count we do after rec time. Trackers picked up on your scent leading to the roof, but then they couldn't track you through the basement because of the magic down there."

"How the hell did I get from the roof to the basement?" I ask, a shiver running through me at the thought of some of the shit down there.

"No idea. I'm just glad I found you."

Rook wraps me up in another hug, and I don't hesitate to squeeze him like he's a lime and I'm making fresh margaritas.

"So tell me more about this whole *you like me* thing?" he needles me as we pull away.

A blush works its way up my neck, but thank fuck the lighting is so bad in these halls that he won't be able to see it.

I scoff. "I was pretty traumatized when you found me. I don't even know if I remember all of the crazy shit that was pouring out of my mouth. I legit thought you were Swamp Thing ready to eat me," I tell him, a teasing lilt to my tone.

"Oh, I'm *definitely* going to eat you," Rook says with a cocky smirk, and then he quickly yanks me against his body as his mouth crashes down to mine.

His kiss consumes me as we parry back and forth, trading ownership of each other's lips and tongues. Everything inside of me heats and melts and gushes as he demands everything I have to give with his kiss, and I let him have it all.

When he finally pulls away, both of us are breathless. It takes several moments for us to come back down to earth from the life-altering make out session.

"So. What were you saying?" Rook taunts.

I clear my throat, my fingers grazing over my swollen lips. "That I like you very, very much," I answer with a sweet smile.

"And don't you forget it," he replies, looking very smug.

"Oh no," I declare, grabbing my head and looking panicked. "It's slipping away. Quick! I need you to remind me again," I announce dramatically and then pucker my lips.

Rook laughs, but instead of kissing me stupid again, he

slaps my ass. I bite my lip as he once again laces our fingers together and leads the way out.

"I can't wait until you're out of here and I can tie you up and fuck that naughty little mouth of yours, just the way you deserve," he purrs.

My stomach does somersaults. "Mmmm, promises, promises," I mock.

"I'm a male of my word, Sunrise," he crows cockily, and I giggle and clench my thighs at the thought of being tied down and dominated by him. He'll find out pretty quickly how much I love to dish it *and* take it.

A steady stream of all the scandalous things I want to do to him starts running through my mind. I stop again and Rook looks back to see what's up. He takes one look at the desire banked in my green gaze, and his pupils dilate.

"You sure we can't find a nice dark, non-haunted corner so I can show you some tongue tricks?" I question, my tone dripping with pure sex and seduction.

Rook's pants tent, and I lick my lips, wanting him deep in my throat. Right. Fucking. Now.

"Oh, you found her! Was she making a run for it?" a guard's voice rings out, surprising the shit out of me as he rounds a corner.

I snap a glare in his direction, and Rook drops my hand like it's a hot coal and steps away from me.

He clears his throat. "No. Turns out the troll on the roof was trying to make a break for it and took her hostage. She got away and then got lost running from him," Rook tells him.

I try not to roll my eyes or rip Rook's pants open and just go to town despite the interruption, while he discretely tries to adjust his hard-on.

"Why don't you call off the search and go fill the Warden in on what happened? I'll get the inmate put back in her cell," Rook tells him casually, and the other guard nods and turns back the way he came.

As soon as the guard is out of sight again, Rook's hand comes down to take mine and we walk in silence. When we make it up to the normal, fluorescent-lit hallways that I recognize, he drops my hand again, and I feel the loss deeply.

For once, I find myself hating the gray prison uniform I'm wearing. I hate the fact that I have to be stuck behind bars and that I'm not allowed to fraternize with this gorgeous male beside me. I did this to myself, but I never thought I'd meet someone in here and that I'd regret losing my freedoms.

Rook broods silently as we walk, and I'm not sure what to do about it. I don't like the constant interruptions of our intimate times either, but this is Nightmare Penitentiary. I'm an inmate and he's a guard, and until that changes, we'll just have to figure out how to make it work.

I don't say any of that though, because if he wanted to talk about whatever is bothering him, he would. When we reach my cell, Rook opens it and motions for me to go in. I turn around, about to ask when I'll see him again, but he follows me in, and I bump right into his chest.

He steadies me, and I lock onto his heated stare. "The cells are monitored, so I can't kiss you the way I want to right now," he says quietly, his face a mask of professionalism aside from the vivid hunger in his eyes. "I can't press your back to the bed and ravish and fuck you the way I want to, or experience the elusive tongue tricks you keep bringing up. And after the hours of panicking when I couldn't find you, I can't hold you and remind myself that you're okay. I can't do any of that right now, and it pisses me the hell off," he says, his teeth grinding with frustration.

I swallow hard at the intenseness of his energy and the rasp of his words.

"But don't worry, Sunrise, I'll figure out a way to make all of that happen and more. Because you're stuck with me now."

The smile he gives me is filled with affection and dirty promises of things yet to come. I return it with my own, and he winks before backing up out of my cell, his gaze never leaving mine.

"Looking forward to it, Glow Worm," I purr as he closes the cell door. "Be sure to check out the camera in my cell tonight after lights out. And just know I'll be thinking about you the whole time I make myself come. Again...and again...and again."

Rook bites his bottom lip. Hard. "That's not right to do to a male, Sunrise," he chastises me as he shakes his head, his eyes lighting up with even more want.

"So, it's a date?"

"You better believe it," he confirms, and then he disappears down the hallway.

My smile is massive, and my heart is fluttery as fuck. I look around my cell and sigh dreamily. Now to get to work on some lingerie to really up the ante for tonight. As annoying as it is that my inmate status is keeping us apart, I can't deny that it ups the naughty factor. I mean, sneaking around is hot in itself, but a criminal sneaking around with her forbidden prison guard? That's a hundred times hotter.

Yo ho, yo ho, it's an inmate's life for me.

14

"Inmate 11764. Get up and put your back against the wall."

I groan, my mind jerking out of the heavy sleep I was having.

"Inmate 11764!"

Wrenching my eyes open, I try to blink the bleariness away as I realize that this is a bad repeat performance. "Go away," I mumble into my silk pillow. "Tell Alpha Bowen I don't want any more luxuries."

"Inmate!" Sandbag snaps. "Last warning. Get up and put your back against the wall."

"Dude, seriously. I'm all luxuried out. Keep it for yourself as a PG perk."

I hear the door open, and I sit up grumpily, ready to wave away whatever new bribe options necessitated this early as fuck wake up call, but my eyes widen when I see the Warden standing there along with several more guards. All of them look grim, and they're definitely not bringing in more silk pillows. My eyes flick over to find Rook standing in the back of the group, his mouth drawn into a thin line.

Fuck, this doesn't look good.

I immediately scramble to my feet, nearly tripping when my legs get tangled in the sheets, and then hurry over to the wall and put my back against it.

The Warden stalks inside, his trench coat slick with shadows curling around his body in ominous waves. Threat. This man is a threat. My cockatrice watches him with wariness while I try not to visibly shake as I stand here in nothing but a pair of panties that I bedazzled and my uniform shirt tied in the middle.

Shit, is this about my little happy hour show last night? Mortification blooms in my chest at the thought of any of them seeing what I was doing. When I notice the other guards leering at me, including Sandbag, I cross my hands over my chest, my face burning. Stupid. I'm so stupid.

The Warden walks around my tiny cell room, his steps short and his eyes assessing as he looks over every crevice. Nobody says a thing or moves an inch. I can feel the Warden's displeasure spiking up higher and higher as he takes everything in.

Finally, after what feels like forever, he comes to stand in front of me. "Where are you, Inmate 11764?"

Is this a trick question?

"Umm...prison?"

"That's right," he says with a nod. "You're in prison. So why the fuck do you think you have a right to any of this shit?"

I shake my head. "I...I didn't—"

"You are here because you were found guilty of crimes, and you're now serving a sentence because of that," he says, cutting me off. "This isn't a fucking vacation. You don't get to have privileges here unless *I* say so."

Awash with newfound humiliation and nervousness, I find myself pressing harder up against the wall. The Warden seems to like the fact that he's scaring me, because he smirks cruelly. "You think this all some big fucking joke? That Nightmare Penitentiary is some all-inclusive resort?"

"N-no, sir."

He narrows his eyes, lifting the cigarette perched between his fingers and taking a long drag off it before blowing his polluted breath back into my face. My eyes immediately burn from the assault, but I don't dare complain or try to move away.

He gives me a hard look until I'm squirming beneath his gaze. "Where is Inmate 57893?"

My eyes dart to the left to Rook for help, but he's not even looking at me. He's just staring down at his boots.

"I'm waiting."

My eyes fly back to the Warden, and I cringe when I see that his shadows have started to float toward me. "I don't know who that is."

"Zen Urlson. Ring a bell?" he asks, his cigarette caught between his teeth.

My stomach drops. Fuck. This is about Zen escaping.

At the look on my face, the Warden takes another step forward until the top of his boots are stepping painfully on my bare toes. I bite my lip to keep from making a noise.

"Where is she." A demand, not a question.

"I don't know," I answer truthfully.

"We spoke with the troll. He claims it was you who was going to try to escape that night."

Fucking Joe.

"Well, he's misinformed, because I'm here, aren't I?" I answer back.

The Warden studies me and then blows another puff of smoke in my face, making my throat burn as I'm forced to breathe it in. "You made trouble for me. I don't fucking like it when inmates make trouble."

I gulp. "I'm sorry."

"I'm fucking done with you and your plush life here. It's all about to end. And if you even think about causing any more trouble or breaking any rules, your ass is mine, do you understand? It'll make your stint in solitary seem like nothing but a holiday."

His voice is like a gavel of judgement cracking down, and my body breaks out in a cold sweat. His shadows curl around me with obvious threat, and my entire body shudders and sways.

He turns to look at the guards. "Remind her that she's an inmate and under our thumbs. And strip it all," he barks out before stalking out, disappearing into his own shadows.

The moment the Warden is gone, my cell is ascended on like a feeding frenzy of carnivorous birds diving into a sea of fish.

Guards, so many guards, rushing and stripping my room all at once. I'm caught against the wall like a fly in a web, watching as they destroy everything.

My mattress is pulled off the frame and sliced with a blade. My pillows are torn apart, making feathers go flying. My fridge is picked up and smashed against the wall, the loud crack filling the air as things from inside come bursting out. I duck and scream as my TV is yanked up and smashed onto the floor, glass shattering. They take all the pretty rocks I've collected and smash them against the ground, and then it all becomes one huge cacophony of smashing, kicking, cutting, tearing, and breaking.

I hug my knees against my chest, trying to protect my head as objects and broken bits fracture all around me, pieces hitting my body while I cower. And then I'm being dragged by the hair, a burst of intense pain flaring from my scalp as I scramble to grab hold of the hand and make him let go.

I'm tossed away like a rag doll for my efforts, and I land

hard against the concrete floor, the side of my head smacking into the broken fridge sagging against me.

Blinking away stars, I look up at Sandbag standing over me. "Fucking shifter bitch, think you can just do whatever the fuck you want?"

Bam!

Lighting-hot pain lances through me as Sandbag lands a kick right into my stomach.

My tear-filled eyes lift up, desperately searching for Rook, and I see him standing by the door, his hands curled into fists at his sides, his fire-filled, furious eyes locked on Sandbag.

"Help," I mouth to him as the first tears track down my face.

But as outraged and angry as he looks, he doesn't help. He doesn't move at all apart from an angry twitch of his tail.

He just stands there and watches as Sandbag delivers another kick to my side, and I dry-heave, a pained cough scraping out of my throat as I curl over into the fetal position.

Someone else spits on me and stomps on my tail, making me flinch in pain.

"Look at this! She's fuckin' writing love notes in a shitty arts and crafts diary," a different guard says, barking out a laugh.

I look over and see him and two others looking at the mock-up journal I made for myself. I have to keep myself occupied in my cell, so I've taken to writing in a journal about my days. Since I don't have a notebook, I take extra napkins from the cafeteria and use those to write on. I even bind them together with a piece of pink thread. I thought it looked fun, and I liked adding a napkin every day, but to see them flipping through my personal words and laughing...my jaw clenches and my face burns.

"That's mine!" I snap.

Everyone ignores me.

"Ooh, she talks about fuckin' some guard in here!" he says as he continues to flip through it, his eyes lighting up in leering excitement. "You think she calls him Glow Worm because he has a worm for a dick?" he asks, and the guards all laugh.

"If you're happy to fuck a worm, just wait until you see my snake," another guard calls out, and acid crawls up the back of my throat.

Humiliated tears burn the skin of my cheeks, and I can feel Rook's eyes on me, but I don't look at him.

"Whore," Sandbag says, nudging me with his boot and laughing when I wince. "I think we're done here. Let's go."

I listen as the guards move out, bringing my destroyed paraphernalia with them. I stay on the floor, not daring to move until I hear my cell door slam shut.

Peeking past wet lashes, I see Rook looking at me from the other side of the bars. A turquoise gaze filled with agonized guilt meets me, but I look away and bury my head in the crook of my elbow.

He...didn't help me.

He just stood there and watched as the Warden threatened me. As the guards wrecked my entire room. As Sandbag kicked me. Spat on me. As they mocked my words that I'd written about *him*, then left me on the floor like a beaten dog.

And Rook didn't do a damn thing.

A sob wrenches out of me, smothered into the skin of my arm.

I don't move until I hear his footsteps turning and fading down the hall, following the rest of the guards.

Gingerly sitting up, I nearly start retching again as the pain in my stomach and side rears up. With a grimace, I manage to pull myself to my feet and look around my disaster of a cell.

There's broken glass and plastic, the last remains of my TV and fridge that are now gone. My mattress, beanbag, and pillows are gone too, leaving only one shredded blanket behind. Even my bedazzled underwear are in ruins.

Hiccupping another sob, I yank the blanket and wrap it around me, before burrowing into the corner of the cell where I bury myself beneath the cover and close my eyes, wishing that I could wake up and this would have all been a shitty dream.

Because all of this—the humiliation, the punishment, the physical blows—it doesn't hurt anywhere near as much as it did to have the male I care about just stand by and watch it all happen.

A tear drips unhindered down my cheek as I lie and stare at nothing.

My thoughts are chaos, and instead of focusing on any of them, I float in the white noise of my mind. I've spent hours playing judge, jury, and executioner over what happened. It's all Alpha Bowen's fault. If he hadn't put a price on my freedom or sent me all the shit I didn't ask for, I wouldn't be in this mess.

The problem with that line of thinking is that it doesn't change the fact that I *am* in this mess and that Rook just stood there.

He couldn't help, part of me argues again. *If they knew what we were doing, he'd be fired. Probably punished. Better for him to stand there and for us to be able to see each other again than for him to be gone.* I've defended and prosecuted him over and over again in my mind, but it all makes no difference to my heart.

I hurt.

And not just because my knight in shining armor didn't get the memo that that's what he's supposed to be. But because it wasn't just my TV, fridge, and ribs that got shattered, it was also my belief that all of this would work out.

I came here thinking that this would be the safest place for me, but I'll spend the next eight months here...and for what? I'm not out of reach the way I thought I was. Alpha Bowen hasn't given up. My situation in Nightmare Penitentiary just got a fuck ton worse. Zen is no longer here to help keep the wolves at bay. The guards are officially out for blood, and the Warden is ready to make my life a living hell.

I finally get the whole *nightmare* part of Nightmare Penitentiary. And doing something to extend my sentence here like I originally planned means figuring out how to survive all of the bullshit even longer.

No matter how I look at it, the future I wished I could have with Rook is impossible. We can't be together in here, and Alpha Bowen will make sure that we can't be together out there either. So maybe it's a good thing that Rook just stood there, because I clearly needed a wakeup call. Like the Warden said, this is prison, not a vaycay spot.

Another tear spills down my cheek. It free falls to the ground, just to be slowly replaced by another. I've accepted my reality, but again, it makes no difference to my heart.

"Inmate 11764, stand up and put your back to the wall."

Fear lances through me at those words, and I shove away the blanket I've cocooned myself with and painfully get to my feet. I press my back against the cinder block wall as my ribs and bruised stomach twinge in protest. I look over to find Sandbag staring at me with both disgust and a gleam of something that makes my skin crawl. His sandy-colored gaze runs down my body and then moves slowly back up my still bare legs.

I suddenly wish I had a suit made of impenetrable metal, as a sick feeling settles in my gut about the thoughts currently swimming in his eyes. He leers at me for a second more, clearly enjoying me being a good little inmate as I keep my body plastered against the wall.

With a smirk, he opens the cell door and walks into the room, and I tense, but he moves to a crumpled pile of gray fabric, picks it up, and then throws the pair of pants at me. I try not to show any relief, not wanting to provoke his inner sadist.

"You have a visitor," he snarls, and I quickly step into my pants and get dressed, ignoring the pain it causes to move so fast.

I don't argue. I don't ask questions. I just silently move to follow him to the visitation room I've come to know so well. I didn't think I'd get visitors when I first landed in here. Dinah swore she'd come visit, but I told her not to. I'd hoped that my parents wouldn't find out where I was, and I didn't want her accidentally leading them to me. I guess that was before I had to move up my timeline and improvise, though.

Sandbag gestures for me to go first, and I'm even more leery of putting him at my back, but I don't really have a choice. I keep alert for threats or any hint that I'm being taken somewhere else. For the first time since I started to serve my sentence, I'm relieved when we stop outside the door marked Visitor Room with the peephole hatch in it. Sandbag opens it, and I step into the room and find a very angry looking mat staring at me from the other side of the plexiglass.

Sandbag shoves me further into the room, deciding I'm not moving fast enough for him, and slams the door shut behind me. I wonder if mat will give him a bonus for roughing me up. Probably.

I sit gingerly in the metal chair and try not to wince when I reach over for the phone receiver, though my entire side feels like it's on fire.

My mat already has her handset gripped in a white knuckle hold and pressed to her ear. I barely pick mine up before she's growling hate and anger at me through the line.

"You had no right to spread lounge business around the way you did!" she screeches at me. "You are *not* the matriarch, and you don't know what's best for *my* people!"

Ah, so she found out. Well, fuck her. I'm not in the mood.

"No," I growl back. "*You* don't know what's best for the people. Look at what you've done. Look what your vanity and thirst for power has done! You single-handedly took down one of the strongest lounges, and for what?" I scream at her, furious tears joining the heartbroken ones on my cheeks. "Out of spite? Because some alpha said he didn't like your hair? Or worse, did he disagree with you, *mother*?" I demand. "You were prideful and stupid. You inherited a whole new lounge and a mountain of debt with it that you had no hopes of paying off."

She opens her mouth to let me have it, but I'm done taking her shit. "The lounge didn't even know they should be watching each other's backs and protecting themselves. All because you're too selfish to warn them that there was a threat. What kind of leader are you? You should be ripped apart for your incompetence," I seethe at her, and for the third time in my life, I see my mom smile.

She stands up and leans toward the plexiglass, and I mirror the movement.

"Well, too bad that you're in there and not out here to challenge me, little girl," she declares, her eyes filled with venom and her words filled with hate. "You won't be there to protect all your little gossiping, disloyal friends. How well do you think people like Cena, Mack, and Stur will be able to survive out in the world after they've been exiled and declared rogue?" she taunts, and my face drains of color.

I look at the sick smirk spread across her thinning lips, and all I see is an evil, vindictive, power-hungry bitch. She wants me to beg her not to do that. She wants me to promise to be good and to go to Alpha Bowen when I get out of here and fix all of her problems for her. But I know her. She'll exile everyone anyway. Nothing I do now other than killing her will change their fate.

I shake my head at her, and a new plan clicks into place. I came here to escape until everything blew over and Alpha Bowen got bored of me. I scoff humorlessly. Rook was right. I was a coward. But that's all going to change.

I stare at my mat's crazed green eyes, and I know exactly what I need to do when I get out of Nightmare Penitentiary. I need to take her out.

And what better place to learn all the ways to make that happen than prison? Yeah, Zen and her protection is gone, and I need to watch myself around the guards. A life with Rook is still impossible, but I knew shit in here wouldn't be all Pop Rocks and meatloaf. I can do this. I can get fiercer and stronger and more brutal. I can become exactly what I need to become to take my lounge from my mat and finally lead and protect them the way they've always deserved.

A determined smile creeps across my face. "I'm coming for you," I tell her, and then I hang up the handset on my side and turn, giving her my back.

For the second time in my visitor history, my mat loses her shit and attacks the thick bulletproof—and probably magic-proof—barrier between us. I hear her claws raking down the glass as she goes into an enraged partial shift, and I revel in the fact that I got under skin.

I mentally start switching up my plans and think of ways I can reach my goals in the next eight months as I bang on the door and Sandbag opens it. His eyes lift over my shoulder at my hissy-fit throwing mat, and he speaks into his walkie-talkie to get people to go handle her instead of forcing me to stay and deal with her vitriol. He gestures me out of the room and motions for me to lead the way.

I move in the direction my cell block is located, but I get a kick to the back of my knee for that directional guess. Stumbling forward with a yelp, I turn to glare at Sandbag, but when I turn, his hand comes down against my cheek, snapping my head to the side.

"Wrong fucking way!" he barks, his slap causing a ringing in my ears.

I taste blood in my mouth, and I tongue the inside of my cheek where I accidentally bit it. Swallowing down my anger, I look in the other direction. There are only two options in this particular hallway—left to my cell block and right to...who the fuck knows where.

I turn right, ignoring my screaming instincts. My beast wants me to let loose and fight this fucker, but I can't. He would just fuck with me even more, and I don't need another reason for the Warden to pay me a visit.

I tell myself that the hallways here are well-lit and monitored. If it looks like Sandbag is taking me somewhere he can get away with hurting me, then I'll fight and deal with the consequences. Until then, I'll endure the kicks and hits and hope that I'm being escorted somewhere safe.

Four knee kicks, two dead arms and a baton slap to the thigh later, I'm stopped at a gray metal door with no distinctive identifiers on it that could clue me in on where the hell I might be. I can hear the faint chatter of people on the other side, and my stomach tangles into knots. Are the voices on the other side friend or foe? Sandbag knocks twice and then waits.

The door opens, and I see the Warden standing there. His eyes sweep over me dismissively, and he gives Sandbag a nod. "Cuff her."

Panic builds in my chest, and my arms are wrenched up and my wrists slapped with heavy handcuffs before I'm turned and shoved into the room. I look around and see a very ordinary space with a conference table set in the very center. People are sitting around the table, and their voices of quiet conversation dry up the moment they see me enter. Everyone is a stranger to me, but they're all paranormals dressed in business suits.

The door is closed, thankfully leaving Sandbag outside, and the Warden motions for me to head to the empty chair at the end of the table. "Take a seat."

With no idea what the hell is happening, I do as I'm told, the chain connecting my wrists jangling as I move. Sitting down, I leave my hands in my lap, my eyes skating over every face in the room. There are eight people, and I pick up the scent of a vampire, shifters, a few elementals, fae, and something else I can't quite put my finger on.

The person presiding over the group seems to be the male vampire sitting directly across from me. He gathers some papers in his hands and straightens them as I take a seat. "Sinclair Denali, this is your parole hearing."

My brow furrows. "Parole?"

He nods. "Yes. You're eligible for early release. We're here to discuss the particulars of it being granted."

My heart suddenly starts pounding in my chest so hard that I know the vampire can sense it. His eyes flash at all the blood zooming through my veins, but my mind is whirling. *Early release?*

I...I'm not ready. Not yet. I need time to figure out this shit with my mat. Now that I know I'm going to fight her for the lounge, I have to be smart about it and prepare, or I have no doubt she'll kill me. And Alpha Bowen...I still have to deal with him too.

"I don't understand," I admit, shaking my head. "How am I eligible?"

A middle-aged male wolf shifter answers. "Quite frankly, Miss Denali, Nightmare Penitentiary is overcrowded as it is, and we have much bigger fish to fry. You've committed minor, non-violent crimes," he scoffs. "I don't know how the prosecutor got away with calling a kiss *assault* or a glitter bomb *assault with a deadly weapon*, but it is what it is," he says with a roll of his eyes. I nod emphatically, like, *right?!* Calling my kiss an assault was seriously overexaggerating.

"Anyway, the point is that the parole board believes adding the time you served in the human jail to the time you served here means you're eligible to be released now. We feel you will be better suited to serve out the remainder of your sentence outside of Nightmare Penitentiary on parole with mandatory counseling."

"What he means is, we need the cell space for criminals worse than you," another shifter adds drily.

I have the vague sense that I should be offended for not seeming like a good enough criminal, but I wisely keep my mouth shut.

"Correct," the vampire says, calling everyone's attention back to him. "We have a letter here from the prosecuting judge with his recommendations for early release with a probational period of your remaining sentence, plus two years. We also have letters from several prison guards that speak of your good behavior."

Good behavior? What the fuck?

My eyes fly over to the Warden.

"Yes, the Warden has also put in his statement recommending your early release."

The shadows shift around the male where he stands, and he nods in my direction with a creepy as fuck grin. "Like I said, I want you out of my prison," he states, echoing his earlier words to me.

He wanted me out of his prison, so he decided to give me early release? This fucker knew my initial plan was to stay for as long as possible. He played dirty.

I'm so caught off guard by this turn of events that I'm not even sure how I feel about it. On one hand, I'm relieved to be getting out now that I know I have to face shit. It also means I can get away from the guards and the Warden. But on the other hand...I haven't prepared for facing my mat or Alpha Bowen. And Rook...I'll be leaving Rook behind for good. My heart squeezes painfully. I'm not ready. I'm not nearly ready yet for anything.

"But...I knocked over some guards while I was in my cockatrice form," I argue. "I made illegal paraphernalia and weapons for other inmates. I should definitely be serving out more of my sentence here. Really make sure I learn my lesson," I blurt, scrambling at straws.

"Sporks and Jolly Ranchers don't count as weapons," the Warden drawls, rolling his eyes. "Child's play compared to the real criminals in the deeper recesses of Nightmare Penitentiary."

"But...I went to solitary confinement," I point out. "How can I be commended for my good behavior when I was sent there?"

The Warden's scowl deepens, and his shadows thicken. I automatically cower in my seat. I probably shouldn't be fighting this, especially not to the Warden's face, but this is happening way too fucking fast, dammit!

"Everyone gets sent to solitary. It's a good learning tool for inmates."

He's good. He's very good.

I look back at the people around the table. "I'm totally up for being released early...but, like, in a month. I vote for that. I get a vote, right?"

Everyone frowns at me. I guess this isn't the normal reaction for a prisoner earning early release.

The vampire clears his throat. "No, you don't *get a vote*," he says somewhat scathingly. He looks around the table. "All in favor?" he asks, and he's met with every single hand being raised in the air. "Good." His eyes land back on me. "The parole board has officially decided to grant you early release, Sinclair Denali. You're to report to the Warden's office to gather your things, and then you're dismissed. You'll have to meet up with a parole officer every week, and you have some other conditions to your parole like counseling, but aside from that, your time is done here at Nightmare Penitentiary."

There's more talking, instructions and rules to be followed, more shuffled papers, and then people get up to leave. I'm in a daze as I'm led away with the Warden, all the way back to his office where I'm suddenly being formally discharged.

It all happens so fucking fast.

"Don't ever come to my prison again," the Warden snarls at me. "If I ever see you standing outside the gates, know that you're not getting out of here alive. I'd rather kill you than deal with the shit that accompanies you. Do you even know what I'm going to have to deal with because your boyfriend made it possible for an inmate to escape?"

I open my mouth to correct the whole *your boyfriend* thing, but he glares at me and grabs the cuffs at my wrists roughly, so I shut the fuck up. He unlocks them and leans down and snaps a smooth metallic anklet around me instead. "Part of your parole," he says with a smirk. I'm too shocked to even process it.

I'm trying to wrap my mind around what the hell I'm going to do now. I need a phone. I need to call Dinah and see if she can help me lay low until I figure out my next move. Fuck, I'm really not ready for this.

The Warden shoves a small bag at me, breaking me from my thoughts. It's labeled with my inmate number, and I suddenly realize that they're not even going to let me get my belongings from my cell because someone already did.

"Am I going to get to say goodbye to..." I trail off to keep from letting Rook's name slip out of my stunned lips.

The Warden gives a humorless snort. "Anyone you think cares about you in there will have forgotten you in a month," he declares callously as he opens his door. "The logs say you came in wearing jail-issued clothes. You can leave wearing what you have on now. Consider it my parting gift."

Oh, gee. Thanks.

"Follow me, inmate," he barks, and I jerk at his yell and robotically fall into place right behind him.

How is this happening? I just came up with a new plan, and it was going to work...but now this. Why is the universe fucking with me? How can they just shove me out of the gates without warning?

I'm terrified, irritated, and hoping somehow that Rook will round a corner and see what's going on. What will he do when I'm just suddenly not here? I shake those thoughts away and square my shoulders. I have bigger things to worry about than Rook. We were always doomed, and my leaving doesn't change that.

All too soon, I'm outside the prison. It's just as gloomy and creepy as I remember. I have to practically jog to keep up with the Warden's steps, and my bag bounces against my thigh as the cuff he forced on me starts to chafe my ankle. My bag definitely isn't heavy enough to contain what's left of my rock collection, so I know they didn't give me all my stuff. I'm going to have to add the pretty stones to the list of things I'll mourn when I'm gone from here.

It seems like it takes way less time to cross the familiar creepy yard than when I came in, but the gates look just as daunting and foreboding on this side as they did when I first arrived and stared at them from the other side.

When they open on a loud creak, I suddenly feel like I can't breathe. I don't want to walk through them yet. Reality and everything I have to face—everything I've been running from—is now slamming into me.

I look behind me, like somehow Rook will hear my thoughts and come running out, but I remind myself that he's not the knight in shining armor type, and I turn to face forward. I'm on my own.

Before I can even take a step, the Warden shoves me. Hard. I stumble forward and struggle to keep my feet under me.

"Get the fuck out," he snarls and slams the gates behind me, cutting me off from the safety and security I worked so hard to acquire in the first place. My plans crumble all around me, and I'm left alone and vulnerable.

I look around, noting the missing element here. "Wait, where's my portal to get me out of here?"

"What makes you think you deserve a portal?" he grins.

I blink at him, worry dragging up my spine at the ominous landscape around me. "But...I don't even know where the fuck I am. Can't I even get a phone call?" I beg from the other side, but the Warden's eyes just gleam with sick satisfaction as he stares into my pleading eyes.

"Good luck out there, Miss Denali," he taunts. "Oh, and I forgot to mention, a condition of your parole is that you can't shift." He gives my anklet a pointed look, and ice-cold panic explodes inside of me with his words.

My wide eyes shoot from my anklet and back to his cruel face. "You can't do that!" I exclaim, his words like a kick to the gut.

How the fuck am I supposed to defend myself without being able to shift? How am I supposed to challenge my mat and claim my lounge? I can't survive in the outside world without my beast—it's too cutthroat and brutal. I can't even make it out of...wherever the hell I am right now without my ability to shift and fly away from here. We're in the middle of fucking nowhere.

I stare at the Warden and the twinkle in his eyes. He just signed my death certificate and he knows it.

I drop my bag and rush up at the gate. I'm not dumb enough to touch it, not with the amount of magic pulsing off it, but I pace back and forth like a caged lion as I scream at him. "I don't deserve this, you piece of shit! I didn't help Zen escape. I never even wanted out. My death is gonna be on your head, shadow eater. And I swear on everything, I'm going to hunt you down and feed you to a foul-assed Drake!" I bellow, irate while I mock-spit on the ground.

The Warden just shakes his head dismissively. "You have five minutes to get away from my prison, or I'll have you tased. And be careful with your threats, Miss Denali. Something like that could get you locked up again, and we both know who would come out on top in that scenario." With that, he turns on his heel and strides away from me.

I wish I could shift and peck him to death, pick him up in my talons and drop him over and over again on a ton of sharp rocks. I want to burn this place to the fucking ground. And honestly, I don't know what's worse: sending me out here to wander aimlessly to my death, or bringing me so low that I envy a piece of shit dragon's fire breathing ability. Fucking Drakes.

I pick up my bag and stomp away on a rage-filled scream that would give a banshee a run for her money. I'm so fucking pissed and helpless. It's like the worst emotion combo ever, and I hate it.

I flip off Nightmare Penitentiary as I start to make my way down the road. There's no sendoff, no time for goodbyes. They didn't even let me go to my cell to grab my own things. Nope, they just tossed me out. Let Sinclair get eaten by whatever fucked up shit lives in the woods that surround this shithole of a prison. I didn't even get to eat first.

Dust kicks up at my feet as I stomp down the dirt road that leads away from the paranormal prison. With a churning stomach, I look back at its looming presence one more time. "Bye, Rook," I whisper. Then I face forward and try to figure out how the fuck I'm going to keep myself alive.

15

I feel like I've been walking forever.

Then again, I thought that same thing when I was in the evil labyrinth basement, and it had only been a couple of hours, so maybe I'm not the best judge.

I check over my shoulder and realize that I can't see the prison anymore, so at least I know my steps have been making progress. But it doesn't change the fact that I'm thirsty and mad, and there's not a sign of civilization anywhere around me.

"Could have given me a bottled water, you prick!" I yell to the heavens, as if the Warden will somehow hear it. "Bet you'd hate it if I died from something boring like dehydration," I tell the shadows around me. "What will you jerk off to at night for your evil spank bank?"

I just need to find a phone. If I can get that sorted, then I can call Dinah. I know she's already off the grid with her rogue parents, and that's exactly where I need to be so I can prepare for everything. But there's nothing out here other than gray clouds, trees, and this never-ending dirt road that I'm just wandering angrily down. It's going to get dark soon, and I have a feeling that being out here after nightfall is *not* a fun place to be.

After another hour or so of walking, I look up at a noise that pulls me from my troubled thoughts. It takes me a moment to peg it, but then I realize it's the distinct sound of tires driving over packed dirt and rocks.

I spin around to find a black SUV with dark tinted windows driving down the road behind me. It's closing the distance fast, and all I can think is, well...this probably isn't good.

I clutch my bag of crap, debating for a minute whether or not I want to make a run for it to the tree line, but I doubt that would help. At this point, whoever is driving can see me, and without me being able to shift, I can't outrun a car.

Then again...I snort at my narcissism in thinking that whoever is in that vehicle is here for me. Nightmare Penitentiary is huge. Whoever is driving probably has nothing to do with me.

As it nears, the SUV starts to slow down, and I curse. Maybe they just want to rubber neck as they pass? Or offer me a phone? I tense and step off the road to let them go by unobstructed, but they stop at my side instead.

Fuck. A second goes by where I just stare at my scraggly reflection in the dark window before it rolls down. And then I'm suddenly staring at Trex, Alpha Bowen's second-in-command.

Fear and anger boils up my throat until I'm spitting mad. "Oh, come on!" I throw my head back and shout up to the sky. "Lube a girl up before you fuck her in the ass!"

How the hell did he find out and get here so fast?

I shake my head at the stupid question. Of course the guards on Alpha Bowen's payroll called him, probably before I was even out of the gate. I take a step back and Trex's eyes narrow slightly. They silently say that if I run, he'll track me, and he won't give up until I'm cornered like prey. I'm pretty much already cornered like prey, and running on a good day isn't my jam, so here I stand.

We just stare at each other. He doesn't say anything, but then again, he doesn't need to. We both know the position I'm in and the scary lack of options in front of me. He doesn't need to threaten or wave the contract in my face. His presence alone reinforces what Alpha Bowen has been communicating from the beginning...I'm *never* getting away from him.

I sigh and switch my weight from one foot to the other as I come to terms with what I'm about to do. I can't shift, and I need to find a way to save my lounge. I may hate it, but I can't logically deny that Alpha Bowen might be my best option. Emotion sits like an anvil on my chest, and my eyes sting as I work to swallow it back down. I look over in the direction of Nightmare Penitentiary and take a deep breath as my heart screams for me not to do this.

But I have to.

I turn back to Trex and give him a nod.

"Wise choice, Miss Denali,"

He opens the door and hops out before holding the door open for me and gesturing for me to get in. I stare at the inside of the car as if it's a whole new kind of prison, but there's nothing that can be done about it now.

I climb into the leather-clad back seat, and Trex skirts the back of the vehicle and gets in on the other side. The driver and the other unfamiliar shifter sitting in the front seat don't even acknowledge me. As soon as both car doors are shut, the SUV resumes its course down the dirt road.

I can feel Trex's weighted stare on the side of my face as I stare out the window. I feel the unspoken words hanging on the tip of his tongue in the air like humidity that's bogging me down. But the inside of the vehicle stays silent.

After a minute, he sets something in my lap, and I look down to discover a thin black blindfold. I pick it up and stare at it, like the inescapable fate it represents. Trex arches a brow, almost daring me to put up a fight.

I sigh and slip it over my eyes and get lost to the darkness.

At least it will hide my tears.

I've never been around much fanciness before in my life.

Being the daughter of the matriarch and patriarch had its advantages of course, but our lounge was stingy. Comfortable, sure, but nothing ever over-the-top.

So the last forty-eight hours have been almost unnerving. After sleeping in the luxury SUV for an indeterminable amount of time, I blinked, bleary-eyed, and found myself at a private airport, sans blindfold. The private plane was small but nice, and Trex had new clothes waiting for me to change into. I tried not to be weirded out by the fact that the underwear, jeans, and T-shirt fit me perfectly. After cleaning up and getting changed, I ate an entire platter of overpriced cheese and wine before promptly falling asleep again.

And now I'm...here.

When Trex put the blindfold on me again to take me from the plane to the car, and the car to...wherever the hell I am now, he didn't tighten it enough, so there's a gap between the fabric and my skin.

Now I'm sitting in a chair, hands tied behind my back, in the middle of an elaborate room—from what I can gather from the fragments that I can see. Peeking around is difficult, because the fabric is only slightly loose, but it's enough that when I tip my head back, I can look down my nose and see beneath the fabric. I probably look like I'm aggressively smelling the air, but whatever. I'm pretty sure I'm alone, so I crane my neck, my head tilted all the way back as I take in the rich surroundings.

I see dark hardwood floors and a plush cream rug beneath my feet. Sparkling wall sconces, crown molding, floor-to-ceiling windows and silk drapes that flutter slightly on a brisk breeze that brings me no scent other than permeating pine.

I can see a glass fireplace burning through crystalized rocks that makes my cockatrice purr as it reflects a dazzling prism of color. The whole room screams wealth. It's warm and masculine, and if I didn't want to gut the male who owned it, I'd appreciate his taste. I inhale deeply, trying to sense if anyone else is in the room with me...and...fucking hell, the dude seriously needs to lay off the Pine-Sol.

I'm not sure why I've been tied up. I haven't put up a fight this entire time, and it feels a bit dramatic. Then again, this is the douche Bowen we're talking about, so I probably shouldn't be surprised.

I hear a faint squeak, like someone stepped wrong on a grumpy floor board, and I immediately drop my head.

Who, me—peeking because my blindfold isn't secure? Never!

The air pressure around me changes, and I know without a shadow of a doubt that someone else is definitely in the room now. They don't talk, which again, shouldn't surprise me, because it seems like what I've met of Alpha Bowen's lounge is the big, over-muscled silent type. Even the pilot of the plane that flew me to my mystery location was ripped and mute. I wonder how he fit in the cockpit.

I want to ask what this motherfucker is doing lurking in the room and watching me, but I feel like whoever talks first loses in this silent battle of wills. I don't like to lose those.

Maybe it's a babysitter watching over me, or someone from Bowen's lounge, curious to get a look at me. Maybe it's the alpha himself. I imagine him looking over his prize tied to a chair and smiling like the smug bastard he is. Well, we'll see how long that smile lasts.

My being here may be conceding to the whole mate thing, but no one said I had to be a *good* mate. After he pays my lounge's debts, I have every intention of being the most annoying mate ever, so that he'll want to return me in no time. Talking and chewing with my mouth open, never closing the door when I go to the bathroom, leaving my clothes all over the floor, doing that annoying exaggerated squeak every time I sneeze...I have a whole list in my head of shit I'm going to pull.

Someone tugs at the tie of my blindfold, and I tense. I didn't even hear the fucker come up to me.

My heart hammers in my chest, and I wonder what Alpha Bowen is going to look like. Maybe he's actually part dragon and that's why he's such an unforgivable prick. I hold my breath, partly because I'm nervous as fuck and partly because I'm pretty sure I'm getting high from the oversaturation of Pine-Sol cleaner in here.

The blindfold drops away from my face, and despite my little peephole, I have to blink as my eyes adjust to the flood of light in the room.

I turn to see who's next to me, and my eyes bug out of my head as my blood runs cold. "*Rook?* What the hell are you doing here?" I demand on a frenzied whisper.

He leans down quickly to untie my hands, and I start hyperventilating with panic. "Rook, you have to get out of here! How did you even find me?" I look around the room, terrified that Alpha Bowen is going to come stomping in at any moment and end him.

"I came as soon as I could. I'm so sorry, Sunrise, I had no idea—"

My hands come free, and I leap out of the chair and

tackle him in a hug. He squeezes me tightly, and we both release a deep relieved sigh at the same time. Tears prick my eyes that he's here, that I can feel him, but as happy and grateful as I am that he came for me, he has to leave. I won't be able to bear it if he gets hurt trying to save me.

"Rook, you have to go," I urge again, pushing out of his arms and grabbing his hand to pull him to the closest door. I pause, suddenly realizing that I have no idea where I'm going.

"Sunrise, wait," Rook calls as he pulls me back toward him.

"We can't wait, Rook! You have no idea what Alpha Bowen will do to you if he catches you here," I whisper-growl. He has no clue how dangerous the situation is that he just snuck into.

"I'll take back everything I ever thought about you being a coward and a piece of shit. Your *knight in shining armor* card will be handed back to you promptly as soon as you get your ass out of wherever we are and get safe!"

"Sunrise, listen to me—"

"No, you need to be listening to *me*! I care about you, and I won't let you risk your life for me. Get the fuck out of here!" I exclaim, wincing when I hear how loud I'm being.

Shit. I have no idea how long we have, but someone is bound to hear me if I don't quiet the fuck down.

Scrambling over to the window, I pull the drapes back to see what floor we're on and if Rook can get out this way, but I go still as I'm met by pine trees everywhere. Are we in a fucking tree house? I shake away the stunned stupor and start looking for a latch somewhere on this wall of windows.

"Come on, come on," I say in a panic, my hands grazing over the glass in my desperation to find a way to open it.

"Sinclair!" Rook suddenly shouts, and I turn on him with crazed eyes and leap at him, covering his mouth with my hand. *Stupid bastard!* I look around and try to listen to see if anyone is coming.

"Are you fucking nuts?" I whisper-yell. "Were you born without a survival instinct? I know you don't know who he is, but Alpha Bowen *will* fucking kill you. I wouldn't be able to come back from that. It would destroy me. Please, Rook…" I beg, my voice cracking with emotion. "If you care about me at all, you will leave right now."

Rook grabs my wrist and forces my hand away from his mouth, while his other hand comes down to hold my hip. "Sinclair, it's *you* who doesn't know who Alpha Bowen is. I get that you have some preconceived notions about him. It's understandable. Cockatrices love gossip almost as much as they love a good rock. But—"

I slice my hand through the air, cutting him off. What is he talking about? Why isn't he taking this seriously? I step back from him and shake my head.

Wait… How the hell did he get in here in the first place?

My mind races as I try to make sense of what's going on. I take Rook in, *really* looking at him for the first time since my blindfold was lifted. He's not in the prison guard's uniform that I'm used to seeing him in. His shirt is white and crisp, his slacks are ash gray and creased. He doesn't look like someone who broke into a house to rescue the girl he loves from the big bad monster alpha.

Rook holds his hands out, and I can see the *wait, it's not what you think* on his lips. My face scrunches up in disgust. "You *work* for him?" I ask, my eyes screaming betrayal and my voice wobbly with disbelief.

"What? No!" Rook declares, and I'm instantly confused again.

"What the hell is going on then? Are you here to rescue me or hand me over?" I demand, my voice suddenly reaching dolphin-level octaves as I grow a smidge hysterical.

Rook's eyes turn pleading, and he takes a step toward me. My body reacts instinctively, and I reach out to take his outstretched hands before I realize what I'm doing. I yank my hands out of his and back up a step.

"Explain without touching me. My body apparently can't be trusted," I admit.

He gives me a small, dimple-filled smile, and my brain gives a dreamy sigh against my will.

Goddamn dimples.

"Sunrise. I'm absolutely here to rescue you," he tells me with conviction.

Relief floods me.

"And I'm also here to hand you over," he adds, and it's like he just poured ice water all over my relief but then set it on fire just to fuck with me.

I open my mouth to yell at him, but he cuts me off.

"Sinclair, my name is Rook Bowen."

My mind hits the brakes so hard that a screech and the smell of burning rubber fills my head and nose. *I fucked my future mate's brother?* Well, shit. Now Alpha Bowen is going to kill us both.

Rook narrows his turquoise eyes at the expression on my face. "Why do I still feel like you're not getting it?"

"Oh, I get it. Your psycho brother is going to take us both out. What the hell were you thinking?" I snap.

"What?" Rook replies, and I feel like my mind is going to explode. I'm getting really fucking tired of feeling confused. He shakes his head at me. "No, Sinclair. *I* am Alpha Bowen."

I blink at him.

He...I'm...what?

My mind stutters to a stop. Just puts on the E-brake and leaves me there to idle.

I stare at him. He stares at me. I can't process it. It's like my brain-computer crashed. I just see that white unfinished circle that indicates that things are loading, only nothing ever does. I need to be rebooted or something.

"Sinclair?"

I shake my head and run my fingers through my hair—my hair that's currently blinking from color to color, like even my strands are confused as fuck and don't know what to do. I realize numbly that my hands are trembling.

I shake my head and drop my hand. "You...you *can't* be Alpha Bowen. He's an evil, conniving prick who goes around claiming lounges because he's a power-hungry douche."

Rook grimaces. "People say all kinds of shit about me. You'll have to make up your mind about all of that. But I *am* Alpha Bowen," he repeats, his eyes wary even though his tone is firm, like he wants to make sure there's no doubt in my mind that he's telling the truth.

Suddenly, the stop sign that my brain's been stuck at implodes. Everything rushes up as the shocking realization of what he's telling me comes flooding through me like a dam bursting.

A choked, strangled noise bursts out of my throat that sounds like a mortifying sob-hiccup.

Rook and I both freeze. We stare at each other with wide shocked eyes. His are asking, *Did that ungodly noise just come from you*? While mine are saying, *I don't want to talk about it.*

No, Sinclair! Just no. Not happening. I will not cry. I will rage and I will rant, but I will not weep. I have a god-awful ugly cry, and I am *not* letting it out.

Despite my inner *knock it off* talk to myself, my eyes grow blurry. I try not to blink so that nothing spills over. I need to get mad. Not sad. I need to fucking tear into him. I need to—

Hiccup!

Fuck.

Rook's eyes widen as he sees my eyes completely

overrun with tears. "Shit," he curses. "Don't cry, Sinclair. Please don't cry."

Why is it that when someone tells you not to cry, it just makes you cry harder?

There's just no containing it now. As if Rook spoke the magic words to release the kraken—which is what I like to call my inner sobbing mess—I start to uncontrollably bawl. My face scrunches up like a used tissue, saltwater runs down my face like a leaky aquarium, and machine gun hiccups fire from my throat.

"You—*hiccup*—liar!" I cry, painful lumps getting stuck in my chest as bubbles of sobs wrench out of me.

Rook looks at me in terror, like he has no idea how to fix this. "Fuck. No, no, no, no, no," he coos and soothes as he pulls me toward a dark gray sectional. He sits and pulls me onto his lap. My hot mess, sniveling self just goes with it because I'm too overwhelmed to function.

"Why are you crying?" he asks softly and that just makes me cry even harder.

"I'm so relieved and...so pissed. This is what you get!" I tell him, gesturing to my face and the red splotchy swollen mess that I know it's turning into. "I didn't know how I was going to do this, but it's *you*..." I add, trailing off.

He wraps his arms around me, and my bawling is so out of control that I don't fight it as he pulls my cheek to his chest to help comfort me. My body molds against his warmth and strength as he holds me. His hands rub up and down my back in a soothing gesture as I try to come to terms with everything.

"I'm not sure how to handle this, Sunrise. I was expecting you to be pissed. To attack me with a hidden shank or some shit. Not...this."

"Oh, I'm *furious*," I assure him as I cling to him and weep. "And—*hiccup*—when my emotions get under control,

I will absolutely be plotting for your death," I tell him with complete seriousness.

He lets out a puff of breath. "I'm so sorry, Sunrise."

"How the hell did you become a guard?" I demand, my uncontrollable tears and snot getting all over his shirt, but since my current state is his fault, I give no fucks.

"Easy," he says with a shrug, his fingers inching up to toss my hair away from my face and run circles over my nape. "I paid the hiring officer off."

"But I asked around about you," I argue.

"More bribes."

"But...the paperwork. I saw your hiring date and your reviews," I cry, my voice more of a whine than I'd like.

I feel his shoulder lift in another shrug. "Forged to make it look like I worked there longer."

"You—*hiccup*—motherfucker."

He starts to chuckle, and I smack him on the stomach to shut him up. He is *not* allowed to laugh right now. Rook lets out a little cough and wisely cuts off his amusement.

Pulling back, I look up at his face. I want to see his eyes when I ask my next question. "Why?"

He takes a breath and works his jaw for a moment, like this is the question he's been dreading. "I intended to take you that first day. I was pissed that you kept evading my attempts at breaking you out. I was going to show you that you couldn't win against me. That I could take you and there was nothing you could do about it. And then I was going to call your lounge out for breach of contract and let your debtors handle you."

Wariness fills my gaze and a clamp of fear twists my gut. "But...?"

His eyes flicker over my face. "But...then the first time we met, you smacked me with a cafeteria tray."

"Should've hit you harder," I grumble.

The corner of his mouth hitches up. "It was an impressive hit."

Pulling out of his arms, I wipe my face and get up, taking a few steps away to give myself some distance. "So...what? I clocked you over the head with a piece of plastic, and you were smitten?"

"Something like that," he says. "My cockatrice liked you immediately."

"You sure it wasn't your other beast that starts with *c-o-c-k*?" I fire back.

He smiles, flashing those stupidly perfect dimples at me. "That too."

Sighing, I run a hand over my tired face. I feel like I could sleep for a month and still need more time to process everything. "I'm so mad at you, Rook," I say quietly.

"Tell me what to do," he says vehemently. "Whatever you want me to do, I'll do it."

I believe him. "You lied to me. I thought..." I swallow past a lump of emotion that I'm still contending with. "I thought I was never going to see you again. And I was so damn mad at you for what happened in my cell—"

He's in front of me in a blink, grabbing hold of my arms. "I'm so fucking sorry, Sinclair. I wanted to fucking kill them, but I knew if I blew my cover, that it would blow up in my face, and I was terrified I wouldn't be able to see you again, that you wouldn't have anyone watching your back if I was gone. You have no idea how much it killed me to watch them do that to my mate."

My startled eyes fly up to him. "I'm not your mate."

He cocks his head, once more bringing up his hand to grasp my jaw. "You are. And not even because of some contract that your matriarch signed on your behalf. But because the moment I met you, I knew you were my match."

Tears fill my eyes again at hearing those words come from his mouth. "Rook..."

"I'm sorry for lying to you," he cuts in. "After I met you, I just wanted to spend time with you in the prison. I knew you hated *Alpha Bowen*, so I wanted you to get to know me just as Rook."

I nod quietly, because I get it. I do. If I'd been in his position, I might've done the same thing. But that doesn't mean that my mind isn't reeling. I'm not sure how to process it all or where that leaves me.

"Why'd you make up that contract?" I ask. "Why me?"

His hand drops away. "You're gonna be pissed."

My eyes narrow on him. "I'm *already* pissed," I remind him. "So spit it out."

"I wanted to fuck with your matriarch."

I blink at him, waiting for the punchline. "Umm..."

"That lounge she took over? The one with all the debt? They were my allies. The mat and pat were good friends of mine. She fucked with them, and I wanted her to pay for it. So I watched. I waited. I knew she took over a shit ton of debt that she couldn't handle. I made all the other lounges stop doing business with her so that she was drowning in it. And then I brought the contract offer when she was desperate and couldn't hold off any longer."

"So I was just a way to get back at my mother?"

"You were just a name on a piece of paper," he tells me. "I didn't know you back then. Never even really thought of you as a person. I was too focused on my plan."

"Which was what exactly?"

His face hardens. "Making the matriarch give up her only heir to me. I figured that would be a blow to her ego, and it was, but I let her believe that was the end. I'd give a dowry for you and that was it. Except I never planned to ally with them. As soon as I had you, I planned to challenge her, kill her, and then take over your lounge."

A whoosh of breath leaves me. He's not a prison guard right now. In this moment, as he explains his cold plan for vengeance, he's every bit the ruthless alpha that everyone knows him as. "And you'd just keep me locked in a tower so you could visit me and gloat?" I ask.

His gaze is unwavering. "Yes."

That's what I thought.

I rear back and punch him in the arm. *Hard.*

"Ow," he complains, rubbing the spot with a frown.

"What am I supposed to do with that, Rook?" I demand, moving away from him. "How am I supposed to be okay with any of this?" I yell as I gesture to his stunning and very tastefully decorated house.

He shakes his head in a frustrated loss. "I don't know. I just know that I lov—care about you, and together, we'll figure this out," he reassures me, trying to close the distance between us again.

I back up until I feel the cold glass of the window against my back. "Did you just drop the *L* word?" I demand, shocked. "First you kidnap me, blindfold and tie me up, then you walk in here and drop the *hey, I'm Alpha Bowen* bomb, and now you *L word me*?" I ask, my voice high-pitched and squeaky.

"No," he answers way too quickly. "I did *not L* word you, I mumbled *care*. I definitely said care," he argues, and I narrow my eyes at the lying liar words coming out of his mouth. "And Trex said you came willingly in the car. I didn't know that you thought you'd been kidnapped. I'm sorry for the tying you up part, but Trex thought you'd take a swing when you first saw me, so he was just trying to protect my face. He lost fifty bucks by the way. He won't be happy about it," Rook tells me, like he expects me to laugh or feel bad or something.

I just stare at him.

"You totally *L* worded me," I insist, not letting him distract me with the rest of his words. I point an accusatory finger at Rook's face when a blush starts to bloom in his cheeks. "See! You know it's true. Admit it!"

He scoffs. "Psh, me? Alpha Bowen, dropping the *L* word after just a handful of months? No, that's not what happened. You misheard," he defends casually as he shifts his weight from the balls of his feet to his heels and back again.

Without warning, I spring at him with a growl. He somehow manages to catch me and keeps me from putting him into the head lock I was going for. He tries to cuddle me against his chest, but I'm not having that shit, so I keep trying to grab him, and he's forced to start wrestling me back. "Tell the truth!" I yell as I pinch at his neck and try to sideswipe his feet with my tail.

"Get your ears cleaned!" he hollers back before plucking me away from his head that I'm trying to squeeze and starts tickling my sides.

"Ah! Stop!" I screech. "This is not funny, and you totally *L* bombed me. Just admit it, you little shit!"

I laugh when he hits a particularly ticklish spot right above my hip bone, but I get my revenge when I find *his* ticklish spot right beneath his armpit.

"Ha!" I crow victoriously as he starts laughing and writhing to get away from me. "The big bad Alpha Bowen is ticklish *and* prematurely drops *L* bombs!"

Wrapping his tail around my ankles, he yanks my legs out from under me, taking me to the ground. His arms cradle the back of my head and back so that I don't fall hard, but as soon as I'm down, he ruthlessly goes for my sides. I squeal and jerk around and try to kick him away from me.

"Confess!" I shout at him in between peals of laughter.

"I'm the one winning. Why would *I* confess?" he argues as he straddles me, using his weight to hold me down as his merciless fingers dig into every ticklish spot I possess.

Knowing I need to play dirty, I lick my finger and stick it in his ear. He jerks back and looks at me with shock and disgust. "Tell the truth, or I'll do it again," I warn, licking a different finger and waving it in his direction as he gets off me and wipes his ear.

"You're twisted," he accuses playfully.

"The truth will set you free, Rook," I retort before lunging at him and extending my drool-laden finger like it's a sword and I'm prepared to duel.

He squeals and leaps away, and the loud ass lady-scream that exits his mouth has me bent over and barking out laughter. I'm dead. Completely finished.

"Alpha Bowen drops *L* bombs and lady-screams!" I shout out between fits of giggles that have my eyes tearing up. "Oh, when people find out..." I threaten as I hold my side and cackle even harder.

"Sunrise," Rook warns as he puts his hands on his hips. "Don't go messing with my rep."

I laugh even harder.

"I will. Unless you admit it," I warn, my eyes gleaming with satisfaction at pinning my prey.

"So vicious," he says, but I don't miss the light or the heat in his eyes as he says it. "Fine. I *started* to say the *L* word before I caught it and corrected myself," he admits, one of his eyebrows going up in challenge.

"So what you're saying is...that I've got you slippin'," I press, my gaze alight with mischief and excitement.

"Maybe," he agrees with a shrug, and there's that adorable blush again.

I walk over to him, my face stretched in a smile so big that it hurts my cheeks. "You totally love me. You're, like, *completely* obsessed."

"That's it," he warns.

I scream as he lunges for me, but before I can get away, he grabs me by the waist and picks me up to throw me over his shoulder. He slaps my ass hard, and I'm so fucking slap happy, I can't stop laughing long enough to fight. He strides down a long hallway and into a massive master bedroom. "You need a time out."

He tosses me onto the bed, and I nearly bounce right off, but he's on me in a second, holding me down. His hands come to cup either side of my face, and then he just looks down at me, his turquoise eyes tracking my features like he wants to memorize every inch of me. My gleeful smile slips at the reverent way he's drinking me in, and the thudding of my heart starts beating in sync with his.

"I'm sorry, Sinclair," he says quietly, all previous laughter and joking wiped away. I can see how deeply he means it. I can feel it too.

"I know," I reply.

"Give me a chance to make you happy. To prove that Prison Guard Rook *and* Alpha Bowen are worthy of you."

I don't take his words lightly. I know what he's asking me. To stay. To live here, as his mate. To get to know him outside of his prison guard uniform.

"You better pay off all my lounge's debts," I tell him sternly.

"Consider it done."

I breathe out long and slow. "Okay."

His eyes light up, as though he didn't expect me to say that. "Okay?"

I nod slowly. "Okay, Alpha PG Rook Bowen. I'll stay with you and do this mate thing. But I want four."

His brow furrows. "Four?"

"Orgasms," I specify. "Right now. On this bed because it's really comfortable. And then I want some meatloaf."

A widespread grin takes over his face, and I stick my fingers in each dimple because they're just too hot not to touch. "When you say meatloaf..."

I dig my fingers into his cheeks harder, letting him feel the bite of my nails. "I mean *meatloaf*. Not your penis. Your dick doesn't get to come out to play. You're still in the doghouse."

I drop my fingers and relax back on the bed, splaying my arms up over my head. "Now gimme four orgasms to start making it up to me."

"You're demanding."

"Yup. Can you handle it?"

His hands skim my sides, making goosebumps scatter over my skin as he lets his gentle fingers trail up the insides of my arms. "I want you," he tells me, his voice deep and rumbling. "And I'll do whatever it takes to have you and keep you."

That dark promise gets my blood pumping, and I feel a flush rise up my chest. "Good," I say, swallowing thickly. "Better get to work then. Four orgasms and counting."

He gives me a devilish smirk. "Nah. I'll give you five."

And he does.

Really, *really* well, too.

16

Over the next week, Rook gets me acquainted with his lounge. Everyone speaks to me with respect, like I've already become his mate in their eyes, and I have to admit, I like it.

His land and his lounge aren't what I would've imagined. Everyone is...normal. Nice. Not at all the bloodthirsty brutes that everyone says they are. Except for his enforcers. Those cockatrices are pretty fucking scary. They look like they eat a dozen raw eggs for a snack and drink human growth hormone during happy hour. They're big, burly, loyal as hell, and somehow, they all seem to have the same wicked scowl, like they practice it in front of the mirror together or something.

Rook has a pretty sweet setup. He owns acres of land, set deep in the forest, for his lounge, and he's basically...obscenely rich. His "house" is a damn mansion. With fifteen bedrooms and bathrooms, three heated pools, a waterfall jacuzzi, a stable, an entertainment room, a gym, a massive garage, and a damn helicopter pad, his house should be a little intimidating. Luckily for me, it's like I was meant for the rich mate life, because I easily embrace it.

Like right now. I'm sprawled out in the sauna, sipping on a strawberry daiquiri that Rook's live-in cook made for me and listening to "Kiss from a Rose" by Seal through the sound system that I currently have hooked up to my phone. The drink serves as a perfect microphone for when the chorus starts, and I sing it at the top of my lungs—as is required by anyone who listens to the song.

Clapping fills the sauna as I close out what can only be labeled as an epic performance, and my eyes snap open to find Rook leaning against the doorway and watching me with laughter gleaming in his eyes.

I sit up from where my head is hanging off the cedar bench, wrapped up in nothing but a towel, so I can bow properly. His eyes dance with mischief. "Hard day?"

"Sorry, I can't hear you," I say.

Rolling his eyes, he snatches my phone and pauses the No Doubt song that just started playing. "Better?"

"Hmm, it's hard to say," I reply, taking a sip of my delicious frozen drink. "Turn the music back on so I can compare."

Laughing, he comes into the steamy sauna and scoops me up, not even caring that his fancy suit is getting all messed up. He pecks a kiss to my forehead. "Sorry to interrupt your...whatever that was," he says as he carries me away from the pool area.

"That was showing Seal that he's still got it...and of course lounging," I tell him. "And you should know this since you're a leader of one."

Rook chuckles as he takes me up the backstairs that lead to our bedroom and heads through the door. The bedroom has an attached drawing room—whatever the heck that means, because I haven't seen him draw in here once—and he sets me down on the couch that he insists on calling a chaise. Again, I've never seen the furniture *chase* anything, so I think the name is silly, but you know rich people. They like to be indulged.

I wait for Rook to get down to business with peeling my towel off and doing very naughty things on his non-chase chaise in the middle of the non-drawing drawing room, but he doesn't. He just...stands there.

"Shit," I say, sitting up and tightening the towel over my chest. "What's wrong?"

"How do you know something is wrong?" he hedges.

"Uh, because you're not ravishing me right now, obviously. And I'm *naked* under here."

He shakes his head with a smirk, but then he sighs. "We have a situation."

My back straightens at the look on his face. "What kind of situation?"

I can tell he doesn't want to tell me. I narrow my eyes. "You knew about this situation this morning didn't you? When you said you had to leave and handle some lounge business."

I can see that I've caught him. "Yes."

I stand up and punch him in the arm. "Ow," he scowls, rubbing the spot. "Mean little thing."

"Don't keep things from me!" I demand. "Tell me right now."

"Fine. It's your mat."

"What about her?"

"She issued a challenge."

"Oh my God, what an idiot!" I tip my head back and laugh. "I knew it! I told you as soon as she found out that I was actually happy here, she'd get pissed off and do something shitty. She has no idea how lucky she is that you paid her debts and that you *L* worded me and decided not to kill her and take her lounge. But nope. She always has to push it." I shake my head incredulously. "She's so dumb. How can she possibly think she can fight and win against you in a challenge?"

Rook says nothing for a moment and just watches me carefully. I stop my rant to study him, and a cold rock of realization slides into the pit of my stomach. "Fuck," I breathe. "She didn't issue the challenge to you, did she?"

He shakes his head no.

My eyes widen, and I begin to pace back and forth inside the room. "Fuck!" I curse. This is bad. Really, really bad.

"She knows, Rook. She knows I can't shift," I say in a panic, pointing to my stupid, useless anklet that I'm still stuck with. "How the hell did she find out?"

"West," he growls.

My brows dip down with confusion. "Um...like, the direction? Or is West supposed to mean something to me?"

"West is the prison guard. The one that assaulted you."

"Ohhhh, Sandbag," I say as I make the connection. "That dude seriously needs his ass beat," I observe, making note to track him down and return all the favors he bestowed upon me while I was in prison.

"Oh, I took care of that before I left," Rook announces casually. "He was thoroughly fucked up. I was just dragging him into a particularly nasty cell in the basement when I was told that the Warden had booted you out."

My eyes widen at his ruthlessness. "Which cell?" I ask, a shiver running up my spine at the thought of the terrifying basement I got lost in.

"One that's magicked to make you live through your worst fears."

I smile at him, my heart all kinds of warm and fuzzy and my mind forming a plan of all the ways I'm going to reward him for this. "You're too good to me," I tell him dreamily.

"I always will be, too," he answers without missing a

beat, his turquoise eyes softening and radiating love and protection.

"So what's her plan?" I ask, bringing our focus back to the issue that's now breathing down our backs like a good for nothing Drake. "Kill me in a challenge while I can't even shift to defend myself? She hates me worse than I thought, but this seems a little extreme, even for her. She never puts this much effort into her daughter. Why start now? Why go through all the trouble to trade me to you just to turn around and take me out?"

"Think, Sinclair," he tells me. "You accepted the contract. You're here, living in my lounge. You're my mate in the eyes of the law, and based on the laws of our people, in issuing a challenge to you, she's issuing a challenge to a matriarch."

My eyes nearly bug out of my head, and I start to pace. Holy shit. "But...But that means..."

"That if you lose, she becomes the matriarch over *this* lounge," Rook finishes for me.

I stop in my tracks as the dread sticks to the soles of my feet. "She's gonna win," I whisper, feeling panic start to grip me. "She's gonna win, and then I'll be dead, and your title will be stripped because of me, and then she'll take over this lounge!"

Rook grabs me by the arms, holding me in place. "I won't let that happen."

"I can't fucking shift, Rook!" I exclaim. "I can't win against her like this."

The selfish bitch played a good hand, one she knew she would win.

He pulls me into him, his arms tightening around me and forcing me to focus on him instead of the alarm bells going off in my head. "Listen to me. I won't let that happen, okay?"

"You can't do anything, Rook," I point out. "Once a

formal challenge has been made, no one is allowed to step in."

"I don't give a shit," he says. "I'm not going to let her touch you."

I raise my hand to let my fingers run over his scratchy cheek. "If you intervene, she can go to the shifter council about it. They could rule in her favor and give her the lounge anyway. You can't do anything, Rook. I have to face her."

His expression turns furious, and his hands drop away from me as he turns and runs his fingers through his electric hair. "You expect me to just do nothing?"

"You've done it before," I point out. His head whips around, and he pins me with a stony stare. Guilt flips my stomach over. "Sorry. That was a low blow," I mumble. "I'm just...freaking out. And we both know you can't do anything to stop this. Not without jeopardizing everything you have."

Silence stretches between us, and I know he's just as worried as I am. His hands are buried in his pockets, and I can easily see the strain around his tightened eyes.

I need to face this and not freak out, because *he's* freaking out, and me being on edge isn't helping. If I don't show him that I can face her, then he'll do something stupid like kill her, and then the council will be on his ass. That's the last thing I want to happen to him. After watching him and his lounge for the last several days, I've seen how good of an alpha he is to his people. I won't let him throw it all away because I'm in a panic and he wants to protect me.

I take a steadying breath. I'm gonna fake it till I make it. "Alright. It's fine. I can handle her."

"Sinclair," he says, exasperated.

"What? I totally can," I defend. "You think I can't?"

"If you could shift into your beast? Yes. But that's not the case. I can't just let you face her challenge and get yourself hurt or killed. You're my fucking mate!"

"Yeah, I am." I stalk over to him and point a finger into his chest. "And guess what? If other lounges find out that I was issued a challenge and you stepped in for me, what do you think will happen?"

He clenches his fists.

"Exactly," I go on. "They'll think I'm weak. That *we're* weak together. If I don't face her, I'll get inundated with so many challenges I won't be able to catch a break until someone takes over this lounge." I graze my hand down his shirt, smoothing out the wrinkles. "I have to do this, Rook. You and I both know it."

Pissed off, he stalks over to a vase that's probably super expensive and chucks it against the wall. "Fuck!" he shouts as it shatters into a million pieces, his face murderous.

"You're cleaning that up," I tell him pointedly.

He narrows his eyes at me. "I have staff."

"It's not your poor staff's fault that you're having a temper tantrum," I tell him. "Now, when is she coming?"

"She's already here," he replies, before clenching his jaw.

Well...fuck.

Fake it, fake it, fake it.

I tamp down the anxiety and rush of adrenaline that are fighting for my attention. I need to think. I need to do what my mat can't. I need to be logical and not let my emotions and pride guide my actions. There's a way to deal with this, with her...I just need to figure it out.

The room is silent, and then an idea hits me. "Is she alone?" I ask.

"Yes."

"Okay. I need my phone," I say matter-of-factly, heading through the doorway toward our bedroom so I can get dressed. The more confident I seem, the less likely he'll be to totally lose his shit, break all the vases in the damn house, and kill my mat with his bare hands.

"How long can we make her wait?" I ask as I head into the closet and grab an outfit from the clothes that Rook had it filled with.

"Twenty-four hours at the most."

Despite how hard my anxiety-ridden heart is pumping, I nod. "Okay. Then let's stall her," I say, quickly getting dressed before heading to the bedside table where I snatch up the phone.

"What are you doing?" Rook asks, watching as my hands fly over the screen as I text Dinah. My friend immediately texts back, and a single kernel of hope pops inside of me.

I smile over at Rook as a plan takes form. "Don't worry, Glow Worm. I got this."

I walk confidently toward the dirt perimeter of the challenge ring. My stomach is already tied into so many knots I don't know if I'll be able to eat for a week. If I'm alive, that is. But I can't show any of that. I need to be cool, calm, and collected —everything I hope I can goad my mat into *not* being.

It's exactly twenty-three hours and forty five minutes since the challenge was first issued. I'm cutting it close, and I just hope everything I've put into play works out as planned.

I look around at the venue for this little showdown. Apparently, this is where Rook's guards and enforcers train in both their human form and cockatrice form. Enough trees are cleared for the length of two football fields, with nothing but dirt and sparse grass on the ground. I can see a couple of buildings in the distance that Rook told me are locker rooms where his enforcers can clean up afterward.

He forced my mat to stay here overnight, which I'm sure

she was spitting mad about. My lips curl up at the thought of her having to sleep without the comforts of a bed. I'm sure she slept like shit, which is good for me. I need any advantage I can have, just in case my plan doesn't work.

There's a crowd of some of Rook's lounge gathered around the perimeter. At least a hundred of them—and not one of them looks happy. In fact, they're all staring daggers in the same direction.

My mat is standing at the end of the ring, her green tail feathers flicking with irritation as she watches me approach. Her hair is pulled back in a tight, proper bun, and she's dressed like she's about to go to work as a CEO in a skyscraper rather than face her daughter in a duel for power.

Rook places his hand on the small of my back as we walk toward her. "Can I kill her?" he mutters.

Despite the circumstances, I feel my mouth twitch in amusement. "Still no."

He sighs, like it's a real inconvenience. "Just say the word."

"Sinclair," my mat says, flicking her eyes over us as we approach. "You're late."

"Not at all," I retort. "I came fifteen minutes early before the twenty-four hours was up. If I wanted to, I could go fuck off for a bit and leave you waiting here even longer."

Her thin lips pull downward. "You see?" she says, motioning toward me with her voice raised so that everyone else can hear her. "This is why you're a poor matriarch. You have no sense of decorum necessary to run a lounge. Although, I shouldn't expect anything else from an ex-convict."

I snort. "I know what you're doing."

"What's that?"

"You're trying to belittle me in front of my new lounge," I

reply steadily. "Trying to form a rift of doubt. But it won't work. Because unlike you, Alpha Bowen, the male *you* sold me to, is a damn good patriarch, and his lounge respects him. They might not know me very well yet, but they know him, and they trust that he wouldn't mate someone who wasn't worthy."

"I think we'll see who's *truly* worthy by the end of this, now won't we?" she retorts as she moves to undress so she can shift.

Rook interrupts her. "Why issue a challenge?" he asks, his strong arms crossed in front of his chest. "Why would you, *her mother*, challenge Sinclair? Like she said, *you* were the one to accept the contract months ago for me to take Sinclair as my mate. Now that she's here, honoring that contract, you issue a challenge within a week. That doesn't read like you had good intentions toward me or my lounge at all."

I can tell that she hates that he's called her out in front of everyone, because her nostrils flare as her green eyes dart around. "My reasons are my own. I don't have to explain them to you or your lounge."

I shake my head. "No, you don't. But you *do* have to explain them to yours."

Her eyebrows draw together in a frown, and then her gaze goes over my shoulder, where my backup just arrived in the form of her entire lounge.

My mat's eyes widen for a split-second before she gets it under control. "What's this?" she demands as she watches Rook's enforcers lead the way, bringing all of my mat's lounge members with them. Dinah shoots me a wink. She gathered everyone in a very short amount of time, and I'm thankful as fuck that she was able to pull it off.

"What are you doing, Meg?" my pat asks, coming up to her. Their entire lounge watches her with confusion.

My mat draws herself up straight, pushing her shoulders back. "I have issued Sinclair a challenge."

Immediately, shock ripples over the lounge, and everyone's eyes dart from me to my mother.

"You issued a challenge without informing me? To our own daughter?" my pat asks. His tone isn't outraged like a father or co-leader should be, but at least he's here. At least he's questioning her, even if his voice is filled with confusion instead of anger.

"Don't question me," she snaps. "I know what's best for our lounge."

"By hurting your own daughter and trying to stake claim to what isn't yours?" Dinah calls out. "How much longer are we going to follow a matriarch like this?" she asks the lounge, her arms raised in question.

The lounge starts speaking out all at once, and even though their words can't be picked apart in the crowd, their meaning is clear: They are over my mat's shit. I suspect maybe they have been for a while now.

My pat raises his hand to get them to settle down. It's the first time I've ever seen him behave like an alpha. And even though the gesture is simple, it holds a lot of weight for everyone, because they all shut up. Red eyes on his mate, my pat shakes his head. "Meg, stop this nonsense. Rescind the challenge on Sinclair and let's go home."

He starts to step forward to tug on her arm, but she wrenches away from his grasp. "No! Now is the time! Sinclair can't shift," she says, pointing at my anklet. "Think what we can do with this lounge," she tells him imploringly. "It's the largest one in the world." Her green eyes are deep set with envy. "This is our chance."

My pat looks at her like he can't wrap his head around her power-hungry words. "But...it's our *daughter*."

My mat levels him with a glare. "This is why I lead our lounge. You're not an alpha. You don't understand."

"Enough, Meg," Dinah calls out. "The lounge doesn't support this challenge. Rescind it."

My former lounge all begin to murmur at the clear disrespect Dinah just showed my mat by using her name instead of her title. My eyes dart between my old lounge, my pat, and my mat. The tension is so thick in the air, it feels like it's wrapped around my neck like a noose. Rook is at my side, incredibly tense, his body poised like he's ready to grab me and get me away from here.

"You issued a challenge, knowing Sinclair was at a disadvantage?" someone asks from behind me, the disgust clear in their tone.

My mat bristles, and her eyes narrow as she tries to identify who just said that. I feel the people behind me move closer together, and their solidarity warms me. Renewed mumbles of judgement and shock ripple through the surrounding crowd, and my mat tracks the noise like it's *the wave* at some sporting event.

I can practically see the list she's making in her head of all the people she'll have to get rid of in this new lounge when she wins.

"We would never follow a matriarch that picks on the weak!" someone from my new lounge declares, and others all around us voice their agreement and nod their heads.

"We would never follow a matriarch that chooses power over their own child either!" another cockatrice calls out.

"You're acting like a backstabbing Drake!" a female shouts out from somewhere across from me.

Every cockatrice present spits on the ground at the same time.

Fucking Drakes.

My mat's eyebrows shoot up in shock and quickly drop

back down into a scowl at the insult. She surveys the crowd's vitriol with calculating green eyes. I had this whole speech prepared about my mat getting her lounge into debt and trouble. About how she sold me to save her ass, knowing that she was going to dishonor the agreement and try to take over this lounge and all of their assets instead of honoring what she agreed to. But from the look of things, I don't need to give it.

The cockatrices from both lounges are oozing plenty of judgement and antipathy out into the atmosphere, and I know my mat can feel it. She's not stupid. She only chooses battles she knows she can win, and this challenge just got a hell of a lot more complicated. She may beat me, but if the entire lounge turns their back on her because of it, she'll have lost in the end. If they won't accept her leadership, she's powerless, and that's not something she'd set herself up for.

"I'm only doing what your alpha was going to do to me. Do you really think he wasn't going to turn on me?" she defends.

"I haven't issued a challenge and had no intention of doing so," Rook counters, and my mat glares at him. I almost feel bad for not letting Rook carry out his initial plans for her. I'm the one that made him agree to leave her alone. I guess this will teach me to be too generous by giving the benefit of the doubt and forgiveness.

Rook watches everything like a hawk. Power and tension radiate off of him like steam, and I wish I could grab his hand and whisper that it's all okay. The plan is working. My mat wants to challenge me, I can see it in her eyes, but we're tying her hands. This is exactly what I was hoping would happen.

My mat has been operating in the shadows for way too long. People who witness shady things are threatened to stay silent about them or are exiled before they can speak out. She's had a stranglehold on everyone and what they know, but that just changed. If she continues to challenge me, she'll be held accountable for it.

It's funny, all cockatrice talk about Alpha Bowen like he's the worst of the worst, when really, he's just strong. Leaders like my mat are the ones that need to be taken out, not him.

The anger in my mat's eyes dims, and her shoulders fall slightly. She knows this isn't going to go down the way she wanted. Frustration and resignation fill her green eyes, and I swallow down the sigh of relief that wants to rush out of my lips. I hoped against hope that this would work, but there were no guarantees.

"I rescind my challenge," my mat calls out begrudgingly. No one says anything, but there's a palpable exhale and release of tension in everyone that's gathered around.

My mat steps to the center of the ring and extends her hand. It's customary to shake hands as a show of faith and renewed trust, but I don't trust my mat. I step away from Rook anyway, because like it or not, I am a matriarch now, and I can't disrespect the cockatrice way.

Cunning green eyes track me as I move confidently closer, and the hair on the back of my neck stands up in warning. I tell myself that she'd be condemning herself to death if she tries anything, but that doesn't do much to make me feel better. But I can't balk or show any hesitation or fear. Just like I told Rook before, to do that would invite endless challenges from rival lounges, and until I get my evil shift-stopping anklet off, we can't have that happen.

I take my mother's hand in mine. It's deceptively soft—probably because she's never done a day of hard work in her life—and unsurprisingly cold, like every other aspect of who she is.

"This isn't over," she tells me flatly as she gives our

clasped hands one hard pump.

I release her hand and step back. "I don't know, mat, from where I'm standing, it looks like the tides are turning."

I spin on my heels to move back toward Rook and the enforcers of my new lounge, leaving her to stew on that. My pulse pounds in my ears as I walk away, adrenaline and relief rushing through me. I can't believe we did it. I mean, I had faith, but to know it's over...I can't help the smile that crawls across my face. I look up, searching for Rook, my eyes filled with victory, but my stomach plummets when I spot the rage pouring off of him.

He shouts a warning as my perception seems to morph into slow motion.

Rook takes a running step forward and then explodes into his cockatrice. But it's the change at my back that I feel almost on a visceral level. I whirl around just in time to see a clawed cockatrice foot headed right for me.

That stupid lying bitch!

I have enough time for that thought to flit through my mind and to get a hand up in front of me protectively before I take a cockatrice roundhouse to the chest. I go flying.

Claws rake down my shoulder and across my abdomen as I get flung through the air. A wing comes slicing toward me, and I'm batted down mid-flight. I slam to the ground with a painful crunch, and dirt plumes around me as I gasp to replace the wind that was just knocked out of me. I watch as Rook surges toward my mother, a call for retribution roaring out of his black beak.

He's less than ten feet away from her and closing fast. He'll kill her. I know this absolutely. Not only is he a hell of a lot bigger than she is, but she just attacked his mate. His eyes are unforgiving and filled with hate and vengeance.

But out of nowhere, another massive cockatrice slams into my mom before Rook can get to her. She screams as she goes crashing to the ground. The massive red cockatrice is on her in a flash, immediately trapping her neck in its maw.

It takes me a beat to figure out who's trying to force my mat into submission, and pure shock flashes through me when I realize it's...my pat.

Completely stunned, I slowly try to push to my feet as my pat clamps down on my mat's neck and thrashes. She roars, but it sounds more outraged than pained. Me, on the other hand, I'm fucking hurting. I quickly give up on my efforts to get to my feet when new strikes of pain light up through my body.

When it's clear she can't break out of my pat's hold, my mat submits with a bitter trill. She shifts back into her human form as he lets go, and I watch, completely flabbergasted, as she begrudgingly lifts her chin to my pat, exposing her neck to him.

My pat snaps down at her, stopping just shy of her flesh. The action is a warning that the mercy being shown could be revoked at any moment. I can't even begin to process what my pat just did. I wouldn't have seen it coming in a million years.

Not only did he come to my rescue, but he put my mat in her place too, and he just promised—in his cockatrice way—to rip her throat out if she crossed him again. My mat breathes hard, seething from her back on the ground, but she doesn't move a muscle as my pat crows out a warning before shifting back into his human form again.

"How could you?" my mat snarls up at him.

"How could *you*?" he growls right back. I've never seen his face hold so much emotion. "Even if that weren't our daughter you were attacking, you dishonor me and our lounge by going against your word to rescind a challenge and attacking when the other person's back is turned! What is wrong with you?" he bellows.

"You didn't hear what she said to me!" my mat defends.

My pat's eyes spark with even more fury. Taking a deep breath, he straightens up and looks around. "I hereby rescind my claim and my mate's claim to...the Denali lounge," he announces.

What the hell?

My eyebrows jump so high they nearly reach my hairline. *Holy shit. He's making them step down from their own lounge!*

"You can't!" my mat screams at him.

He looks back down at her. "I can, and I do. Enough is enough. You made me ashamed to be mated to you today," he tells her, and whatever she was about to say dies on her lips. She stares at him, completely astonished, and she's not the only one.

My pat has *never* stood up for me against her before. If I hadn't just witnessed it with my own eyes, I wouldn't have believed it possible.

I feel hands on my body, and I look up to find Rook's furious and concerned gaze moving over me. I give him a weak smile and a completely nonsensical thumbs up as he moves to pick me up. My hip pops back into place as he helps me to my feet, and I bite back the scream that wants to escape, but it comes out like a gurgled screech.

Rook freezes. "I'm going to rip her apart," he threatens as he moves to cradle my dirt-smudged face in his hands.

I huff out a laugh and then wince, because I'm pretty sure I have a broken rib or two. Damn, she really did a number on me. I know I'll be fine with no permanent damage, but that doesn't make it hurt any less.

I look down at my chest and see gouges through the tatters of my shirt. "Dammit, I really liked this shirt. It hugged me in all the right places," I whine.

"Come here so *I* can hug you in all the right places,"

Rook growls as he gets his hands under me and picks me up. He holds me close, and I can feel his heart pounding hard in his chest.

"I'm fine," I reassure him, lifting my hand to his face. He's got this sexy scruff thing going on—now that he doesn't have to pretend he's a clean cut prison guard. I'm torn about liking it though, because it hides his lickable dimples.

He levels me with a look. "You are *not* fine. I can smell the blood, Sinclair, and you wince every time you take a breath."

"I'm fine-ish," I amend.

He huffs and then starts walking over toward my pat. "Put me down," I whisper, not wanting to be carried like a baby in front of the lounges.

"Not a chance in hell," he replies, his arms continuing to cradle me.

We walk up to my pat—wait, no. He's not a patriarch anymore. He just stepped down from that role. My *father* bows his head. "If you wish to issue a challenge, I will bear the responsibility of my mate's behavior."

My eyes fly up to Rook. He might be my mate...but this is new between us. And he's a strong, incredibly proud alpha. He could very well demand that my parents face him in a challenge for my mother's disrespect today. No one would judge him for it. *I* couldn't even judge him for it, even though it's my parents and the thought of him hurting my father makes me a little sick.

Rook studies them, sending a low growling noise at my mother who's standing behind my father with her head lowered. My mate's eyes shift from her to me, his expression immediately softening. I feel his fingers lightly circle my skin where he's holding me. "No," he says, answering my father. "I won't issue a challenge. You controlled your mate and made her submit, and you stepped down as alpha leaders of your lounge. I'm satisfied with that if Sinclair is."

Pride swells in my chest at his words. Not just because he's choosing to let it go, but because he's including me in his decision. I give a nod. "I'm cool as long as I never have to see her again."

My father accepts my words with a tilt of his head. I wriggle in Rook's arms until he puts me down, but the stubborn cockatrice keeps a hand around my waist, even as I lean in to hug my father. "Thank you," I whisper.

"I'm sorry," he replies before pulling away, his eyes misty and filled with so much regret it makes my breath catch in my throat. He addresses his former, now leaderless lounge. "I'm sorry to all of you. We are not the leaders you deserve. But maybe...*they* are," he says, motioning toward Rook and me. Then he turns to leave, pulling my mother along with him.

I watch them walk away, but I don't feel even a twinge of disappointment that I'll probably never see her again. I'm pretty cheerful about it, actually. I'll try to keep in touch with my father, but she just became nothing to me the moment she shifted and attacked.

Rook turns, his arm still steadying around my waist. "If any of you wish to join our lounge, we will welcome you," he says, and my heart squeezes at his generosity.

There's an awkward pause as my old lounge sizes up my new one, probably wondering how well they'll mesh together, but my purple-haired friend lets out an obnoxiously loud whistle, her face beaming. "Woo! That's what I'm talking about!" Dinah says with an excited clap. "Baby!" she shouts over to her mate. "Go get our daughter. We're moving in!"

I laugh, shaking my head, but the pain steals my smile

away and replaces it with a grimace. "See? Not fucking fine," Rook says at my side.

Before I can respond, I'm scooped up in his arms again and he's stalking away. "Party tonight to celebrate our new lounge members and my mating with Sinclair," he calls out, and whoops and catcalls sound out all around us. "Now, I'm going to take care of my mate."

"You're so hot right now," I purr as I run a finger over his pec.

He cocks a brow at me, but I see his blue and green hair begin to glow. "Sinclair. You're torn the fuck up from your mother's claws, and you're beat to hell from your landing. How the hell can you be turned on right now?" he says with exasperation as he walks us toward his car to drive us back to our mansion.

"Uhh, duh. You're naked from shifting, and you went all wise and benevolent alpha in front of everyone. It was totally sexy."

He rolls his eyes, but amusement dances over his expression. "What am I going to do with you?"

"Hopefully take me into a dark room and have your wise and benevolent way with me," I quip.

"I'll be giving you a bath, after which you'll be tended to by a healer, and then you'll be resting for the remainder of the day until the party."

My bottom lip sticks out as he yanks open the car door and places me gently on the seat before shutting me in. "But somewhere between all of that, I'm getting orgasms, right?" I holler as he walks around the hood to get in on the other side. He still hasn't answered by the time he starts up the car and begins to drive away. "Right?" I demand.

He puts a hand on my thigh and squeezes. "You're injured," he points out.

"You're naked," I fire back. "Also, your cockatrice?

Fucking epic. My cockatrice wants to tail flick all over him."

His hair glows to epic levels of glowiness, making me trill in excitement. "I love your colors," I sigh dreamily.

"You're looking at my cock," he says drily.

My eyes lift from his lap. "Yeah, so? It has nice lighting on it right now from your hair glow."

He chuckles as his hands shift over the steering wheel. "How'd I end up with such a perfect mate?"

I smile, because I was thinking the exact same thing. "Prison. Apparently, all the awesome people are in prison," I say with a playful shrug. "I met this hot prison guard in there, and it worked out for me."

He snorts. "How convenient for you."

"Yep. Now let's go play convicts and captors. Naked," I say, wagging my brows.

"*You* need a bath and a healer," he counters.

"Ugh, Rook, don't get stingy on me now," I whine.

He gives me the *alpha eyes* that radiate *what I say goes*.

"Fine," I relent. "I'll take a bath...but you have to take it with me."

"Done," he agrees. So easy.

"Ooh, we can totally play hide the submarine," I announce with a clap. When he doesn't reply, I spell it out for him, thinking maybe he doesn't know this game. "You know, hide the submarine? The submarine would be your dick. And it would be hiding in my pus—"

"I got it," he drawls with a smirk before reaching over to lace his fingers with mine. In a tender move, he brings my hand to his lips and kisses it. "I love you, Sunrise."

"Love you, Glow Worm," I chirp back, a smile overtaking my face.

Who knew prison would be the best thing to ever happen to me? Me, actually. I totally called it.

Best idea ever.

EPILOGUE
THREE MONTHS LATER

I'm dead asleep, drooling into a silk pillow and living my best life when a rooster crows loudly enough to make me jolt awake. I sit up so fast my head spins. Disheveled and out of it, I swipe my hair away from my face just as another *cock-a-doodle-fuckin-doo* sounds out.

With a squeal, I slam my hands over my ears and glare over at the wide-open doors. The whole damn wall is made up of accordion-style sliding doors that lead to a massive balcony. A balcony where my mate and fearless lounge leader is currently perched, making that god-awful sound in all his cockatrice glory.

I glare at him. I'm not even distracted by his super pretty green and blue comb on the top of his head or the matching feathers at the end of his long tail right now. It's too early for this shit.

"You asshole, the sun isn't even up yet!" I tell him crankily.

In response, his head wobbles at me. I scoff. "Don't try to be cute. You woke me up."

He lengthens his neck and lets out another ear-splitting crowing noise. I lift a pillow and chuck it at him, proud when it smacks him right in his face. He looks down at the silk fluff and then steps right over it, heading inside.

Eyes wide, I scramble off the bed and try to rush toward him, shaking my head with my hands out. "Oh no you don't. We've talked about this. No coming into the bedroom in your cockatrice form!" I tell him.

He stops in front of me, but he's already crossed the barrier. He has to duck down so he doesn't hit the ceiling and tuck his wings in since his beast is so massive. The once giant room now seems way too small with him in it.

"Out," I say sternly, pointing toward the door. His cockatrice gives a sad little trill, but I hold firm. "Your claws are wrecking the hardwood, and your feathers are—wait," I stop, my eyes narrowing. "Do you have something in your mouth?"

His head bobs excitedly, and then he leans over, tipping his beak open. Huge rocks come spilling from his mouth and slam onto the floor with loud cracks, as pieces of sand fall down with them in a dusty rainfall. I have to jump back before any of the big rocks land on me and crush my toes.

Now the hardwood is definitely wrecked by the damn *boulders* that he just dropped at my feet like an offering. But honestly, these rocks are dope.

I gasp when I spot one in particular. "Oh my God, is that a basanite?" I ask, leaning down to snatch it up.

I *try* to snatch it up. It's really fucking heavy and big, so I have to settle for wrapping my adoring arms around it and giving it an appreciative hug. "Pretty," I purr as I stroke the rock. My cockatrice is so flattered right now.

I stare at the boulders dreamily for another second and then look back up at Rook. "That's super sweet, but seriously, no cockatrices in the house. You know the rules. Either shift or get out," I remind him, my arm extended and my finger pointed out toward the balcony. "And take your rocks—"

Rook shifts before I can finish my sentence, and despite his glorious nakedness, I glare at him. "Oh sure, just leave the boulders in the middle of the room," I snark.

He rubs at his chest and looks over at today's haul proudly. "Got you some basanite," he tells me with a self-satisfied smile and an eyebrow wag.

I roll my eyes at the cocky cockatrice. "I see that. Couldn't have found a smaller sample to impress me with?" I ask, pointing to the massive rock that will now be a permanent fixture in our room until his cockatrice gets over himself and hefts it out.

"This one was so pretty, though," he defends, and I shake my head at him, trying not to smile.

"It's super pretty," I reassure him. "But you have to be logical about it. What the hell am I supposed to do with these massive things? I can't exactly put them on a shelf like a knickknack. Not to mention, this will be the third time we'll have to refinish the floors in the last two months! Why can't your cockatrice just put them in the rock garden and take me down to see them there?" I offer. "Remember *all* the things we did on the obsidian boulder when you put it in the garden instead of fucking up the house with it?"

His eyes gleam, and I know he remembers really well.

"So only let your beast bring me nice, hand-sized rocks indoors, okay?"

"I like the big ones," he argues. "They call to me."

"Well, then answer the fucking call in the rock garden!" I snap suddenly. I pause and give myself the side-eye for that one. I take a deep breath and release it slowly. "Sorry. I'm cranky. I really do love the basanite."

His smug smile returns. "I know. It's awesome. But I have a few more rocks to give you."

I give him a look. "Rook, I know I'm your amazing mate and everything, but you've gotta slow down on the rock-giving. You're going to make my cockatrice spoiled rotten."

"I like spoiling my mate," he says as he walks over to his bedside table. He opens a drawer and digs around before grabbing something and heading back over to me with his hands behind his back. "Close your eyes."

I humor him, closing my eyes as he walks up to me. He grabs my hands, making me hold them palm-up in front of me, and then places something on them. It's definitely not a rock, though. I open my eyes and find a box filled with a variety pack of Pop Rocks. A happy gasp spills from my lips. "*OhmygawdIloveyousomuch*," I half babble on a girl-squeal as I tear into it.

"I haven't had Pop Rocks for months. Not since the prison!" I say as I rip open the first packet and dump the entire contents in my mouth.

"I know," Rook tells me, still wearing his self-satisfied smile. But he earned that look this time. "You've even been talking about them in your sleep."

"Can you blame me? They're awesome," I say, mouth full as the candy goes off like mini-explosions so loud it almost drowns out my voice. So. Good.

I moan a little from the watermelon flavor and notice Rook's dick jump between his legs. An idea sparks in my mind, and I lift my eyes back up to his.

Whatever expression is on my face makes him instantly wary. "What?"

I shrug, trying to be all nonchalant, but he just looks more suspicious. "Sunrise, I know that look. What are you thinking?"

I crunch the last of the candies and swallow them down. "I'm thinking...that I want to reward you. For being such a nice mate and bringing me so many rocks—the candy kind *and* the boulder kind," I say suggestively.

Heat immediately banks in his eyes. "Hmm. Reward me? How will you do that?"

I trace my finger down his sexy, chiseled chest. "Do you trust me?"

"Always."

"Good."

I lean forward and kiss him, tilting my head and plunging my tongue deep into his mouth, just the way he likes. My tail curls around his leg, my feathers stroking up his skin with soft, teasing movements.

"Mmm, you taste good," he says huskily as he pulls away and starts grazing his mouth along my neck.

"You're about to taste real good too," I tell him. And then I drop to my knees.

His cock jerks upright like a student who just got caught slouching in class after the teacher called on him. I wrap my hand around it in a friendly greeting. "Mmm, I just love your cock...atrice," I smirk before leaning forward and licking over the head.

Rook jolts where he stands. "Every time I see you on your knees for me, it blows my fucking mind," he says, his hand brushing away some of my hair.

"I'm about to blow your mind even more," I reply before reaching forward and snagging another packet.

"What?" he asks.

"You said you trusted me. I've been wanting to do this since the prison," I admit, and then I rip open the packet and dump some candy in. As soon as it hits my slick tongue and starts popping, I open wide and sink my mouth over Rook.

Holding my wet tongue against his length, I lick and

slurp and bob over him, letting him feel the rock candy popping all over his thick dick.

"Holy fuck rocks," he says with a strangled grunt. "Shit. That's weird."

I start to pull off, thinking maybe he doesn't like it, but he shoves my head back on him so fast I gag. "No. Don't stop," he pants. "Don't fucking stop."

Smiling around his dick, I suck him with enthusiasm, and when the popping fades, I pull off and put more candy onto my tongue and then do it again and again and again.

I suck and swirl and go as deep as I can, driving him totally out of his mind until he can't take it anymore and starts fucking in and out of my throat. I love it. I love that I make him so out of his mind with need and lust that he loses control. He makes noises that I've never heard him make before, and those growls make me wet as fuck.

I get through green apple, a blue raspberry, and a cotton candy packet before he finally tenses.

"I'm going to come," he says, and I hum my acknowledgement around him.

A few pumps later, he's spilling into my mouth, his molten cum hitting the back of my throat. I swallow it down with the remnants of the candy, everything tasting sugary sweet.

I lick him up, cleaning him off, and then let him slip from my mouth. I look up at him with a sly smile. "Good?"

"Fucking incredible," he says, pulling me to my feet and crushing me against him. "Your turn."

He hauls me over his shoulder and snatches up the box of candy before striding into the bathroom.

"Wait—" I start to say, but he's already turned the shower on and dropped me onto the bench. I squeal at the icy cold water. "Fuck! That's freezing, Rook!" I snap as goosebumps prickle all up and down my body.

"Sorry, Sunrise," he says, though he doesn't look sorry at all.

I glare and cross my arms in front of my chest as he steps into the shower, stuffing a few packets of Pop Rocks onto the elevated stone shelf. "I'll warm you up."

He kneels down in front of me and takes my sopping wet shirt, pulling it over my head. He eyes my rock hard nipples. "Mmm. Cold looks good on you," he says, plucking the distended peaks between his fingers. I hiss at the sensitivity that borders on pain.

"Up. I need these pants off," he tells me.

My teeth are nearly chattering, but luckily, the water is slowly heating up. I stand, my hands going to my leggings, but he pushes them down before I can and tosses them in the corner of the shower where my shirt is already waiting.

His eyes roam over my chilled body. "You're goddamn beautiful, do you know that?"

"I'm goddamn cold, actually," I grumble, making him laugh.

"Ah, Sunrise. You need my mouth to warm you up?"

"Yes," I gripe.

He grabs one of the packets, pouring the candy into his mouth, his eyes widening when he feels the popping start to blast against his tongue. He leans down, gathering my breasts into his hands like he's offering them up to himself to feast on, and he closes his mouth over a cold, firm nipple, sucking lightly.

The heat of his mouth, the swirl of his tongue, and pops of the candy make a gasp slip out between my lips. "*Oh.*"

Rook feasts on my nipples, back and forth and back again, until my breasts are heavy under his attention, aching and needy. The popping adds a whole other element to the sensation, making me writhe beneath him. I need him. I need him so badly.

"Rook."

"What do you need, Sunrise?" he asks, kissing a trail up between my breasts.

"You," I say. "I need you inside me."

"Not yet."

"Rook..." I whine, and he bites me lightly on the collarbone.

"Be patient. You'll get my cock when I'm ready. But I'm not done playing with you."

He goes right back to his teasing ministrations, his scorching mouth mixing with the now-hot water that cascades over our bodies. Everywhere he licks and nibbles and kisses is like flint, casting off sparks along my nerves.

Slowly, he makes his way down.

So. Damn. Slowly.

When he's made it to my belly button, I finally snap, growling at him as my tail wraps around his arm and tries to yank him all the way down to his knees. He chuckles, his own tail coming out to pull mine away. "Such a naughty mate, trying to rush me."

"Stop teasing me!" I grouse, my tone needy and flustered.

Placing one last kiss on my navel, he finally drops down to his knees. "You need me, Sunrise?"

"Yes," I groan. "Please."

"Hand me that packet."

I shake my head. I can't handle that now. "It'll be too much," I tell him.

He cocks a brow and waits. Fucking stubborn cockatrice.

"Fine," I say, snatching the packet and handing it to him.

"Good girl." He rips the top off with his teeth and dumps the contents in. Lifting my right thigh to balance over his shoulder, he attacks. He goes straight for my clit, licking and sucking with the explosions going on in his mouth, and I explode right along with them.

So fast.

Like, embarrassingly fast.

My eyes grow as wide as saucers as the orgasm detonates through me. It's as fast and intense as a firework, arcing up with a flare and then fizzling out. "Holy fuck. Oh shit. Goddamn," I pant, rambling as my head drops back against the wall. "I totally get the Pop Rocks panties trend now. I could've made a fortune."

I think Rook will stand up and get to business now that I've come, but I'm mistaken. A strangled choke of a breath whooshes out of me as Rook's mouth closes over my clit again.

"No, no. It's too sensitive, I can't," I tell him, my nerves still throbbing from that spectacular orgasm.

"You can," he says. "You're gonna come again on my mouth, and then I'm gonna bend you over and fuck you against the wall."

Warmth floods me at his demanding, dirty words. "Oh God…"

Closing his mouth over me, he licks and laps and holds his popping tongue against my clit until I come apart all over again, hard enough that I see little Pop Rocks stars bursting behind my eyes.

Only then does he toss the packet away, flip me around, and sink his dick into me from behind with one hard thrust. We both let out obscenely loud groans.

"Fuck, Sunrise. Your pussy gripping my cock is one of the best feelings in the world," he growls sensually.

I moan, and he grinds against my ass. His tail slicks up my leg, the feathers tickling my sensitive clit. I feel him everywhere, and it's too much and not enough all at the same time.

"I can feel you so wet and ready to cum all over me again."

He's right. It's like he jump started my pleasure, and now I'm just in an endless wave of need as his dick saws in and out of me, drawing everything out into blissful ripples.

He fists his hand in my hair and tugs up, arching my back as I brace my hands flat against the wall.

"This is gonna be rough," he tells me against my ear, the steamy water pouring over us. "I need to fuck you hard and fast, and I'm not gonna stop until you're screaming my fucking name. You got it?"

"Yes, yes!" I say, nearly incapable of speech.

"Good."

He's a male of his word.

He starts powering into me, and all I can do is hold on and take it. I feel every inch of his dick as it buries into me balls-deep before whipping out and thrusting right back in again. Over and over, he propels his hips forward until smacking skin and my own garbled moans and incoherent words are all that I can hear. His hold on my hair keeps me in place as he gives me everything I can take.

I'm so wet that I'm squelching around every drag and push of his cock. He moves so fast that I can feel his sack slapping up against me every time he moves. He fucks me hard. Savagely. Without holding back. He's fucking me like an alpha. Like a dominating, possessive, lust-crazed mate, and I *love* it.

When he reaches around and pinches my clit between his fingers, I come with a scream. "My name," he snarls against my ear, and I have just enough wherewithal to be able to accomplish his demands, and his name tears from my lips.

He roars out his release on the backend of my own, burying himself so deep inside of me that it's like he wants to take up permanent residence. I collapse against the tiled wall, feeling completely wrung out, almost high from the back-to-back orgasms he just gave me.

I blink as his mouth trails kisses up my spine. "Love you, Sunrise," he purrs, and I smile.

"Ahluuurvvooooo," I mumble, too blissed out and satisfied to speak any kind of intelligible language.

Rook laughs and splays his hand on my chest to stand me upright. "We're...sticky," he observes, and I chuckle.

"Candy sex requires good hygiene practices," I slur out.

"I guess the shower was a good call."

"Mmm-hmm," I agree, and he pulls out of me and reaches for the body wash and loofah.

He lathers it up and starts washing and massaging my entire body with adoring tenderness. Seriously, if we could get the *boulders in the house* thing in check, I'd have the best mate ever. Fuck it, even with the boulders, he's the best mate ever.

I melt against him, and he chuckles, knowing exactly what he's doing to me. Bubbles streak over my breasts and down my stomach as he draws little circles with the soaped up loofah across my belly.

"I want to put a baby in here soon," he declares completely out of the blue, and my mind skids to a stop, hits reverses, and honks out a *say what?*

The pool of post orgasmic calm I was just floating in is replaced by shock. I study his face for a moment, and he does the same as we both attempt to silently hear what the other is thinking.

"Um, that's not going to happen," I mumble awkwardly.

His brows immediately dip. "I'm not saying now. Obviously, it's all about whenever you're ready. I'm just letting you know that I'm ready. Whenever you are," he tells me sweetly before he drops the loofah between my thighs.

Fuck, that feels good. *Focus, Sinclair!*

"No, I'm saying that can't happen bec—"

"Just forget I mentioned it. It was stupid. I don't want to fight, and if you keep saying it can't happen, we're going to argue about it," he states, cutting me off.

I growl in irritation.

"See? It's happening already. I knew I should have waited for you to bring it up. I totally owe Trex twenty now."

That admission makes me pause. Why are Trex and Rook betting over baby talk? Males are weird. I shake my head to clear those thoughts away.

"Rook," I start, but he drops the loofah and starts playing with my clit again.

I hiss and then moan as he pulls a now squeaky clean nipple into his mouth. "Let's do more of this instead," he murmurs in between flicks of his tongue against my peaked breast.

I get lost to the sensations for a beat before snapping myself out of it. I push his hands and head away from my body.

"Will you stop interrupting me and distracting me with your mouth and fingers? Let me talk, and then we can get to the *more sex* portion of today's program!"

He chuckles and keeps his mouth closed as I once again collect my thoughts and focus on what I'm trying to say. "When I say that it can't happen, that you can't put a baby in me soon...I say that because you can't put a baby in there when there's already one calling dibs on the place," I tell him, feeling shy about the admission. I've only known myself for a couple of days and I've been debating how best to go about the big reveal.

Rook just stares at me, blinking.

"It's early, only a couple months I think, but the little squirt seems to like it in there. Other than the missed periods, I haven't even felt any differently. Dinah was sick as fuck with Verity, but so far so good for me," I ramble.

Rook's mouth suddenly crashes to mine, and he kisses me stupid. He cups my head and pours all his love and excitement from his lips to mine. By the time he pulls away, happy tears are slipping down both of our faces.

He smiles the most beautiful dimple-laced smile ever and raises his hands in victory and whoops at the top of his lungs. "I'm going to be a daddy!"

I laugh as he goes running out of the shower. "Where are you going?"

"I have to tell everyone!" he shouts back over his shoulder, almost slipping and falling in his hurry to go spread the good news.

"Rook Bowen, you get your fine ass back in here!"

He immediately comes squeaking back. "Is it the baby?" he asks, suddenly all concerned.

I laugh and roll my eyes. "No, I just need you to finish what you started," I tell him with a seductive smile and a finger pointing down toward my vagina, just in case he missed my meaning.

His eyes heat, and he prowls back toward me. He picks me up, and I wrap my legs around his waist as he carries us out of the shower.

"Hey, I liked it in there!" I protest.

"Nope, showers are slippery and dangerous. From now on, we fuck in the bed only. Much safer," he declares, heading right for our massive bed.

I groan and laugh. He's going to be insufferably protective, I can already tell. I smile at the thought. Meh, there are worse things.

I spot the new boulders decorating the room. My cockatrice loves the sight. "I don't know, Glow Worm, I bet sex on rocks would be pretty safe too," I mention casually. "I see a couple that my amazing mate just brought for me, and I bet they could use a good breaking in."

Rook growls approvingly and switches directions, beelining it right for the basanite. I laugh and grind against him as I nip at his neck.

Happiness envelops me, and I wouldn't be able to wipe the smile from my face for anything. If someone had told me seven months ago that Alpha Bowen would become everything to me, I would have junk punched them. But now, life is sweeter than Pop Rocks and nineties music, and I wouldn't have it any other way.

The End.

PARANORMAL PRISON

Welcome to Nightmare Penitentiary

Siren Condemned by C.R. Jane and Mila Young

Delinquent Demons by K. Webster

Conveniently Convicted by Raven Kennedy & Ivy Asher

Noir Reformatory by Lexi C. Foss & Jennifer Thorn

Blindly Indicted by Katie May

Stolen Song by Autumn Reed & Ripley Proserpina

Prison Princess by CoraLee June & Rebecca Royce

Succubus Chained by Heather Long

Wraith Captive by Lacey Carter Andersen

ALSO BY IVY ASHER & RAVEN KENENDY

Dystopian Romantic Comedy Standalone

April's Fools

Hellgate Guardians Series

Grave Mistakes

Grave Consequences

Grave Decisions

Grave Signs

ALSO BY IVY ASHER

The Sentinel World

THE LOST SENTINEL

The Lost and the Chosen

Awakened and Betrayed

The Marked and the Broken

Found and Forged

SHADOWED WINGS

The Hidden

The Avowed

The Reclamation

MORE IN THE SENTINEL WORLD COMING SOON.

Paranormal Romance

THE OSSEOUS CHRONICLES

The Bone Witch

Book 2 coming soon

Dystopian Romantic Comedy Standalone

April's Fools

ALSO BY RAVEN KENNEDY

Paranormal Shifter Romance:
Addie: Pack of Misfits Book 1
Reese: Pack of Misfits Book 2
Jetta: Pack of Misfits Book 3

Fantasy Reverse Harem Romantic Comedy:
Signs of Cupidity: Book 1
Bonds of Cupidity: Book 2
Crimes of Cupidity: Book 3
For the Love of Cupidity: Book 4
Cupidity Box Set

Fantasy Romance
Gild: The Plated Prisoner Series Book 1
Glint: The Plated Prisoner Series Book 2

Romantic Comedy Stand-Alone:
Can't Fix Cupid
April's Fools

Dark Contemporary Romance:
The Girl Who Cries Colors
Cruel: Savannah Heirs Book 1

Tame: Savannah Heirs Book 2

Wild: Savannah Heirs Book 3

Dark Paranormal Romance:

Void

Wicked Webs

IVY ASHER

Ivy Asher is addicted to chai, swearing, and laughing a lot—but not in a creepy, laughing alone kind of way. She loves the snow, books, and her family of two humans, and three fur-babies. She has worlds and characters just floating around in her head, and she's lucky enough to be surrounded by amazing people who support that kind of crazy.

Join Ivy Asher's Reader Group and follow her on Instagram and BookBub for updates on your favorite series and upcoming releases!!!

- facebook.com/IvyAsherBooks
- instagram.com/ivy.asher
- amazon.com/author/ivyasher
- bookbub.com/profile/ivy-asher

RAVEN KENNEDY

Raven Kennedy lives in California with her family. She is most known for her international bestselling Heart Hassle series about a quirky cupid who wants to find love for herself. RK writes in a range of genres, including romantic comedies, fantasy, dark romances, contemporary, and paranormal. Whether she makes you laugh or cry, she hopes to connect with readers and create characters you can root for.

You can connect one-on-one with RK on Facebook in Raven Kennedy's Reader Group and on her Instagram. Click the icons below!

- facebook.com/ravenkennedybooks
- instagram.com/ravenkennedybooks
- amazon.com/author/ravenkennedy
- bookbub.com/authors/raven-kennedy